SEARCH
FOR TRUTH

The next step...

Bryan Radzin

SEARCH FOR TRUTH

The next step...

ISBN#   978-0-578-16600-1

UNRELENTING POSITIVITY

AUTHOR: BRYAN RADZIN

COVER ART: SANDY FACTOR

I DEDICATE THIS TO ALL THE PEOPLE WHO HAVE EVER STRUGGLED OR WHO CONTINUE TO STRUGGLE FOR EQUALITY AND BASIC HUMAN DECENCY. YOU HAVE NOT STRUGGLED IN VAIN. YOUR STRUGGLE IS MY STRUGGLE, IT IS EVERYBODY'S STRUGGLE. WE CAN MAKE THE POSITIVE CHANGE WE ALL SEEK, BECAUSE THE CHANGE IS US.

ACKNOWLEDGMENTS

Thank you mom for not only being my biggest cheerleader, but also the peace of mind that I never have to question your support. I wouldn't be the man I am today, if it weren't for your love and motivation. I only hope I can make you proud. Thank you dad for giving me the best base of understanding about life that a boy could have ever hoped for. I also wouldn't be the man I am today, if it weren't for your words of wisdom.

To Grandma Laurine for always being my example of what love and family should be about. Even if you aren't around anymore in the physical world, mom and I know you are always with us. We love you with all our hearts.

To Grandpa Mel for always making me smile when I think of all the fun times I had with you when I was younger. I only hope that when I'm a grandpa one day, I can live up to your example.

To Grandma Yona for giving me a love of my culture that nobody can ever take away. To Grandpa Herman you have instilled in me an undeniable desire for a better life no matter the odds. I will find out the true story behind Radzyn Poland one day.

To Aunt Suzie who has never failed to show love from the bottom of her soul. Thank you for showing when I feel the love and support of those around me, there is nothing I can't accomplish.

To Cousin Hillary for becoming an ever evolving, critically thinking and conscientious member of the human race. Society will progress for the betterment of us all because people like us know there is a better way.

To Uncle Eugene for always taking an interest in what I'm up to because you actually care. To Uncle Garry for providing me with the knowledge to never take life too seriously, but also to tell people what you really think.

To Aunt Lisa for proving that women are just as capable and probably more so then men at making a good life for their kids. To Cousin Shawna for following your dreams and for proving to me that the sky is the limit, if we want it to be.

To Ryan for showing that somebody who works their ass and plays their ass off, can also love their ass off. To Sean for always having your priorities straight, and for always caring what I'm up to. To Tim for not only being my oldest friend and my biggest fan, but also for "getting it." People like us can create a better world.

To Mackey for not only buying the 1st copy of my book before it was even out, but also for proving in real time that somebody can do anything they set their mind to. To Laurie for not only always having words of wisdom for my life and for my writing, but also somebody I can collaborate with intellectually at any time. To Jaime for having the determination to live a better life, and for being my friend; you have the power to accomplish whatever you dream.

To Diane for being one of my biggest fans and supporters. Thank you for all the help editing this book, and constructive advice to make it better. I only hope that each successive novel after this lives up to your expectations. To Ed for proving that knowledge and clarity comes with life experience. Thank you for your help editing this sequel, I hope that it clearly shows the consciousness both you and I know the world so desperately needs.

To my neighbor Jen for always having a smile and a kind word when I'm feeling blue. You are the best neighbor and friend a guy could ask for. To my neighbor Jeff even if safety meeting isn't in your vocabulary at the moment, I will always cherish the intellectual curiosity that stemmed from our conversations. To my neighbor Amber for always lending an ear when I needed to talk because you genuinely cared, you deserve all the success and happiness in the world.

To Lisa for not only being the best boss a guy could ask for, but also for creating a work environment that I could never be miserable in. Without you I surely wouldn't be the writer I am or the human being I am. Thank you for being exactly who you are.

To Robert for being the biggest Kings fan, I mean the biggest Sharks fan I know. Don't worry, with each other around making the other laugh, it ensures we will never pull a Kapernik ☺ To Cedric for always having a warm smile and a warm heart. You are one of the most authentic people I know, and you've shown that somebody can overcome anything if they really want to. To Andrea for always greeting me with a smile and a "how are you" because to you it wasn't just something to say. Your writing will progress, because you are one of the most honest and down to earth people I know. Thank you for the Brigadieros.

To the 4th St market guy, (who I should know your name) I will always remember your awesome shirts that take me back to my childhood; and for the motivational musings that you so often release. To the other 4th St market guy. I should also know your name. Thank you for the kind words about my writing, and the encouragement that went along with it. You have shown me that it doesn't matter what religion you are, but what kind of human being you are.

To the bank ladies for not only making me feel welcome, knowing my first name and smiling at me whenever I came in, but also for showing that big evil banks would be less evil if their CEOs followed the humanity of their employees. To the lady at the Co-op for always smiling at me when I come in, and showing me warmth that goes to my very soul. I can only hope that one day I learn your name. To the lady at Safeway that smiles the depth of her soul every time I come in, and rekindles my faith in humanity.

It might be weird to say thank you not to a specific barbeque, but the act of barbequing, but I don't care. Thank you for giving me the Zen pleasure of stepping back in time hundreds of thousands of years. To the Marsh once again for being my refuge, my Walden Pond, the place I can always count on to wash away my worries. Thank you for reminding me of all the beauty in the world, no matter how much I forget.

To Mr. Estrada and Mr. Soderholm thank you for being the two teachers I've remembered and will continue to remember my whole life because you had the biggest impact on me. You both cared about your students to the point, that you taught them the best way they actually learn, not how bureaucrats thought they should learn. You are both the reason my critical thinking skills are what they are and I am eternally grateful.

Thank you to the earth for always providing whatever I need, even if I think it has disappeared. You give beauty, sustenance, life, love and everything else a human needs to survive and flourish. All you ask is to be taken care of, like we do. Through all the wars, famine, disease, natural disasters and people messing with you because they think they can; through all of that you have more than proven your resiliency. I only hope that all the generations that come after me are able to see the beauty in you that I see.

Thank you to my life, thank you to my life, thank you to my life. I am so grateful that I have made it this far, and I am very excited about everything that is still ahead. Thank you for proving on a daily basis I have the ability to not only surprise myself, but also to far surpass my expectations. I feel gratitude from the bottom of my feet, to the top of my head, to the deepness of my soul for everything and everybody that is in my life. Without you, I wouldn't be the person I am today. Synchronicities have become part of my life simply because my gratitude has become authentic. Thank you, thank you, thank you.

INTRO

Life is like trying to get up on water skis. If you want to ski, you have to let the boat do the work and pull you up. Your intent has to be there to get up on the skis, but you can't pull the boat no matter how hard you try. You just have to let it happen, you have to let it pull you. Much like life, the best we can do is move forward with intent and purpose while putting ourselves in what we think is the right place at the right time; but we still have to let it happen. What's supposed to happen, will only happen if we let it.

Challenges arrive when things aren't happening fast enough for us. When we've put all this hard work into something, that why on earth hasn't it bared fruit yet? We deserve it, don't we? Don't we? We try our best to be the best people we can, why hasn't it happened for us yet? When is it going to be our time?

The only thing I can say is we have to keep loving, striving, working, fighting and dreaming. The minute we forget about what we want out of life or what our dreams are, all those things trying to keep us down will succeed in their mission. If we're honest with ourselves and seek the truth that's all around us, we can succeed. Sometimes truth is screaming at the top of its lungs in our face. Will we listen, or will we mindlessly move forward, forcing things to happen because we see the person next to us being much more successful? Will we continue to try pulling the boat, forcing it to go the direction we want, believing we actually can? Or will we just relax, prepare the best we can, and let the boat take us where it's meant to take us?

Unhappiness can be derived from simply waiting on life to happen, thinking everybody else is more happy and successful than they actually are. This is a trap we find ourselves in when things don't work out as planned. We overcome this by constantly asking ourselves what we're thankful for. Instead of cutting ourselves down by only seeing how much more our neighbor has then us, we need to build ourselves up by realizing there are always people much worse off; and they wish they could be in the position we're in.

If life is all about perspective, then how we see life can determine what we get out of it. Do we look at life like it owes us something, or do we look at it and see all the beauty within it? The more beauty we see, the more it comes back to us. The more it comes back to us, the more thankful we are for what we have; causing the cycle to start all over again.

Right now you might be asking yourself, what does all this have to do with a boat pulling me up when water skis are strapped to my feet? What does a pleasure activity have to do with succeeding at life, accomplishing goals or even finding love?

We have to pay attention to what's happening, realize forces will appear more powerful than us if we try to muscle past them. We can put on skis, we can get in the water, we can even have friends cheering us on, including that cutie giving us the eye; but we can't make the boat pull us. However, if we put on the skis, relax and let life happen, the forces trying to keep us down won't seem so powerful.

When we're stuck and feel like we're going nowhere, we must ask ourselves if we're getting stuck in the mud of indecision and uncertainty. Is the overwhelmed feeling coursing through our veins so vivid because we're thinking of all the things we should be doing, instead of all the things we are doing?

When we trust the process and we let it work, we're allowing the boat to pull us.

PROLOGUE

"The smell of unbelievably juicy, melt in your mouth pork can bring the strongest man to his knees, not to mention the perfectly cured ham, the yellow mustard, the sliced pickles and the ooey gooey melted swiss cheese on that perfectly toasted bread, coming together to bring an ecstasy of taste to the tongue. It's a great thing to have the most amazing sandwich on the planet, in the birthplace of the people that came up with it only after immigrating to another country. Crazy world we live in."

This is what Jason read on the postcard, which he thought was odd because the reverse side had the most generic beach scene he ever saw. He smoothed back the tail of his hair which was a bit greasy from waking up, which usually wasn't an issue when his hair was in a ponytail; but his hair tie broke while he was sleeping and he needed to go the store to buy more.

Christina was still tossing and turning, not wanting to get up because of the late night she and Jason experienced. Of course a Netflix marathon will do that to a person. She rolled around for another minute or two in a nightgown top which consisted of one of Jason's old shirts when he was a lot heavier. He always thought it was sexy when she put on his shirts, it made it easier for him to see the deep burning passion behind her eyes.

"Jason?" Christina called out because she rolled over and felt the empty space on the bed next to her. "Where did you go sexy man, don't I get a good morning wakeup?"

"I'm in the living room, I'll be there in a minute honey," Jason answered as he imagined a Cuban sandwich because of the postcard he received out of the blue. Who could have sent it he wondered?

"I was walking to the kitchen for a drink of water, and this was slipped under the door," Jason stated as he walked back in the bedroom and showed Christina the postcard. She was still under the covers not wanting yet to see the light of day.

"What is this, somebody sent you a postcard?" Christina inquired with a curiosity that caused her eyebrows to rise. Her hair was as greasy as Jason's from having just been asleep, but hers was longer, brown and reacted better to the silk sheets on their bed.

"Yeah, no return address, just a description of a Cuban sandwich so vivid it made my mouth water immediately."

Still half asleep, Jason handed Christina the postcard. She tried very hard to focus because the writing on it was too small for anybody to read, let alone somebody just waking up.

"This does make it sound pretty amazing, even makes me hungry for one. Which says a lot because you've always been a much bigger fan of them than me," remarked

Christina. She was alternately wiping the sleep out of her eyes, and trying to read the very small, but very neat writing.

"Hello, you still with me?" Jason asked because Christina had been staring at the postcard for what seemed like five minutes. "You're really enjoying that description eh?"

"I was just thinking about this part at the end," Christina reflected as she pointed her unpainted fingernail at the end of the paragraph. "This part here, having a sandwich in a place that gave birth to the people that didn't come up with it until they immigrated somewhere else. I think it's some kind of code."

Jason quickly snatched the postcard out of Christina's hand which caused her to sneer at him a bit. "We just woke up, it's too early for that code talking stuff," Jason expressed as he rolled his eyes.

Christina and Jason had spent a lot of time lying low since taking down the President, because they knew anybody and everybody could be after them. The old man, Marty, the security guard from the tea party rally, any one of them. They hadn't produced one shred of material or evidence to take down anybody in the few years since it happened, and Christina was getting antsy. She read all kinds of magazines and newspapers which wasn't abnormal because Jason did the same thing, they were both addicted to information which was one of the things that attracted them to each other. The difference being

Christina was becoming obsessed. She told Jason she saw patterns in everything, and he noticed she was trying to outline them on the actual material. Christina's parents talked a lot about codes when she was a kid, and about how much information is hidden in plain sight. This worked great when she worked for Shane corp., but since she and Jason had been underground, Christina was trying to cling to anything because she felt like she gave up on her dream. She loved Jason, but sometimes Christina felt he was inhibiting her.

"I know I've been on edge the last few years being out of the game, and it's dragged up all this stuff from my childhood. My parents forced me to read specifically so I could tell them what I saw behind the words. It drove me nuts, and took all the fun out of a good book or article. I had it under control when I became an adult, and especially after I met you. Ever since we took down the President and I left my job, I haven't felt useful, I haven't felt like I mattered," lamented Christina, unloading on Jason who smiled back. He knew this was one of those times when the glowing light from his soul would greatly help the beautiful woman lying next to him.

"I love you babe, you're one of the most intelligent people I know. Words can't describe how much you do count and how much you do matter," Jason asserted as he put his arm around Christina and slid his fingers gently though her hair. "I'm sorry about the code talker remark. You know how I am when I wake up sometimes."

"It's ok babe. I'm just trying to move forward and feel gratitude for what life has given me, and I think I've been doing pretty well so far. I just need to be reminded of it from time to time, so thank you," Christina replied. She gave Jason a kiss that made it plainly true to the entire universe, that pure love was emanating from a small cottage tucked away in the trees of Northern California.

"I love you, and I'll tell you as often as necessary. So now that we have that out of the way," Jason quipped with a loving smile that always made Christina melt. "What do you think the postcard means?"

"I think somebody is telling us where they are, and that we should come find them. There's no return address, but from the description of the Cuban sandwich, they had to be talking about Cuba. The person who wrote it would have wanted this description to reach somebody who really understood it. Somebody who loves Cuban sandwiches just as much as them."

"Bryan?"

CHAPTER ONE

Succulent Cuban pork and boisterous 55 Chevys backfiring provided smells and sounds so thick you could cut them with a knife. The buildings looked like something out of an old movie, where time never caught up and the whole city was on hold. This is what Jason and Christina experienced when they walked through the streets of Havana for the first time. Both of them had been out of the United States a few times, but this was the start of a whole new adventure, and they both could feel it.

"The food from these street vendors smells insanely good, my mouth is watering," Jason uttered with a huge smile on his face.

"It does smell good, but let's not forget why we're here," replied Christina who loved food just as much as Jason, but knew he had a habit for getting sidetracked; she had to help keep him on point.

That postcard, how did it get to them when only a few people knew where to find them? Even if it was Bryan, what connections did he have to find where he and Christina were? Jason knew he could trust Bryan because they had been through so much together, at the same time he knew a lot was left unsaid.

"You still with me, it looks like you got lost in that unwieldy brain of yours and were floating away," wondered Christina with a caring, but nervous look on her face.

"How could Bryan have possibly known where we were, if he could find us who else could?"

"Something tells me we'll find out when we find Bryan. The way we do that is by following the synchronicities. That's what led us to take down the President, and that's what led us to a place that's been the home of so many dissidents and rebels over the years. Anyway, let's also try to have some fun, how often do we take vacations?"

"You're so right," agreed Jason as he leaned over and gave Christina a deep kiss that kept their souls intertwined, giving them the ability to delve into whatever the next step was going to be.

"We should stop and get something to eat, and maybe even listen to some music, I'm sure that will get our brains moving in the right direction," Christina mentioned as she steered Jason into the small restaurant on the corner.

"That's a great idea my mind always works better on a full stomach. Besides, there's no way I'd come here without roaming amongst the people," Jason shot back. He eagerly followed Christina into the Paladar with a joy he hadn't felt since the leader of the free world, became just another proven criminal and liar.

What became of Charles Bowman? Since a mysterious group made up of the world's most powerful people were hiding him, there was no telling where he was. The only thing Jason knew for certain was that they must enjoy this moment, at this point in time. Just like Ridell happened on them in the bar out of the blue, somebody could tap them on the shoulder in this neighborhood place, and it could be the beginning of the end.

The lights were dim, and the small crowd consisted of the usual lunch rush. When Jason and Christina sat down at one of the only ten tables in the place, he knew this was the spot they would plan their next move.

"They're here, do you want me to engage them or just wait to see if they lead us to Bryan?" asked the graying man in his early fifties behind the bar.

"Wait and see what develops, they might lead us right to him. We know Bryan is hiding somewhere in Cuba, but we can't openly look for him; we bourgeoisie Americans aren't exactly welcome here. Bryan being lured here by that postcard was just the first step. Using Jason's skills to our advantage is exactly the mind game I want to twist him up with. We have so many surprises in store for him amigo," stated the confident man on the other side of the phone.

The blue clock on the wall said 1pm, even though Jason thought it was only about 11. Jet lag was catching up with him. "Do you think we could buy some old baseball cards while we're here since everything is from the fifties, I'll bet they have some?"

"Are you crazy, we're still underground looking for somebody that doesn't want to be found," Christina responded, dragging Jason back to reality.

"What do you mean he doesn't want to be found, what about the postcard?" queried Jason with a smile because the love of his life was still pushing him to think after all these years.

"We only assumed the postcard was from Bryan, but what if it came from somebody who only wants us to think it was from Bryan?" asked Christina anxiously.

"Why didn't you mention that before we came all the way down here? Why are you bringing this up now, are you getting one of those feelings again?"

Just as Jason was adding fuel to a growing fire of an argument between two love birds, a woman in her late fifties walked up and spoke in perfect English with a perfected fake smile. "What can I get you folks? Sometimes good food can aid the decision making process."

"How did you know we're trying to make a decision?" Jason speculated as his antennae perked right up.

"I could hear you from the kitchen, this place isn't that big. I can show you some really nice postcards we have," replied the waitress who hoped these crazy white people would just order something and leave before her husband returned. "So are you going to order something or what?"

"Yeah hold on," retorted Jason. He was growing testy because the lady wasn't very welcoming to somebody who was about to be her customer. "We'll have a couple of

Cubanos with everything, and some Cuban coffee afterwards. We need some thinking juice." Jason winked at the lady to see if he could crack her hard exterior.

"Sorry I snapped, so many fishy white people have come through here in the last couple weeks. I don't know what to think anymore," answered the lady who was starting to sound more human, but still very guarded. "My husband and I run this place, he will be back soon. He's grown weary of all Americans because of how they carry themselves. He knows they are up to something, and said he'll do whatever he can to stop them."

"He sounds like a standup guy, and I'm sure you both just want to make some money so you can survive. The world needs more people willing to put in the hard work required to build something. Just out of curiosity, what kind of fishy people came in here?" Christina asked with a caring aura that was hard for anybody to resist because they felt her pure humanity.

"There were a couple guys in here the other day that I never saw before. They walked in and were very rude to my bus boy who was only trying to clear tables. They harassed him and asked him all kinds of questions."

"Like what?" Jason wondered, because he knew something important was about to be divulged.

"They asked where they could find the rebels, the atheist commies trying to bring down America; something you'd see straight off your Fox News."

The three of them had a good laugh. It's amazing the common ground that can be found when people laugh at obvious stupidity. "And what else?" Jason inquired, trying to get back on topic because he knew this was one of those times he must be present in the moment.

"The leader was the loudest and most obnoxious of the two, and looked like he'd kill the other if he didn't laugh at his jokes. Anyway, he starts asking if I know where to find a guy named Bryan. Besides the European tourists that come through here once in a while, I never met anybody named Bryan. He said they needed to find him because he hadn't shown up for work in a while, and were concerned about his well-being," explained the waitress who was starting to feel a little more at ease; maybe all Americans weren't the same she thought.

"Did they say what kind of work he was doing, how long he's been here, or how they knew he was here in the first place?" questioned Jason. He was starting to feel Bryan had something up his sleeve.

"The boss guy was vaguer than vanilla ice cream. All he said was that Bryan messed up, and caused some sort of fracture within his company by taking sides; which led somebody at the top to no longer be the boss."

This was starting to sound way too familiar. Christina and Jason were walking down the street in a country they had to sneak into. They randomly entered a small restaurant on the side of a rock strewn dirt road, only to find a waitress say some rude American customers were asking about the guy they risked coming out of hiding to locate.

"What else did they say?" Christina probed. She saw the wheels inside Jason's head were spinning. She also wanted to get to the bottom of this synchronicity. She knew it had to be happening for a reason.

"That was about it really. Oh, they did ask about postcards," revealed the waitress, trailing off as she walked back to the kitchen because the cook was yelling for her assistance.

Jason pondered for a moment as he looked around the room. On the walls were beautiful paintings for sale by local artists, along with pictures of some of the restaurants tastiest dishes, and awards they won for them. He thought it was weird that the register where people paid looked exactly the same as in any American diner.

"For somebody who is weary of Americans, they lay out their Paladares just like our diners," Jason blurted out with a skeptical glint in his eye.

"Maybe, since Cuba and America were so closely linked before Castro, it kind of makes sense. This place is stuck in the time before the revolution, because of the embargo they've had a hard time catching up to how fast society is changing," Christina fired back. She was trying to agree with Jason just enough, so he wouldn't get on one of his soap boxes.

Jason and Christina's stomachs began to growl because they hadn't eaten since the day before. The flight over had been long, especially since they had to fly out of Mexico City posing as a minster and his wife just to get into Cuba. However, they were here now, and if they were going to have any hope of figuring this out, they needed some nourishment.

"Your food is almost up, please accept these fried plantains in the meantime," pronounced the waitress as she set down a steaming plate of the most exquisite fried snack Jason had ever seen.

"Thank you, these look good," expressed Jason as his mouth began to water.

"Here's some sweet sauce to dip them in, but be careful, they're very hot." The waitress knew burnt tongues meant people couldn't talk as easily. Something inside was telling her to help this random guy who walked into her place searching for truth.

Jason eagerly grabbed a piece of a plantain and blew on it, which caused a lot steam to rise. "You can't beat fresh."

"Just don't injure your tongue, I might want to utilize that later," Christina sniped with a sexy look in her eye that made Jason do anything she wanted.

"Of course, as long as you use yours," Jason responded with a smirk.

Christina loved messing with Jason, because he completed her just as much as she completed him. The hard part was figuring out where to go from here, but that was also the exciting part.

As Jason was alternating between blowing on the plantains and slowly trying to eat them without melting his tongue off, Christina scanned the room. Showcasing local artists was nice, she wondered if they would get to meet any while they were there. Her eyes stopped when she got to the cash register Jason mentioned. Right beside it was a rack of postcards with one on the top looking very familiar.

"Jason, take that hot thing out of your mouth and look over there, by the register," exclaimed Christina with laser focus because she spotted something.

"I would never tell you to take something hot out of your mouth, unless it wasn't mine," chuckled Jason because the woman next to him never failed to turn him on.

"I'll bet," winked Christina with a sultry look that always made Jason melt. "See those postcards over there?"

With a steaming plantain hanging from his mouth, Jason looked to where Christina was motioning. "That postcard on the top does look familiar," pondered Jason as things started to click, causing the plantain to fall out of his mouth onto the floor.

Jason got up from his chair, not noticing his first step ground the plantain into the carpet under their table. He sauntered over and picked up the postcard. He looked at the picture and just shook his head.

"What is it honey?" Christina asked lovingly. She had seen this look on Jason's face before, it was the same as the one he had when he began his quest to bring down the world's powerful.

"It's this postcard, you see the picture? Look at this space on the back, perfect place for the description of a Cuban sandwich huh?"

CHAPTER TWO

"Do you think the six entities sent this to lure me out so they could finish what they started? Do you think Bryan is here and they can't find him?" theorized Jason. He was talking a mile a minute out of hunger because their sandwiches hadn't arrived yet.

"Maybe, could be the old man, could be any one of the faceless entities that make up the six," replied Christina. She got pretty worked up looking into them since Bowman went away, but knew that some good food would help them think more clearly. "They knew you'd come looking for Bryan. Once we find his trail whether they sent the postcard or not, I'll bet they'll try following us right to him."

Jason thought for a minute, yes, he cared about his friend, yes, he wanted to find him, but there was a chance he could lead the bad guys right to Bryan. Dilemmas were something Jason was used to, what he didn't know was what step to take next.

When all hope was starting to fade, the sandwiches arrived steaming and smelling so good, that if Jason died at that moment, he would be a happy man.

"Ahhhh, this is better," Jason declared as he took a big bite out of the Cubano, the swiss cheese oozing out the sides. "Food is just what I needed to think clearly, I know we can figure out this quandary now."

Jason knew Bryan had been in the game for quite a while working for Marty, and uncovered some big schemes; along with doing whatever Marty needed done. Bryan didn't question his tasks because Marty was the boss, and the boss was supposed to know what to do at all times.

After spending so much time and energy taking Ridell and Bill down, Jason knew Bryan needed some time to himself. He was always so focused on the task at hand, that Bryan couldn't see anything else; to blow off some steam was just what the doctor ordered.

Cuba was a place that accepted all people fighting for a righteous cause Jason thought. Even though Bryan wasn't directly running from anybody, Jason knew he'd want to be among people and a society that stood for justice, and against corporate control.

Cuba welcomed all manner of Communist, Socialist and other political prisoners that needed a place of refuge with like-minded people. Jason discovered this immediately upon arriving.

Bryan would have had to go undercover, which wasn't too hard in a place stuck back in time sixty years. For him to stay hidden however, Jason knew he needed friends. Even if Bryan made it on the island, there was no guarantee he'd be safe.

"Man this sandwich is good. Those Cubanos in New York were good, but nothing like this," Jason stated because he was almost done with his before Christina even finished half of hers.

"I'm glad I tied my hair back before I started eating this thing because food would get all stuck in there," remarked Christina. She was certainly having a moment of enjoyment, just not as much as her love that was sitting across from her. "So what's the plan?"

"I thought we could talk to some of the locals and see if they can point us in the right direction."

"That sounds good, but how do you know it won't be a trap we're being led into by some secret CIA agent or something that will rendition us to Guantanamo?"

"After all the stuff we pulled, they probably would send us there. Taking down the President can get some people pretty pissed off."

Out on the street it sounded like a parade going by, a soccer team celebrating a win or some holiday Jason wasn't aware of. He felt in the deepest part of his soul that he must go outside and see what was going on.

"Let's hurry up and pay for these, something tells me we have to be out there for this," Jason blurted out. He was starting to get one of those feelings again that Christina knew would lead them to their next risky undertaking.

"You know I'm never one to stop you when you have feelings like that," Christina loved the way Jason got so passionate, as long as there was a point to it. Somehow she always knew there was. "This is beginning to feel like that time we flashed back to the water park murder. Then when we came back to reality, Marty called and offered you a job in New York."

"That's true, so this has got to be leading somewhere right? We came to this Paladar, and had an amazing Cubano. We discover the postcard we received might have been purchased here, by some guys looking for Bryan. I'd say we're hot on the trail."

"You're so sexy when you're on a mission. I could have had any guy I wanted when I was growing up. After I met you under that Japanese maple, I knew then that you were the one for me, because you always go where your heart tells you; it's one of the most attractive things I can think of."

Christina decided she would pick up the bill this time because food was cheap in Cuba compared to the U.S., so she thought why not. The U.S. embargo had greatly cut off food and everyday goods from this small island only ninety miles from the mainland, a whole ninety miles away. Jason knew the situation had to change, before he or anybody else would be able to see the true freedom they all dreamed about.

After setting some money down on the table which included a very nice tip, Christina and Jason thanked the waitress in the Paladar for her hospitality.

"Thank you for your service, it's really nice to meet somebody that is so welcoming to people they don't know. Thank you and we will be back," Jason expressed to the mid-fifties waitress that he knew could cook anybody under the table.

"Thank you for coming in, we don't get too many Americans in here. When we do and they're as down to earth as you two, it really makes my day. That guy you were looking for, what was his name again?" inquired the waitress with a look on her face that said she really wanted to help.

"Bryan. We used to work together and I haven't seen him for a while," Jason replied. He was very curious where this was leading, as was Christina who was ready for some action because they were in the activist capital of the world.

"I don't know this guy Bryan, but those guys that came in, the ones that were rude and asking about postcards?" continued the waitress.

"That's actually what led us to this place," answered Jason.

"You better steer clear of them, they looked like trouble. However I can tell you and this lovely lady are meant to be here. I know a guy that could help in your search. He is American, very secretive, but trustworthy. He's helped me out of a couple of jams I got into with the government, and with the rebels. People don't like that I'm an independent businesswoman trying to eke out an honest living."

"Who is this guy?" Christina asked, feeling this was the start of their next step.

"I think he used to be CIA or something, he gives off the vibe of a tough guy with military training. He always seems to know what's really going on. He has uncovered illegal schemes that unscrupulous people pulled and brought them to justice, which is one of the reasons he helped me. Those guys looking for your friend are bad guys, trust me, I've been around. This Bryan guy must have really pissed them off somehow."

"I'd tell you what he did, but I don't want to implicate you, probably better you don't know," Jason quipped.

"You're probably right. Anyway, this guy goes by a pen name," divulged the waitress trying to give all her information before another customer walked in. She needed all the business she could get.

"A pen name, did he used to be a writer or something?" Jason asked very curiously, still wondering who this guy was. It wasn't every day that things fall into place, but he knew it happened a lot more often when you put yourself in the right place at the right time without knowing it's the right place and the right time.

"He might have written something, I'm not sure. He goes by the name Madman for Good."

"Really, that's his name? Nobody will find him with that name," reacted Christina very sarcastically because even though this was starting to sound too easy, she was intrigued at the same time. What else was she going to do she thought, take Jason home and be stuck always wondering if they could have found Bryan? If this was a trap that Moonsystems or the Six Entities was trying to lure them into, Christina didn't know; but she was really starting to feel it was worth their time to find out.

"He's always been nice to me. Even though he can be a little abrasive with the way he talks, I've seen him produce results. He once took down a corrupt government official who was pocketing money that was supposed to support poor families. The official was playing both sides, trying to be friends with Castro and the U.S. at the same time. Anyway, a Madman for Good is a new concept for me, so I thought I'd give him a try. I first heard about him through a friend who had issues with a guy who was some kind of fixer," exclaimed the waitress speaking a mile a minute because she didn't want anybody to walk in and hear her, but still wanted to help the nice young people standing in front of her.

"So a Madman for Good huh, that intrigues me too, I must say," retorted Jason who often thought of himself as a Madman for Good, but never fully took on the persona. He thought he was one when he took down a corrupt Congressman and then the President, but this was different. This guy was doing the same thing he and Christina were doing, only for longer; and possibly for hire.

"Where can we find this guy? He probably could help us with everything you just said," Christina queried because she wanted to get the show on the road. She had grown very anxious for action since she left Shane Corp., and didn't want to go back to only searching for coded messages in newspapers. She wanted to step into the real world and fight the good fight.

"You see all that commotion outside?" asked the waitress as she wiped sweat from her brow because the heat outside combined with thinking about the Madman for Good was stirring up her passion. He was a force to be reckoned with she thought. Maybe he could help these people find what they're looking for, while at the same time find what he's looking for.

"Yeah I see that. I thought it was a parade or something. What is going on out there?" Jason inquired with a happy but determined feeling that he hadn't felt since he decided to randomly take a trip. This led him to randomly finding a blog, and then because he trusted the process and let it work, he was led to Christina who helped him take down the President. Would this lead to something like that, who knows? The only thing Jason was sure of, he needed to check it out.

"It's a weekly protest and teach-in that one of the worker parties holds around here. You want to talk to the

Madman and see if he can help you? Walk right outside there and ask him yourself, he's about to step up to the microphone."

Jason and Christina thanked the waitress profusely and hurried to try to see the Madman. They walked outside and wove their way through the crowd, trying to catch a glimpse of the stage; which happened to be the back of a pickup truck that would make for a quick getaway if need be.

A man with a thick greying beard climbed into the bed of the truck, but before he could speak, Jason blurted out something he'll never forget. "Hey Madman, how good are you?"

"I'm really good, as are most people when it comes down to it. The fact that you showed up here today, means that things are finally coming together. Maybe this time we have a chance to take these bastards down, you with me Jason?"

CHAPTER THREE

The crowd was growing all around Jason and Christina who were starting to worry the government's secret police were going to come round everyone up, but the madman wasn't deterred.

"So how do you know my name?" Jason asked. He was very concerned this was yet another person portraying themselves as somebody they're not, just to get people to follow them. Also, had he been following them; and for how long?

"I know a lot about you. I know about Moonsystems and how you helped take down Bowman, that was some good work. Of course if it wasn't for that old man, things might have turned out differently," sniped the Madman trying to gauge Jason's reaction.

"That's true, but you still haven't answered my question. How do you know my name?" questioned Jason who was growing testier.

"Have you been following Jason and me for that matter? Do you know about everything we've done, because that's exactly what the people at Moonsystems claimed," Christina pried. She not only wanted to throw in her two cents, but also wanted to know if she should be worried.

"Well not following you per say, but just keeping up on your accomplishments. I like to follow up on people around the world who shake things up, and are willing to risk everything to bring accountability and end corruption. I keep track of different activists and people that make a difference, so I can see who is worthy of joining my cause."

"And what exactly is your cause?" Jason wondered. He knew this was leading somewhere because the hair on the back of his neck stood straight up. The intense heat and humidity was making the crowd miserable waiting for the guest of honor to speak. They had been waiting a long time for this rally to happen.

The Madman for Good used to be someone who followed everybody's guidelines of what a perfect citizen and productive member of society should be. His change happened when he woke up one day, and started asking himself what the hell he was doing. Was he becoming just one more pawn in the game of how badly can we screw over the little guy? Once he realized he didn't want to help the new breed of ultra-free market capitalism evolve, he had to change, and he had to help others change as well.

"My cause you ask, my cause is to bring as many like-minded people as I can together so we can finally demand some change. There is so much work to do, and the only way we have a fighting chance is if we grow our numbers; which requires me to do some recruiting. My goal is to show people that they don't have to put up with the same old thing. Things can and will get better. First they must believe its true, then they must go out and make it happen."

Jason stood there and thought for a minute. He was starting to sweat because Christina didn't tie the end of his braid tight enough. What was this guy's plan? Build a group big enough to put the "powers that be" on notice? Was he just building a cult of personality so he could use this group of people for his own nefarious interests? Jason knew that either option could be a possibility. Since he and Christina had learned a few things fighting the good fight, they decided to stay and listen because this guy might come in handy.

"If I don't go on stage now and start speaking, these people will take me down instead of the six entities controlling the whole ball of wax," insisted the Madman as he motioned for Jason and Christina to take their places for the speech, but be close by so he could talk to them afterward. He didn't want them to get lost in the crowd because he wanted to discover their motivations, and if they were authentically down for his cause.

"You think we can trust this guy, his words make him sound like he's down for the same cause we are of ushering in accountability and ending corruption, but I'm not sure. I'm nervous around people that have an answer for everything," Christina whispered gently into Jason's ear so nobody else could hear her. Of course with the crowd noise nobody could hear anything, even the two random guys in unassuming suits who were scanning the crowd.

"Trust him? What like the old man on the beach who just happened to be Marty's brother and friends with the

President because they were all dorm buddies in school? As long as we stay on our toes and keep our eyes and ears open, I think this guy can be useful in finding Bryan. Any more than that, we'll have to wait and see. We've followed our passion of conscious evolution to an adventure in Cuba, in order to find a friend that may or may not have sent a postcard after five years of no word. We need to play this one out, but don't worry we're here together," Jason responded as he gave Christina a deep kiss that always warmed her heart, and bear hugged her soul.

The Madman for Good grabbed the microphone for what was sure to be a rousing speech. Jason and Christina took their places by the truck so they were close, but could still look at the crowd to gauge reaction.

"My friends and fellow truth seekers, how you all doing today?" asked the Madman whose smooth voice welcomed the crowd like a cozy blanket on a cold day.

"Sounds normal so far," Jason remarked as his eyes widened at Christina like here we go.

"It does but remember until we know we can trust somebody, we can't trust anybody," Christina expressed in a very concerned voice. She knew that until they figured out this guy's motives, they could only trust themselves. "Let's see what this quote un-quote Madman has to say, see if it's an earned title, or just a marketing ploy."

Just as Christina was about to let out another snide remark, the Madman started to speak. "I've gathered you all here today for a specific reason, which I'm sure you're aware of if you've been following me on Facebook and Twitter." The Madman had built up his following mostly through social media, and specifically designed public spectacles; which proved he wasn't just words, but action, or so Jason thought.

"Enough buildup, get to it already," yelled a random guy in the crowd, who seemed to represent the entirety of the people there, who were all losing their glossy gazes and growing skeptical looks on their faces.

"I'll get to it, because I want us all to get to it. There are those fighting tooth and nail to keep up the status quo, people looking to privatize every resource we as humans need to ensure our survival for generations to come. I'm here to talk to you about that, and what we can do."

"He's beating around the bush, I hope this is building towards something," Jason seethed under his breath in Christina's direction.

"Whether it's good or bad, it's leading somewhere. Nobody calls themselves a Madman for anything unless they're relentless," Christina replied.

The Madman was scanning the crowd and noticed many people carrying signs for the different issues they cared about. Privatization was by far the most popular, and he knew faceless entities didn't like people who stepped out of line. He needed to know who was truly interested, and who was faking interest so they could tear others down.

"There might be a limit to their greed, and there might not be. What I can tell you though, is that I'm a relentless hunter and gatherer of unadulterated truth. Whatever ugliness lies behind the scenes, I'll be there to uncover it. Many politicians, appointed and elected officials all cower to somebody. Our goal is to find out who that somebody is, and bring them down so they can never hurt anybody again."

"Still sounding pretty vague, but at least he's getting closer to a point," Christina retorted who was trying to listen because she liked his philosophy. Now that she thought about it, he sounded familiar.

"How do we find these people who make huge profits off the cleanliness of the water we drink, the quality of the food we eat, the chemicals we buy and produce, and the thoughts we may or may not have in our heads? We start by realizing that to truly succeed we must all become "Mad People for Good." We must ensure unrelenting positivity runs through everything we do. Because although the people we're up against will stop at nothing to hold us back, we must show them that their power is illusory because we've allowed them to have it.

We must let go of the idea that all people are out to do us good, and also the idea that everybody is out to do us harm. Discernment is the key to all interactions. If we believed everybody in the world was out to get us, we might never trust anybody. If we want to build a worldwide coalition to end the destruction of our species, then we have to upend their worldwide movement. They might have bigger guns and more money at their disposal, but we have something much more powerful. We the people have the will to see them pay for what they've done. We have the will to see their false promises and silver tongues are just a means of gaining more power and control. We need to show them we have the real power because there are way more of us than there are of them."

Christina and Jason began looking around to see how the Madman's message was being received. Some Europeans were roaming the crowd, but most were local Cubans who needed something to light a fire under them; because no one had been screwed over more by both sides than them. They had a revolution and installed what they thought was the answer to American imperialism and control of the world.

The world shunned Cuba because the United States government made them. This caused the Cuban government to be focused on control, stamping out dissent, and firming up their grip on power by telling the people just enough of what they wanted to hear.

"You think this guy means what he says?" Jason asked Christina, no longer in a whisper because the crowd began to scream and cheer for the Madman who finally made a point they could get behind.

"I believe he does mean what he says, that it's possible to bring everyone together around a common cause that's in all their best interests. I believe he believes that," explained Christina who was going from skeptical to a little less cynical.

"So you're not totally on board, you think it's a line of b.s.?" Jason wondered.

"I've heard a lot of people say a lot of things, and most of the time it turns out the exact opposite of what they say. How can this guy be truly as good and passionate for collective uplift as he says? Or should I say as relentless in pursuit of positivity?"

Jason knew she might be right, but he noticed the look on her sun soaked face was the same as his when he thought he saw Aaron for the first time. Did Christina know this guy?

"The more we raise the issue of being treated like pawns and worker bees, the less smoothly it goes for the "elites". The less smoothly it goes, the less profit is made; the less profit that's made, the more lives that can be saved.

Once they see we've been reading between the lines and can spot what's hidden in plain sight, they'll realize we have the upper hand. Our purpose is to bring real people together." The Madman was staring directly at Christina with no attempt to hide himself. "I love you all. I love humanity, that's why I do this. That's why I'm a Madman for Good."

The Madman for Good then exited the back of the truck, walked up close to Christina to take one more look at her, before he was driven away by one of the vague looking men in suits that had been scanning the crowd.

Christina was in the front clutching Jason's hand very tight, scared to the point of almost pissing herself, but also excited and anxious like she had just seen a ghost.

"So you want to tell me what that was all about? Why was he staring at you like he was trying to tell you he loved you, and everything has been in preparation for saving humanity, and you?" inquired Jason who was starting to feel uneasy.

"I wasn't sure who he was at first, but then he said a few things so familiar I knew I had heard them before. Many people talk about the evils of privatizing resources so a few can make profit off the many, which is something I've always been down for putting an end to. When he looked at me I knew, he might have been wearing sunglasses, and that shaggy and greying beard made him look old and out of the loop, but I could tell he's still in the game. He was obviously trying to disguise himself, but then he lowered his sunglasses just enough so I could look into his eyes. Like he wanted to show me who he truly was, if only for a second before his driver sped down that back road over there," Christina fired back while pointing to the unmarked and heavily wooded road right behind them.

"You obviously feel like you know this guy. I've felt like I've known a lot of people, and then it turned out I was only relating to them because our beliefs and thought processes were the same. How can you say you know somebody through a disguise and words strong enough to stir a crowd, but just vague enough that he wouldn't have anybody chasing him? He didn't precisely say what the problem was or what he was going to do." Jason was concerned for Christina's state of mind because of her history of taking things to the absolute limit.

Christina stood there for a minute before she spoke. She knew she could trust Jason. Hell, he was the only man that understood all her quirks and eccentricities but loved her anyway. She slowly started to open her mouth to speak, but had a very dry tongue from the heat and the thoughts swirling in her head.

"I know that look, as if something is weighing on your mind. Just tell me," Jason whispered softly as he looked into Christina's soul to let her know he loved her and always would.

"That Madman for Good or whatever he's calling himself these days, I think he's my father."

CHAPTER FOUR

The Madman for Good, aka Jay Sherman always wanted to do the right thing, but sometimes there was a roadblock preventing his forward progress. He would question and question and question, and nothing seemed to ever come from it.

When the Madman met Julie, everything changed. Not only did he begin looking at everything differently, but now his endless questioning had a focal point that Julie helped to shape.

Julie and Jay were inseparable. They finished each other's sentences and seemed to complete each other where the other was lacking. This went on for several years until they married, and eventually had a baby girl named Christina.

"What do you mean the Madman is your father? I thought your parents were back in Michigan," pried Jason, a little concerned this was the start of another one of Christina's episodes. He also knew she would never tell a lie, even if it hurt.

"I mean he is my dad. I don't know how much clearer I can say it," stated Christina whose fuse was shortening.

"I didn't mean to upset you, I just think it's crazy that we traced some secret postcard that may or may not have been sent by Bryan, to a country we had to sneak into because of a travel embargo. Then all of a sudden we run into your father," asserted Jason whose love for Christina was always on display; especially when he needed to get to the bottom of so many different synchronicities.

"I'm sorry I didn't mean to snap at you, I'm just in shock. I could really use a joint right now, something to calm my nerves and help me think rationally. They also have some of the best rum in the world here, even though whisky has always been more our thing, and the green. I so wish I could imbibe right now."

"I feel you on that, but we're in a place where we don't really know anybody. Since the United States has one of the most feared prisons in the world here, we don't want to end up in it because somebody spotted the stoners who took down the President. Cuba might not have any extradition, but I'm sure the CIA or any number of other spy agencies both government and private would love to get their hands on us. We don't want to give them an excuse," retorted Jason a little scared, but feeling a surge of energy because he knew they were being led somewhere they needed to go.

Just as Christina leaned over to kiss Jason because it always grounded her with warm sustaining energy, a note fell out of her pocket.

"What's that?" asked Jason pointing to the crumbled up piece of notebook paper that tumbled out of Christina's pocket and onto the scorching hot asphalt below her feet.

The words "honey bear" were scrawled across the note that was lying on the ground. She started to cry as she picked it up. "What's wrong sweetheart?" Jason asked because he never liked to see a woman cry, let alone the one that made his soul sing.

"Honey bear is a nickname my dad gave me when I was young. I'd be playing with my toys in the living room and watching cartoons early on a Saturday morning, when my dad would come out and say, honey bear want me to cook you a special breakfast this morning?"

Jason just stood there and didn't say anything. Could this be true, could this guy really be her father? Or was it another ruse perpetuated by some random person that had been following them, and put this note in Christina's pocket to throw them off.

"So you think this was the Madman?" Jason inquired, trying to help them step out of the emotional mess they seemed to be sinking into.

"Yes. I think my dad the Madman slipped this into my pocket, for what reason I don't know," wondered Christina, stumped by what on earth the note could possibly say.

"Open it, aren't you curious, I sure am. You've told me a lot about your parents while you were growing up. How they pushed you to your limit in finding what they thought was the truth, while at the same time pushing you to find your own path.

You two must have had a falling out. Where was your mom in all this? Anyway, whatever this note says, I'm here for you. Something tells me it will give you some of the answers you seek."

Jason and Christina were on the same wavelength of finding truth and what was really going on. Now a clue was slapping them in the face saying, hey look at me.

"Can we go sit under that tree? I need some shade, the sun is making me sweat like a pig," revealed Christina. She just wanted to be comfortable while she was being shown what she needed to see.

"I always like to make you sweat, but usually it's followed by moans and joyful screams," Jason joked, trying to lighten the mood.

"That's true," replied Christina as a miniscule smile broke out on her face. "We haven't had an outdoor adventure in a while, and the woods over there would be perfect; but first this note."

The trees behind where the Madman's truck had been parked provided some shade, but not much from the sweltering Caribbean sun. Locals were roaming around as the crowd had pretty much dispersed. People actually seemed to be getting back to their daily lives, like a spontaneous protest hadn't just happened. Which seemed a little odd to Jason, but he was sure the answer would come in time.

Jason and Christina sat under a tall wispy tree that provided a rather sweet sound from the wind blowing through the small amount of leaves that were on it.

"So what does it say?" Jason persisted, almost as anxious as Christina to see what was said by somebody who claimed to be her dad.

"Hold on, hold on. Don't get your panties all in a bunch," Christina jeered. She was trying to regain her composure, and crude sense of humor that always made Jason fall in love with her all over again.

"I love when your panties are in a bunch, but only when they're crumpled up on the floor," Jason chuckled with a look in his eye that made Christina tingly.

"Ok, ok; plenty of time for that later." Christina gave Jason a look back that said I'm going to tear you up, but not now.

"Are you going to read the note, or are we just going to eye fuck each other all day?"

"I'm getting to it, hold on." Christina opened the note and began to read. "Dear honey bear, I know it has been a long time since we've seen each other, and I'm very sorry for that. I abandoned you when you needed me most, and it's been the biggest regret of my life. I've spent the last bunch of years wracking my brain about how I could make it up to you, and then it came to me. Hello to Jason by the way☺."

"How does he know me, I've never even met the guy, I've barely heard you talk about him at all," Jason exclaimed. He was now very intrigued because this note was the beginning of something that would take them exactly where they were needed to go.

Christina kept reading. "I can explain everything if you and Jason will meet me. I know a safe place where we won't be watched or recorded. Follow the dirt road you saw my truck drive away on. About a half mile down, there is a road on the right hand side you want to take. Follow that for a few miles, until you get to a stand of four trees that look unnatural because they're all growing together; but trust me, they're very real.

Once you get there, a small trail right behind it will lead down a hill and eventually to a cabin with a chimney on top. You'll know it when you see it, there's something on the side only you would know about. Hope to see you two soon. We have much to discuss and catch up on. Love Pop."

"That was quite a note. What do you think we should do? Should we follow the path he laid out for us?" questioned Jason who didn't want to make a move without Christina's input. He didn't want anything to come between them. He couldn't handle any more time apart from her, and neither could she.

"Yes, I think we should go. We've been following synchronicities since we met back up after you randomly answered that blog post. It led us not only into each other's arms, but also to take down the leader of the free world. We've made it this far because we've followed the signs in front of us. Sometimes I've taken that to an extreme, but that's why I have you to balance me out," Christina exuded with as much honesty as she could provoke.

"Well, that's it then. It's so hot out here. Let's grab a couple bottles of water for the walk. I don't want to get so dehydrated before we get there that we don't see somebody following us. We have a history of being watched," exclaimed Christina who never spoke truer words.

The Trafficante liquor store existed for the traveler that didn't want anybody to know what they were buying, or for what reason. Cuba had been the home to countless militants, activists, radicals and revolutionaries since long before Castro. Its history would dictate that such a store existed.

Jason and Christina walked in the front door, which was only a couple hundred yards from the tree they were sitting under. Customers were milling around the aisles trying to decide what kind of munchies they wanted. Most of the stuff looked old and outdated, very much like the bodegas in America. When Jason grabbed a couple bottles of water out of the cooler, he was relieved they were ice cold.

"This water is just what we need. Is it really that hot outside, or is it just me?" Jason quipped with an evil smirk as he and Christina walked up to the register.

"Oh it's just that hot outside," volleyed Christina as she gave Jason an equally evil smirk that caused them both to laugh out loud.

A few people turned around to see what was so funny, but when they saw it was just some American tourists being dumb, they went back to finding their temporary happiness.

"That will be one dollar," barked the grizzled early sixties Cuban man whose untrimmed beard was scraggly, because he always had something more important to do.

Christina reached into her sweaty pocket and pulled out a very crumpled and soggy bill and gave it to the man behind the counter.

"Sorry about that, sometimes these things get pretty messed up," Christina acknowledged wanting to come off as the friendly person she really was. She knew the calmer she stayed, the clearer she could think.

"That's okay, in this heat I've seen it all," relayed the store clerk who spoke with a Cuban accent, but in very good English as he put the money in the drawer.

"I was just curious," inquired Jason as Christina worried about what might come out of his mouth. "Do you know anything about the guy that spoke on the back of that truck? He was really inspiring. We'd like to find him and ask him some questions."

"That guy, you don't want to mess with that guy. He showed up about twenty years ago, said he was running from somebody or something I can't remember now. Since Cuba has been refuge to all sorts of people in the last half century, I didn't think anything of it. Shortly after he arrived, all these shadowy looking people appeared asking what was he up to and what his goals were," declared the store guy with fear in his eyes.

"It's okay, you can tell us, what happened then?" asked Jason because his inner journalist was begging to come out after lying dormant for so long.

"There isn't much more to tell, I don't want to get involved with somebody like that. I don't want to end up in Guantanamo. Americans don't like us already. I don't want to get them more upset by helping a guy they're chasing. I've said enough. You two should leave now," responded the clerk, more nervous than he was before.

"No problem, we don't want any trouble. Do you know where we could find him?" wondered Jason who needed to know. He felt deep down that this would not only lead to Christina's father, but would also lead them to Bryan.

"I don't know too much, except for rumors of a hideout in the woods. I'm not going to look for it though, with my luck some no named death-squad would disappear me.

Then I couldn't get lovin from the woman that makes my soul sing; just like your lady does for you."

"Thank you for your help, stay strong. These people can't win forever," Jason dispatched, channeling his inner Guevara.

Christina led Jason out of the store so fast, they didn't notice the two people looking at magazines had been spying on them the whole time.

"Where do you think they're going, do you think they're going after the Madman?" asked the dark sunglass wearing forty year old man near the register.

"I don't know. You asked me to keep tabs on them with my contacts and I have. What more do you want from me?" inquired the clerk who was obviously being pressured.

"We'll let you know when we've had enough. Those are some of the most dangerous people in the world. They've messed with our operations enough already. We can't let them do it again."

Jason and Christina walked along the path looking for the right hand turn the note mentioned. It seemed like they had been walking forever because of the sweltering heat and humidity, but in actuality was probably about twenty minutes.

"Are we there yet, I don't see any evidence of a road," queried Jason. He was starting to feel they were being led on a wild goose chase.

"Wait, what is that up there?" pointed Christina to an odd looking rock on the right side of the road.

They walked up to it, barely able to make out a message written on the front. "What does it say, I can't read it," asked Jason very curiously.

Christina bent down to look and saw the words honey bear written on the side. The nickname was in barely legible writing produced by some kind of plant or other natural substance in the area, because it definitely wasn't a pen or pencil.

"It says honey bear," read Christina who looked at Jason to see what he thought.

"This has to be a clue, it's too coincidental."

Christina looked behind the rock and saw a bunch of needles and branches had been piled up to conceal something. She motioned for Jason to help her clear some of it so they could see what it was.

"What do you think is back here?"

"I don't know, but we'll find out sooner if you help me."

Just as Christina uttered those words, she saw a small road the overgrown brush had been hiding, but very much still travelable by truck.

"This has to be the way, my dad always covered his tracks well; something he always trained me to do as a kid."

Just as Jason and Christina started walking down the path they heard some voices.

"Where did they go, do you think they know we're after them? They've never been to Cuba before and are randomly walking through the jungle to find somebody they may or may not know," wondered one of the men who had interrogated the clerk back in the liquor store.

"We've been tailing them for the last few years. They found their way all the way down here, they must be up to something," the senior operative insinuated.

The voices sounded very close so Jason and Christina hurriedly put back as many of the branches as they could, and hid in a nearby bush.

"They got to be close, I can smell them."

"Shhh," whispered Jason trying to keep them both quiet so they wouldn't get caught.

"What's this rock doing here, that's kind of weird," observed the junior operative.

"Well, rocks have been here for millions of years, what's next you going to ask me what a tree is for?" bantered the senior operative very sarcastically. "Come on, let's keep going." With that the two mysterious men continued to walk down the dirt road.

"That was close," Christina whispered to Jason as they got back on the path and continued walking. "I could really use a joint right now, especially after that. Maybe my dad will have some good stuff when we get to his house."

"Your dad smokes weed?" Jason asked very surprised.

"I know he used to when he was younger. But since he's been absent from my life for a long time hiding in Cuba, I wouldn't be surprised."

The next hour was long, neither Jason nor Christina said a word. They alternated taking sips of water and watching their feet move forward in a hypnotizing cadence. It almost prevented them from seeing the four trees growing together right in front of them.

"Look, I think those are the trees he was talking about," Jason pointed to the abnormally tall and strange looking trees that were all growing together.

Christina hurried to catch up, and saw there was a path right behind the trees that led down a pretty steep hill, but one they could manage. "I think the path is that way, leading down that ravine. This reminds me of those crazy hippy trails going down to the beach. College Cove and

Baker Beach were always my favorites, sometimes you had to bushwhack; but when you finally made it to the beach, you were always blown away no matter how many times you had been there." Christina was filling up with energy again like she was when Jason and she met back up.

"Well then let's go, this is yet another synchronicity we must follow, they haven't steered us wrong yet."

The hillside was a little soft, but rocks were stuck into the cliff acting as a crude staircase. From the footprints in-between them, Jason and Christina could tell this path had been used recently.

After about twenty minutes of switchbacks, they finally got to the bottom of the ravine. There stood a small cabin with a chimney protruding from the top just like the note said. Christina ran up, not noticing Jason was having a hard time catching her; the love of his life was presently finding her destiny.

Christina saw a big Winnie the Pooh that had been carved with a chainsaw, and hung by one of the windows as a display.

"This has got to be it, I'm sure of it. Winnie the Pooh was my favorite cartoon growing up, that's why my dad was calling me honey bear," Christina explained excitedly, anxious for the next step.

"You're thinking of what the next step is going to be aren't you," Jason theorized.

"How did you know?" wondered Christina with a smile.

"Come on now, after all we've been through, you're asking me how I know you so well," Jason replied, trying to reassure the love of his life that he'd always be interested in the person she was, and the person she'd evolve into. "Aren't you going to knock?"

"Don't get you panties in a bunch."

"Haven't we been through that before?" sniped Jason with a smile that conveyed he wanted nothing more than to make the beautiful woman in front of him scream out in ecstasy. However, they had more important things to do at the moment.

"Hold on I'm going."

"I know, it's okay, it really is. Just knock."

The two of them walked up to an old rustic door that Jeremiah Johnson himself would have been proud of. With sweat rolling down her face Christina gave a big knock, very nervous about who might be on the other side. After what seemed like an eternity, the door creaked open and a man came into view.

"Honey bear, you made it."

"Hi dad."

CHAPTER FIVE

As if being in a communist country on the list of state sponsors of terror wasn't bad enough, seeing her dad after so many years was almost too much for Christina to handle.

"You coming in, or are you just going to stand there with your mouth open?" sniped the Madman, who very lovingly wanted the daughter he missed to once again be a part of his life.

"Yeah I am, I'm just a bit in shock," expressed Christina who was having a million emotions flow through her all at once. "This is Jason by the way."

"Hello sir, it's nice to meet you." Jason nervously stuck out his hand, but was quickly put at ease because of a hearty handshake that conveyed mutual respect. "Quite a place you got here."

"Thank you, I've been working on it for some time. It's nice to have a place tucked away, where you can only be found by those you want to be found by. Call me Jay."

The three of them walked inside the cabin and shut the heavy door, or maybe it just seemed heavy considering the emotion of the moment. Jay motioned for them to sit at the handmade wooden table sitting in the middle of his modest kitchen. He put a kettle of water on the range for tea.

"So why all the secrecy, and why after all these years did you want to meet up with me? I thought about you so much when you left. You have missed so many of my life's experiences. There are so many things I want to tell you," Christina blurted out. She was doing her best to keep her composure, but the emotional roller coaster she had been on was coming to a head.

"All that will come in time." Jay didn't want to divulge too much right away. In a world of mysterious worldwide conspiracies, you couldn't be sure what to believe or who to trust; even if they were your own flesh and blood.

The cabin was like something right out of a novel. Simple and cozy with a smell of wood polish, potpourri and firewood from the wood stove; which seemed strange to Jason considering how hot it was outside.

"So what's up with the protesting, how long have you been leading those?" Jason inquired not wanting to sound imposing, but when you randomly see your girlfriend's father after randomly following a secret postcard to a random country you've never been to before, the brain naturally has lots of questions.

"I've been doing those for a while, even more since I left the states." Jay anxiously waited for the water to boil. He knew the energy to fully articulate his thoughts would only come once he had some tea in him. "It's quite a different story down here, life is so different."

"That's true, the mixture of poverty and natural beauty is unlike anything I've ever seen," acknowledged Jason who was excited because he was starting to feel that this was no accidental meeting.

"You get a great snapshot of humanity when the extreme from one side, fights the extreme from the other side, while keeping everyone else in the middle from coming together."

Tracking through the woods to find her dad's secret hideout, feeling he was hiding something once she found him; Christina watched the whole scene play out in her head.

"I have a question," interjected Christina, interrupting Jason and her dad's back and forth about the problems with a sixty year embargo. "After the protest you stuck that note in my pocket, how did you write it so fast? I saw you speaking, you stopped and talked to somebody for a minute, walked close to me and then you sped away in that truck. How did you have time? How did you know we'd be here?"

"Come on babe let the guy ease into it. It's been a long time," exclaimed Jason who knew that no amount of comforting would make Christina feel better until she got her answers. He wanted to comfort her anyway because he loved her that much.

"It's okay, I know I have a lot of explaining to do," retorted Jay whose mind was spinning a million miles a minute.

Jason was beginning to see where Christina got it from. The tea kettle started to whistle, so Jay got up from the old wooden chair he was sitting in and turned off the burner on the stove. He grabbed three mugs out of the cupboard, while looking out the window to see four of his armed guards patrolling the perimeter.

"So, you going to start explaining? What's all that security outside, who are you?" Christina seethed. She knew exactly who she was talking to, but wanted to know who the person she previously knew as her father had become.

"Ok ok," Jay answered with a slight smile. He knew his daughter was someone he could be proud of once he got to know her more than he already did.

Jay put three mugs on the table, one of which was a Winnie the Pooh mug meant for Christina.

"I've been following your exploits for some time now. I saw how you took down the President, that had to feel good to root out corruption at that high a level," Jay divulged, trying to start off light and loving. "There must have been a lot of people after you. Did they ever find his plane?"

"I don't think they did, at least it wasn't talked about on the news or social media. Jason and I were laying low for a while, trying to stay under the radar until the dust settled. When you take down the leader of the free world however, the dust never really settles, it just kind of re-accumulates."

"So how did you find your way to Cuba, I still want to know the answer to that question," inquired Jay already knowing the answer. Jason wanted to prove to this man that he was worthy of his daughter, but he knew better than to get in the middle of something that had been brewing for some time.

"Jason and I woke up one day and discovered somebody slipped a postcard under our door." Christina was happy to see her dad, but still cautious about revealing everything too quickly; after everything that happened to them so far, her trust level was pretty low.

"You traveled all the way here because of some postcard with a generic beach picture on it," Jay questioned. His antennae went up because he didn't believe in coincidences, and believed everything happened for a reason.

"Yeah, but I never mentioned a beach picture," Christina realized. "Jason had a partner named Bryan when he worked for this magazine in New York."

"Oh yeah, the one that he was working at when he took the Congressman down?"

"Yes that one," Jason responded, very proud of his accomplishments, but also very curious. "How did you know that?"

"They have media down here too. It's much harder to get when you don't have an open internet, you have to use all sorts of proxy servers so the government doesn't spot you, but it can be done."

The sun was lazily hanging in the sky, waiting for its final descent which was sure to produce colors of unimaginable richness. Jay didn't have much time to enjoy them however. He always had to stay inside with a bunch of guns and trusted people around him.

"Bryan had been chasing Congressman Ridell for years with no success, and really needed a break after he and Jason finally brought him down," Christina revealed with a growing energy. "So Bryan called and told Jason he was going away for a while."

"How did that lead you here to Cuba?" Jay persisted. He was pretty sure of the answer, but wanted it spelled out.

"While in New York Jason grew very fond of Cuban sandwiches. He always liked them before he arrived, but they made them really good in New York. Having been in the Big Apple longer than Jason, Bryan grew quite fond of them as well."

Jason and Jay looked at each other, thinking of how comforting a good Cubano was. "Hey if you like them that much, I know a great little place that makes them. It actually isn't far from where I was speaking."

"Yeah, we know; we just finished eating there when we heard a crowd gathering outside and asked the waitress what was going on. She said the Madman for Good was holding a rally and always had good things to say, so we should go out and hear him," Jason interjected who wanted back in on the conversation. He always loved talking about food.

Christina and Jason sat there and stared at each other, they knew the person sitting across from them wasn't telling the whole truth. "So again about the postcard," Jay hammered. He knew this was leading somewhere, but wasn't sure if he'd like the answer.

"Yeah sorry," Christina acquiesced who wasn't really sorry, but knew her dad was holding something back, just as she was. She truly felt at that moment that she was her father's daughter. "Bryan called Jason up and said he needed a break after taking down the Congressman, Jason thought nothing of it; besides the fact that he wouldn't be seeing somebody he grew very close to for a while."

"And the postcard?" Jay repeated because he knew Christina was good at going off on tangents because he invented the act.

"Jason got up that morning to get a glass of water, and saw it slipped under the door. Written on it was one of the most beautiful descriptions of a Cuban sandwich he ever read. Everything from the toastiness of the bun, down to the juiciness of the pork and ham, the tanginess of the pickle and mustard, and then the way the swiss cheese melted, you could totally picture it."

Jay looked at Jason and realized they were both picturing Cubanos, and smiled at each other because their love for them knew no limits.

"Cuban sandwiches are good, I eat them at least a couple times a week," remarked Jay with a grin because he had the man who shared his love for his daughter and his love for Cubanos sitting next to him. He was feeling things were now possible, kind of like when Jason was open but didn't know where to go and randomly met Christina.

"So Jason is reading this Cubano description, and really loving it, but not thinking more of it than that. He brings it in the bedroom to show me, because he thought it was weird to receive something with no return address when we were underground. Nobody was supposed to know where we were."

Some Grateful Dead switched on and a slight buzzing sound was heard during this impromptu family reunion. "What is that sound? I see you have guards out there, which I'm sure will be explained in time. But what was that, is somebody else here?" wondered Christina a little startled.

"Yeah, but don't worry. It's just my good buddy trimming some of the finest weed I've been able to grow since I've been down here. He really knows his way around a garden," Jay shot back as he winked at the both of them.

"See I told you, my dad would have some weed. I was just telling Jason on the hike in, that I could really use a joint," blurted Christina as the three of them shared a smile and a feeling of mutual admiration and respect. Even if they weren't 100% comfortable with sharing everything yet, they knew they would get there.

"Cool, I can't wait to try some. I haven't had any great weed since I was in New York with Bryan. He always seemed to have the best stuff," Jason mentioned with a slight feeling that something was about to happen that he couldn't explain, so he just decided to roll with it.

Christina didn't want to break up this moment, but wanted to get things back on track because they still had a mission. "So, Jason comes into the bedroom to show me this postcard."

Jason knew this was leading somewhere so he piped up, "I love Christina more than anything in the world. We're on this island for a reason. Tell him about the postcard sweetheart."

Christina lovingly looked at Jason, knowing she was loved for all that she was, and was reminded of it on a daily basis. "Ok ok, the postcard." Christina took a drink of tea. "So Jason brings in this postcard and starts talking about the Cubano description; I asked him to show it to me because there was probably some coded message in it. Jason reminded me of problems that began sprouting up again with seeing patterns in everything. Thanks dad."

"Sorry about that, I only wanted the best for you."

"We'll talk about that later. Anyway, I looked at the postcard, and agreed with Jason that it was a very detailed description of a Cuban sandwich. Then I noticed a line at the end about how amazing it was to be in a place that birthed a people who immigrated to a completely different country to invent this food," Christina relayed to her dad just to gauge his reaction.

"Sounds like you're hot on the trail," inferred Jay, anxious to see what else his Honey Bear figured out about the postcard.

"It was the exact story of Cubanos. Since they were first made in Miami, I knew Cuba had to be the place."

"Okay that makes sense, but what else? Are you saying you risked coming out of hiding, and traveled all the way here because of a description of a sandwich? I thought you didn't like them as much as Jason."

"I don't, but I knew who did, Jason's friend and partner Bryan. He was somebody who had been in the game for a long time, and knew how to write coded messages."

"I knew that if Christina was right and this was Bryan, he'd only contact me if he wanted to be found, or if he needed help. That's when Christina and I came up with cover identities, made our way into Mexico, and then boarded a flight here. Marty helped bury our true identities so much, that it would be hard for anybody to catch us," Jason chimed in, wanting to prove to Jay he was worthy of his daughter.

Christina was watching Jason with admiration because he wasn't only sticking up for her, but trying to earn respect from her father at the same time. She knew that some special play time was just how she wanted to reward Jason, but that would have to wait. A sudden thought appeared that she couldn't ignore.

"We made our way down here because we thought his friend might be in trouble. Since neither of us had been here before, let alone been on any kind of vacation in a long time, we thought it sounded like a good idea. There's just one thing that's bothering me," wondered Christina with a very puzzled look on her face.

"What's that?" wondered Jay with complete attention to the words that were about to spill from his daughter's lips.

"Earlier, when we started talking about the postcard you said oh yeah, the one with a generic picture on it, how would you know that?" inquired Christina starting to worry something not right was going on.

"Honey bear, there's a few things I have to tell you. I've been on the run for quite some time. Here in Cuba it's pretty safe to hide from the United States, or should I say it's somewhat easy to blend in. Anyway, I followed your experiences and achievements. I have hacker friends do things I need done." Jay shot Christina a smile, and she winked because she also had hacker friends. "I've been keeping tabs on you for a while, so I could still feel like I was part of your life in some way."

"You were keeping tabs on me, why didn't you just pick up the phone?"

"I was scared and didn't know what to say. Keeping tabs on you kept me close. Once I realized my daughter and this great guy were inseparable, I started keeping tabs on him too."

"You were keeping tabs on me?" Jason stammered with much surprise.

"Yes, but only with the best intentions in mind. I wanted to know you, like I knew her; that way if I ever met back up with Christina, I'd know what drives her."

"That sounds reasonable to me, but continue, sounds like there's more to this story," stated Jason who took a big sip of tea, which was now cold, but provided just enough energy to keep him on point.

"I wanted to meet you and Christina, but I didn't know how, and then it hit me. Put something in code that only she would understand. Since I knew you'd be with her, as any man who worships my daughter should, I put in the clue linking to your friend. Yes Christina, I sent the postcard."

The three of them just sat there, not sure what to say. A thousand bombs could have gone off, but none of them would have noticed because their minds were focused on what was in front of them. Jason wanted to always be with Christina, and she always with him. Since they were both seekers of the truth, they knew they couldn't ignore a message that was obviously meant for them. After everything they'd been through to this point, they didn't know where to go, except to keep moving forward.

"This is almost too much for me to take. You lured us down here with some fake postcard telling us through a coded message that Bryan was in trouble, just because you wanted to say hello? Again, why couldn't you just pick up the phone like a normal person? I hope you have an untraceable satellite phone like we do for those kinds of situations." Christina fumed at her dad for not being truthful, because she knew they weren't lured there just because he wanted to say hello.

"Yes, but I had a good reason," replied Jay as calmly and lovingly as he could.

"I sure hope so." Christina was overcome with emotion because a zillion thoughts were blasted through her head all at once. She and Jason knew what the cure was. They both had the same intellectual affliction of over activity of the mind. "What about some of that weed you mentioned earlier? Is your friend trimming some of it in the other room or what? Have him bring some out. I'd love to meet him and smoke. If I needed it when I was reading that note you snuck in my pocket, I really need it now."

"Yes some good herb would help ease the current situation," related Jay. He smiled because he knew it was a special moment when you smoke a joint with your daughter, and connect on an intellectual level. He wanted this moment to last forever, as he knew there were great things in store for them all.

"Hey man, can you bring some of that stuff in here? I think we all could use a safety meeting. I don't think any of us are feeling quite safe enough," Jay yelled into the other room as Jason just smiled at Christina, thinking it was pretty cool that Christina's dad used some of the same phrases as they did.

As the tension broke, and the thought of imbibing some good weed entered into the minds of the trio, they got a fourth. Jay's friend came out of the back room with a big tray in his hands. It was mounded over with some of the stickiest, stinkiest and most beautiful buds Christina and Jason ever laid their eyes on.

Sunlight poured through the window, blinding Jason and Christina from seeing the face of Jay's friend until he set the tray down on the table.

"Holy shit, Bryan???"

CHAPTER SIX

If there was ever a time the beautiful island of Cuba would lead to answers, then now was the time. Jason and Bryan parted ways some years ago, but it was past time to reestablish their connection.

"Hey Jason, how you been? It's been a long time," Bryan asked as he and Jason shared a caring but curious hug because they both didn't know what to expect.

"I'm good man, I'm here with Christina, so life isn't too bad," replied Jason. He gave his love a kiss on her forehead to remind her they had a lot to be thankful for. "After you left, I drifted around for a while looking for ways to take down Moonsystems, and to find out who was paying the Congressman. I randomly met up with Christina in California because I followed what was true to my heart."

Jason and Bryan looked at each other without saying a word. Their friendship knew no bounds when they were together in New York. Now that they were both in a foreign country that the United States didn't particularly like, they knew this had to be leading to something big.

As the sun began to set, a deep pink and orange hue shimmered through the giant front window of the cabin. Jay always needed a beautiful place to end his day in peace, and with the beautiful surroundings of the most secluded place he could find, he knew it was the perfect place to set up shop for the next step.

Christina was witnessing two old friends who needed some alone time, so she motioned her dad to the front porch where they could enjoy a nice joint and catch up themselves.

"Come on dad, let's leave these two alone. I'm sure they have a lot to catch up on, just like you and me," Christina expressed with an admiration and love for her dad that never dissapeared. She had her own thoughts because she was now an adult, not some kid he could order around anymore.

"Sounds good to me, we can catch the sunset on the porch. Let me grab some of the good stuff Bryan just trimmed so we can have a safety meeting of our own." Jay grabbed a cd case from the table to roll on, and some of the super stinky nugs from his stash.

As Christina and her dad exited the French doors onto the porch to sit in two of the world's most comfortable deck chairs, Jason began to speak. "So what's up man, what happened to you, how did you end up in Cuba?"

Bryan didn't want to totally blow his cover, it had been a long time since he had seen Jason and he wanted to tread lightly. "I left New York because I needed a change of scenery. Ridell and my brother Bill were in jail, and I didn't know if their higher ups would send secret henchmen to come find me. I came here because it's a place that's always supported revolutionaries and activists of all stripes, especially ones the United States aren't fond of; it seemed like a good place to go, and then there was the delicious food."

Jason shifted around in his chair causing the wooden floor beneath his feet to creak like a teenager sneaking into the house after curfew. "I want to tell you what led me here," blurted Jason who didn't know what to expect, only that he needed to be here at this exact moment. "So if you can roll a joint I'll tell you how I came down here, and you can fill in the rest of your story."

Bryan put some buds into the grinder he kept on his trimming tray for whenever he needed to imbibe. Since he knew his joints were 1000 times better than Jason's pregnant ones, he knew this safety meeting would put everything more in focus. As Bryan finished rolling the doobie with ease, he grabbed a lighter to start it off and handed it to Jason like a microphone to speak into.

Jason took a big puff, and as he exhaled he started talking with a raspy voice. "I woke up early one day and went to the kitchen for a glass of water. I walked by the front door, and saw a postcard somebody must have slipped under the door; which I thought was weird because nobody was supposed to know where Christina and I were."

Bryan grabbed the joint from Jason's outstretched hands and took a puff of his own before he answered. "That's something I wanted to talk to you about." Bryan took another big hit and passed it back to Jason. Through the cloud of smoke that just left his lungs, Bryan continued.

"When I came to Cuba, I didn't know anybody; I didn't even really know the language. I knew some basic Spanish to get by with, but not enough to help me melt into the background."

"So how did you run into Christina's dad, she hasn't seen him for almost twenty years?" Jason inquired because he got the feeling this interaction was leading to the next big mission.

"Like I said I didn't know anybody, so I went into a little café because they advertised that they made the best Cubanos in town. I felt like a good place to start was filling my stomach with something I liked very much," Bryan reminisced as he and Jason started picturing Cuban sandwiches. If the scene was a cartoon, bubbles would be above their heads with floating Cubanos inside them.

Things started to click for Jason, but he wanted Bryan to fill in the blanks. "Then what happened?"

"As I'm sitting there anticipating my food, they bring out some fried plantains because the wait was longer than the lady expected. I was hungry enough to eat a horse, but it was a nice gesture none the less," remarked Bryan who saw that Jason was happy to see him, but knew his former best friend was in truth seeking mode and needed some answers before they could fully reconnect.

"When did Christina's dad come into the picture?" Jason persisted while taking two big drags off the doobie before passing it back.

"Just as the waitress walked away from my table after setting the plantains down, a guy sits down at the table next to me. He orders food in perfect Spanish, even though you could tell he was American from his bad accent. After he was done ordering, I leaned over and said, "what's up?" I hadn't seen anybody that looked even remotely American since I stepped on the island, at least ones that didn't seem like secret agents.

We started talking about sports and the weather. You know the usual ice breakers. Once he felt comfortable, he told me that he came to Cuba some years back because he was investigating a guy named Bill who was Washington's best fixer."

"That's crazy. You left the country to get away and immediately find somebody who is investigating your brother?" Jason questioned as his ears perked up.

"Tell me about it. After this guy fills me in on investigating my brother, I told him how a friend and I just took him down, along with a Congressman he was a fixer for. He seemed very intrigued by that. Once our food arrived, we talked for hours about politics, the problems of the world that were hard to fix, but easy at the same time. We started to really connect, I thought now this was a guy I could hang with. He was glad we took down my brother, but he came to Cuba because investigating Bill had led him to more legs of the spider web."

The joint was now half gone, and past the point where either needed any more; they were just enjoying each other's company. "So then what, you just decided to team up? Did he tell you that he was Christina's dad?"

"He didn't. He talked about a daughter that he felt bad about leaving when she needed him most, but he was trying to take down some of the most powerful people in the world, and feared for her safety. Something called the six entities, remember them?"

Jason immediately went into a flashback of eating a Cuban sandwich after Bryan and he took down Bill and Congressman Riddell. He remembered how Bryan told him just to enjoy their victory. "It's interesting that you took time off to decompress, and because you were purposely trying not to think about something, it comes right back up again. What you resist, persists, sounds like there is work that still needs to be done," Jason stated. He knew he was hot on the trail of something, just like when they attended the anti-immigrant rally.

"That was my thought. Jay told me that he disguised himself as the Madman for Good, because he had to build a movement to even have a chance at taking these bastards down."

"If so much of our work has to be done in secret, why come right out in the open and say hello world, come get me?" Jason asked like it was the 800 pound gorilla in the room.

"I had the same question, especially since you never really know who was on the entities payroll. He said he didn't want to hide anymore, and wanted to really take it to them. Even though he was putting himself at risk, he felt the more authentic he was in what he said and what he wanted to accomplish, not only would just any people flock to his side, but the right people. These would be the people that would provide him the connections to do what needed to be done."

Jason knew that he felt the same, but wasn't at the point in his life yet where he could just say "fuck it, I'm going to do what's right. Yeah the people who want to stop me are way more powerful, but if I get enough people on my side, then maybe we have a shot."

"We talked for a little while longer before he asked me where I was staying. I said I didn't really have a place yet because I didn't know who to trust," Bryan muttered with a little trepidation because he knew the fear that melted away since he had been with Jay, would return once Jason and he got going again. Since Jason and now Christina were on the scene, he knew they would soon be off on their next adventure to save humanity.

"Why did you think you could trust him?" Jason quizzed, trying to test if Bryan still had what it takes.

"I didn't but he told me that he picked the moniker Madman for Good, because he had unrelenting positivity for everything he did; and was a madman for making good things happen. I knew he was somebody I could accomplish great things with, especially since he was trying to build a following. He told me about a little cabin he had, and I don't know if it was because of the way I looked or what, but he could tell I liked weed. He told me I could crash with him for a little while because he needed help trimming his new crop. So I thought what the heck. That was 3 years ago now, and I couldn't be happier. We've tried to investigate things down here without much luck, but now that you're here, I'm sure we'll all get to where we need to go."

Jason was trying to process his thoughts. Did his good friend and partner leave New York for Cuba, and really just randomly meet up with his girlfriend's father who he didn't even know about? He remembered everything changed when Christina and he met an old man on a beach, just because they decided to smoke a doobie on that exact beach at that exact time. He knew anything was possible.

"What about the postcard?" Jason drilled, still wondering how that fit into the story, since that's what led Christina and him there in the first place.

"Well, Jay and I were talking one night about what we could do to fix the generational problems that seemed easy but so hard at the same time; how everything was being privatized, and how it was causing the downfall of society. We both agreed there are some things that should never be done for profit," replied Bryan like he was trying to stall and not give the full answer.

"That's very true. When the only thing on a person's or company's mind is profit, they won't care who they step on to get to the top. But again, what about the postcard?" quipped Jason who could talk about privatization for hours, but wanted to get back to the point.

"We talked about how privatization of natural resources could control food production. Privatizing water systems, food systems, basically every way humans fuel their body, and allows them to be alive. I started thinking of anybody who could help with our investigations. I mentioned a friend I used to work with that always hyper-focused on anything that had to do with privatization.

I didn't know where you were, but Jay said he had some connections back in the states that could help find you. He made a couple of phone calls, and then got an address. I came up with the idea of the postcard with a vague enough picture anybody would think it was just another postcard. But once you read the Cuban sandwich description, I knew you would figure out who sent it."

"That's the funny part man I didn't figure it out at first. My mouth was watering from the picture in my head, but I didn't know what it meant. I brought it into the bedroom and showed Christina, and she figured out it must be you. She was the one that put the pieces together," explained

Jason who was feeling so happy that he and Christina were on this adventure side by side.

"You would always talk about her and how much you missed her. Now I can see why, she has just as good an eye for this stuff as you do. Since she's Jay's daughter, I can see how the apple doesn't fall far from the tree. I hope you don't mind me luring you down here, I figured it had been a while since we hung out and worked together, and it was time to get back to it. I knew what you always said about following synchronicities, even if you don't know where they lead."

"It's all good man, I'm glad to see you and get back to work. I've never been to Cuba before, but with the food, the weather and the best team a guy could ask for, who's going to stop us?" Jason inquired feeling an immense energy flow through his veins that told him everything would work out, the more authentic he was.

Jason and Bryan were red eyed and clear eyed at the same time. Red eyed because of the amazing weed Christina's dad grew, but also clear eyed because of what was in front of them. If the six entities were able to control resources, Jason knew it would very bad for everybody. He opened the French door to see the sun had set, but still showed a beautiful night sky. Jason always loved this part of the day, as the day itself was transitioning to the next step in its own evolution.

"How are you all doing out here," Jason asked the love of his life who was just as red eyed and clear eyed as he was. "Bryan filled me in on what he and your dad have been up to. He told me he sent the postcard with your dad's help. He was trying to decompress so he could figure out his next move, but the synchronicities were slapping him in the face saying hey, there's more work to be done."

"We're doing great and also ready to get to work," exclaimed Christina who shared a smile with her dad that filled up her soul in a way that she thought was gone forever. "We are all here for a reason, one that will be felt through the ages. We must show these six entities that we have four entities here. Four people they don't want to mess with. The question isn't are we ready to take these people down, but are they ready for something they'll never see coming?"

"I couldn't have said it better myself," agreed Jay as he gave Christina a look of deep admiration. "We should start with somebody I've been looking into for a while who moves a lot of money around. He could always be trusted to do the right thing, until he started buying municipal water systems and tripling the rates, while stuffing as much as he could in his pockets. He figured that by controlling the water, he could control what food was grown and how much of it could be grown."

Jason, Christina and Bryan's ears all perked up at the same time. They looked at Jay, then back at each other with the same thought. They had their team and were ready to attack the next leg of the spider web. Their gaze went back toward Jay, but only Jason could manage any words.

"So who is this guy?" Jason inquired very curiously.

"Ever heard of Marty Jackson?"

CHAPTER SEVEN

"Excuse me, am I just really stoned or did you say you've been tracking Bryan's and my former boss?" Jason questioned with a very suspicious look on his face.

Jay took a deep breath before he answered. He knew he might not have an opportunity with his daughter again, and he didn't want to mess it up. At the same time, the truth that flowed through him, was the same that flowed through Christina. "Yes I did. I began to keep tabs on Christina some years back, just to keep an eye out for her safety; and in turn, your life and Marty's."

"So you've been spying on me? Like I said earlier, why couldn't you just pick up a phone like a normal person? It's kind of stalker-ish to follow me," rebuked Christina as a great uneasiness settled over her, causing her hands to shake.

"Yes, I was watching you, but only because I wanted you protected. I just couldn't step foot back in the States with all the people that are after me. That's why I found my home here in outcast's paradise." Jay stretched out his arms to showcase the immense natural beauty all around them.

The strict control of land use caused there to be almost no development anywhere on the island. Since they were cut off from almost all outside fuel sources because of U.S.

sanctions, the Cuban population had to be rather creative with how they generated power.

"There is something important I must tell you though," Jay insisted as he wanted to test the three people standing in front of him to see if they had his back.

"What is it man? I worked for Marty for a long time. You're telling us that he was loaded down with dirty money. You're saying he was a complete hypocrite who said one thing and did another?" Bryan fumed. "He was like a father to me."

"Look all I'm saying, is that when I was looking in on Christina, I had to look at all aspects of her life. This guy Marty has an interesting past, I'm sure you know about how he was roommates in college with the former President and some guy named Terrance Shipley?"

Jason immediately looked at Christina like what the hell did he just say. They both instantly thought of the old man on the beach and how he said Marty, President Bowman and him had all been college dorm buddies. Could Terrance Shipley be the old man that not only helped them take down the President, but also threatened them afterwards?

"Holy shit, Christina and I met this old guy on a beach in California who said he was roommates with them. You think it could be the same guy?" wondered Jason whose mystery solving powers were kicking in. "It all started because we wanted to smoke that joint."

"No, I think it was because you wanted to fondle me in the sun, hoping we'd get caught," Christina remarked with a devilish smile.

"You wanted to smoke a joint with me on a random day too man, did you want to fondle me in the sun?" Bryan quipped with a snappy comeback that caused all four of them to fall out of their chairs laughing.

"Okay in all seriousness," interjected Jay trying to get ahold of the situation because he was barely able to keep a straight face himself.

"I am being cereal, super cereal," chuckled Christina, which caused their laughing fits to go on for the next ten minutes.

After the laugher dust settled down, they all sat there and eyed each other. Could they trust one another, could Bryan trust Jay, the man who spied on him these last few years because Jay was investigating the guy he used to work for? Could Christina trust her newly located father that abandoned her? Could Jason trust any of them to do what was best for the world, let alone himself? Time would answer all queries.

Just when the four of them were ready to talk again, a huge bird flew over their heads with colors none of them had ever seen before. "What kind of bird is that?" asked Jason whose inquisitive mind always strived to know the logic behind things, even if he might never understand their mechanics.

"I don't know. It sure is weird looking, and it sounds like its making a humming sound," answered Jay who was just as perplexed. By now the day was done and it was almost dark. "You know if somebody wanted to make people think they were dead so they could hide somewhere under a new identity, it would look something like that."

"Hey Pop, I think you've had a little too much of that good stuff you're growing out back," sniped Christina because she missed giving her dad crap, and was making up for lost time.

"No, I think there's something to what he said," Jason added as his hamster started to run on its wheel. "The President we took down, or should I say that the old man took down."

"Yeah what about him?" asked Christina who always thought Jason's inquisitiveness was attractive, but she was beginning to wonder if he had smoked himself stupid.

"The metaphor your dad just mentioned, The President resigned, he fakes his death immediately afterwards in a plane crash, then he hides in plain sight under an assumed identity," blurted Jason who was trying to make a point. "The President is probably hiding out with the old man since he threatened us that day. Hell, since Marty was their old drinking buddy, they're probably all in cahoots. Hell, Marty might be one of them. What would you do Bryan if Marty was working for the six entities? What would you do if all the work you've done was to support a lie?"

"I would want the truth, I would want to know why all this happened," Bryan snapped back with a forthrightness and a passion for doing the right thing that Jason immediately picked up on when he came to New York.

"I did think it was weird that I didn't talk to Marty after the President went down. I mean I didn't talk to him much after I went underground, but this is just all too coincidental. I mean what if the money he was sending was part of the water scheme Jay was talking about?" Jason asked with a calm smile on his face despite the groups rising anxiety.

"That's why I want to find out the truth," replied Bryan, feeling like he was repeating himself.

"Okay boys, let's all calm down." Christina felt like she needed to inject some female energy into the situation. "Let's not turn this into a pissing contest of who knows more or who cares more. Hey Pop, tell us more about Marty and his buying up of city water systems."

The four of them sat around a table that was a beautiful stained redwood, which reminded Jason and Christina of back home. It also caused them to forget about the bird that was now hovering a hundred feet above their head.

"Don't move the controller too fast, you'll crash the thing," *demanded a mysterious voice in the back of a non-descript*

office situated in a common office park you'd see anywhere in America. "I knew I shouldn't have let you fly this thing."

"Okay okay, we just got out of jail. I just want to have a little fun, you remember what fun is? Or did all the male attention in the can make you go soft?" responded the confident man who was wearing shorts and a t-shirt with an American flag lapel pin over his heart.

"You want me to get hard for you wouldn't you? Just fly it straight, and keep an eye on them. Who would have thought little brother would lead to the Madman for Good. If we get him, then the entities might take us back after we screwed up last time."

Back a hundred feet below, the four unlikely heroes were deciding their next moves.

"So, Marty invested in all these water systems? Seems like a smart investment in a business sense, even if it's completely heartless considering he could cause the next big drought," Jason stammered, wondering what they should do. He forgot that the best way to figure out a problem was to clear your head so you could truly see what's in front of you.

"Yes, I traced his investments all over the world. Basically any major city that was having budget problems, Marty offered to buy their water and then sell it back to them at a discounted rate. Little by little over time, he'd raise the rates which caused the cities to go into more and more debt, but with him," Jay explained with a slight smile. He now had the brain of his amazingly beautiful daughter, and the guy who made her heart sing sitting in front of him; not to mention his new friend and Marty's former right hand man.

"Did you know about any of this when you were showing me around New York, or at any time we worked together? During the meeting with Marty in his office after the anti-immigration rally, did you know then?" wondered Jason because he was beginning to question his trust for the guy he always thought had his back.

"No man, no. I didn't know any of this. Are you asking me if I can be trusted, seems like we've been through this before. I'll cut to the chase, I don't think Marty was intentionally leading you away from him, but he wasn't exactly leading you towards him either," Bryan replied cryptically.

"What are you saying man?" asked Jason, beginning to wonder if he could trust anybody.

While the small argument was going on, the bird above them had begun to take pictures and video with almost perfect sound.

"I think we need to get back to the point at hand. Marty bought up many cities water systems, including Detroit's," Jay interjected. "You guys have plenty of time to talk about your trust issues later. I'm trying to tell you Marty had a secret headquarters in Detroit built into on one of the many rundown warehouses. Since they were all over the place, he thought nobody would find it. He thought he could control his operations better by being in the middle of the country."

"I hope they keep talking down there, this is kind of fun. I'll bet we could spy on all kinds of people with this, it looks identical to any number of birds."

"Maybe we should go there and see what we can find. Maybe we can discover who Marty really is, I'm guessing it will blow this whole thing wide open. Of course I'd hate to leave this amazing place," Bryan expressed. He looked around at the beautiful surroundings, but also at the group like what are we waiting for, why haven't we left yet?

"That sounds like a great idea," Jason and Christina quipped in such sarcastic unison that it caused them to kiss each other long and deep.

"Gross, get a room," Jay remarked with a laugh.

"I'm sorry, it turns me on that the most beautiful woman in the world has the same passion for uncovering truth and collective consciousness raising as me," Jason divulged as he looked lovingly into Christina's eyes.

"Looks like she raised something," Bryan joked as he started laughing at the very obvious tent in Jason's pants.

The animals were starting to come out of their hiding spots because night fall was upon them, which signaled Jay to grab a small cherry wood box from below the table they were sitting at.

"I think we should go to Detroit and see what we can find. We came to Cuba for a reason Jason. We met up with your good friend and former partner, and I met up with my dad who I hadn't seen in a very long time. Even though we still have a lot of issues to work out, there is plenty of time for that. You should come with us dad," Christina insisted as she looked at Jay because she wanted to give him another chance.

"I don't think I should," replied Jay. He was almost done breaking up some of the stinkiest weed this side of Havana, even stinkier than what they smoked when they first arrived. "Marty and his gang, they're looking all over the place for me; that's one of the reasons I came to Cuba. I still wanted do some good, but I needed to hide out. I built a small movement so I'd have good people around if something happened to me. I wasn't using these people, I was helping them become what they always dreamed of, people who did great things for humanity."

"I agree that they, Marty, the entities or whomever or whatever they're calling themselves now are probably after you, but you are using these people; like you used me to further your own ends when I was a kid. You knew I had above average intelligence. You knew that I didn't get along with other kids because I was always thinking of the millions of things going on in the world. Isn't that why you left me, because you couldn't use me anymore?" Christina blasted. She started to cry until Jason put his arm around her.

"I never used you, I was only doing what I thought was right. I knew I had to nurture your intelligence, and push you to be even better than you imagined. I only wanted the best for you, I always loved you; hell, that's why I followed you and kept you safe. You think people didn't follow you after you investigated that lady from Shane Corp. who was murdered? I'm the one that stopped them. I'm the one that slowed them down."

"Let's all settle down here," Jason bellowed, trying to bring a little calm.

"Jason was always the great mediator, I see why Bryan wanted him as a partner; that's okay though, we'll have the last laugh."

"You're right, let's all take some deep breaths. So Jay, you said Marty had a secret headquarters in Detroit?" questioned Bryan, trying to introduce some civility back into the conversation. "Do you think we should go there?"

"Yes I do, I think you should all go and see what you can find. I need to stay here for now. Christina, I will always look out for you, I will always protect you." Jay lovingly looked into Christina's eyes and whispered a number in her ear. "That number is how you reach me. It will lead directly to me no matter where I am. Don't forget it."

Christina looked into her father's eyes with tears streaming down her face. "No matter how much I hate you for leaving, I can't deny that Jason and I followed synchronicities to this island. We have to see it through, we will go to Detroit."

"You're coming with us right man?" Jason asked Bryan trying not to sound desperate to have his friend by his side, but also wanted to portray how he truly felt.

"Do I want find out if the guy I trusted for years was really one of the vile bastards we tried to take down, 1000% I'm in," clamored Bryan with the most enthusiastic expression Jason ever saw on him.

"Great, now let's smoke this joint and relax so we can get a good night's sleep. We have a big day tomorrow we'll need all the energy we can get." Jay smiled as he lit up a perfectly proportioned joint.

"Well I see where you got your rolling skills from," responded Jason to Christina with a laugh.

"And her good looks," quipped Jay as he tried joining in on the fun by flipping back his thick grey hair.

The four of them smoked and laughed and smoked some more until they could barely keep their eyes open, which meant it was time for bed. The Owls, frogs and spider monkeys were coming out and making a lot of noise, which signaled it was their time to play.

"Those poor stoners are so out of it, they'll never see us coming."

The next day started earlier than anybody wanted with a pounding on the door. Jay stumbled from his bed and slowly walked to answer it. "What's up man?"

"Sir it's time to go. If we want to get them out safe, we must go now. We heard some chatter last night that there is a new kind of drone in the area. We can trace most of them, but this one, we couldn't tell where the signal was coming from because it bounced around so much. We must hurry, we don't want to get ambushed," demanded the heavily armed man in full fatigues that looked like Rambo's brother.

"Thanks Jerry, I appreciate you rallying your troops. I know I haven't been here for long, and you're risking your lives to extract them, I just want to say thank you," remarked Jay with immense admiration.

"The pleasure is mine, sir. You have such passion for making positive change that anybody can feel it within thirty feet of you. We're only doing our small part to help change society and the world. You're our conduit, we're with you. Meet at the landing strip in ten minutes."

Jay walked into his spare room, and woke up the three people who were about to go deeper into harm's way than they had ever been before; but he knew that the light at the end of this particular tunnel was very bright. "You guys ready? We have to meet up with my men in ten minutes if we want to make this happen, and get you back to the U.S."

"Ok, no problem. You ready for this babe?" Jason inquired as he blearily looked at Christina who was beginning to come back to life.

"I've been ready for this, let's do it," responded Christina. "What about you Bryan?"

"You don't need to ask me, I think we should have been on that plane yesterday," Bryan blurted out with an instant confidence faster than those energy shakes that pawned themselves off as breakfast.

Jason and Christina didn't have much, and Bryan was quite the minimalist since he left the states, so it didn't take them long to get ready.

Knowing that Jay's guy might have been telling the truth that somebody could've been watching and listening to everything they said the night before, Jason knew it was very important they do this quick. In the age of instant communication, coupled with weapons that could be fired from anywhere in the world, threats could come from all sides.

"You okay, pop?" Christina asked her dad, feeling strange, but good that she actually cared about his well-being. "You look like you're a thousand miles away."

"I'm fine, let's just do this," retorted Jay. Jason, Bryan and Christina all grabbed a bug out bag that Jay provided them with. The four of them walked out the back door of the cabin and onto a trail that was well covered with bushes. The thorns told all four of them they better be careful. "I should trim these, sorry if you get snagged."

"It's okay, with whomever might be after us a little snag is the least of our worries. Besides, if I've learned anything, it's that you have to move forward with what life gives you; because more often than not, you'll find what you're looking for," remarked Jason. He followed the group down the path towards the little air strip on the other side of the next hill.

"I can see why you love this guy, always a positive thing to say, while at the same time down for anything. I said Detroit, and he was the first one to jump on board," expressed Jay with caring towards Jason, who he thought might make a good son-in-law one day.

The four of them walked for what seemed like forever, like the next bend would never come. The bushes and trees were as beautiful a place as they ever saw. The plant life was so thick, it would have been very energy fulfilling to be around if it weren't for the fact they were about to embark on a mission that would change all their lives.

"Okay brother, this is it, were going to get you this time."

"Finally, geez I must be out of shape, that walk seemed a lot shorter the last time. I should cut down on the Cubanos and plantains," Jay kidded, trying to elicit some laughter.

"That sounds so good right now," Jason remarked as the four of them crested the hill after what seemed like an hour, but was only fifteen minutes since they left the cabin. The small airstrip was a big open field completely surrounded by trees. The way it was designed, it looked to Jason like only the best pilots in the world could fly in and out of there. "I'll bet this place is hard to trace."

"It is, but with the technology we have at our fingertips these days, anything anywhere is possible. You three would all do yourselves a lot of good to remember that," Jay retorted as he led them towards the plane that had ten men surrounding it holding guns bigger than anything Jason had ever seen up close.

"Are those real, or are they trying to compensate for something?" Jason sniped trying to lighten the mood.

"A little from column A and a little from column B," replied Jay because he knew this type of humor like the back of his hand. "Plus you never can be too careful."

Just as they were twenty feet from the plane, bullets started to rain from the sky.

"Who the hell is shooting at us?" yelled Jason like the rest of the group didn't realize bullets were falling all around them.

The four of them ran towards the plane, while the men standing around it gave them cover by firing into the air. By the time they reached the plane, the gunshot decibel level was deafening.

"I love you Christina, we will meet up again. I will be a part of your life. Remember, call if you need anything," shouted Jay at the top of his lungs as fast he could, like his life depended on it; because it did.

"I love you too Pop," Christina expressed as she leaned over to give her dad a kiss. The guards were providing good cover they thought, until a bullet landed three inches from Bryans head.

"Let's get out of here, hurry," demanded Bryan who was in just as much danger as any of them; even though in his mind, he was the only one acting with the level of urgency the situation called for.

Jason, Christina and Bryan barely got onboard the plane as a missile exploded three feet to their left. "We've got to get in the air, I think they got a drone after us. I can't see where the shooting is coming from," screamed the pilot who was scared that he wouldn't make it home for dinner with his family, let alone get them off the island.

Several more missiles landed near the plane as it started hauling-ass down the runway trying to pick up enough speed to take off. Through the smoke and flying debris, Christina looked out the window and saw her dad waving, before he got into a vehicle that looked like it had a 50cal.

on the roof. She couldn't be positive though from how far away she was.

The plane was trying to ascend as the firing intensified. The wheels barely left the ground as three more explosions hit right in front of them. They had built up just enough speed to fly up and over it. The missiles seemed to stop, causing Christina to look back towards where her dad had got into the car. Just as she saw what looked like the vehicle, a missile rocketed down and exploded the car he was in like it was target practice.

"Oh shit, I think my dad just got hit," Christina cried out because she witnessed a massive explosion down on the air strip. "I think since they didn't get us, they got him instead. Oh dad, I'm so sorry I came here just to get you killed. I'll always remember the things you taught me, I won't let you down."

"Oh baby," deplored Jason as he put his arms around a crying Christina. Bryan had a weird looking smile on his face the whole time as they flew further and further away from the air strip. He realized this was his chance to see what Marty was up to, and from the look in his eyes, he knew he would get to the truth by any means necessary.

After crying for twenty minutes, Christina wiped her face on her sleeve and was able to find her words again. "My dad told me I could reach him through this secret phone number he said I couldn't forget." Christina whispered the number into Jason's ear.

"I don't think that's a phone number, I think those are coordinates. It sounds like a place Marty used to hide stuff," stated Jason, beginning to wonder why he was brought to New York in the first place.

"Marty had places like that all over," interjected Bryan whose anger was growing because he was thinking more and more about how he was deceived. "He was looking through it just before he brought you to New York. He said he went through some papers, and really wanted to get ahold of somebody he left behind."

"What, he didn't even know me. How could that be why he brought me to New York?" Jason speculated, starting to question if he should trust Bryan like he had in New York. Of course it turned out okay then, so this time it might too. Jason decided to give him the benefit of the doubt.

"He didn't know you, but he wanted to. He gave me this envelope, and said I would know the right time to show you. Since we almost just got killed trying to escape from Cuba, I mean like Cuba the country, I think this is the perfect time," stammered Bryan. He was stumbling on his words, but was looking at Jason like the caring brother he never had. He handed Jason the envelope who was very eager to see what was inside.

Jason opened it to find only a single piece of paper, that from the looks of it had been through hell.

"This is a birth certificate," Jason exclaimed, reading the words at the top.

"What gave it away, the fact that it says birth certificate in big bold letters at the top?" quipped Christina. She cracked a slight smile, which made Jason smile as he looked deep into her eyes.

"We'll be back in the states soon, and then you guys can ravage each other till the cows come home. For now, I want to know who that certificate belongs to. Marty never told me, he just handed it to me to give to you. I thought it was weird, but like I said before, when Marty gave orders, I didn't question," replied Bryan with an anxiousness that needed to be resolved.

Jason looked further down the page and noticed the name on it was his. "This looks like my birth certificate. My mom said she lost mine which is why I never saw it, but why would Marty have it?" Jason mused. He was growing very uneasy, but as his eyes continued down the page there it was, the answer staring him right in the face.

"Well what does it say?" Bryan and Christina shouted in unison because they were both equally excited and anxious to know.

"This says Marty is my father."

CHAPTER EIGHT

If there was one thing Jason was always sure of, it was that he knew where he came from. Now, he wasn't so sure. "I always had the same parents from when I was little. I don't see how Marty could possibly be my father." As if being shot at and having missiles attempt to blow him up wasn't bad enough, now Jason had to deal with his childhood being thrown into question.

"It's okay, just one more mystery we have to figure out," Christina remarked in a very loving, but determined tone. She had been very anxious to do things for society ever since she left Shane Corp. Christina was hurt when she and Jason went underground, but now she simply saw it as training for her next evolutionary step.

The flight seemed like it took forever, but since they were being rescued it didn't much matter. They couldn't fly into the regular Detroit airport because they weren't supposed to be in Cuba in the first place. Wherever they touched down, there was no telling who would be waiting for them.

Since the pilot was expecting the drone to be following as they flew out, he was quite surprised they were free and clear a few miles out from where they took off.

The weather was clear, not a cloud in the sky; which was a good thing considering Jason, Bryan and Christina were being thrown into a fight they hoped they had the energy to finish. Marty was somebody that Jason and Bryan trusted, and they both knew they had to get to the bottom of it.

"Does this plane have a bar? I could really use a scotch right now," queried Jason needing some liquid courage.

"I think it does, but since you're going to a meeting with the boss, it might be a good idea to go in clear eyed and sober," revealed Bryan, feeling déjà vu from the sentence that spilled from his lips.

"Wait, haven't you said that before?" inquired Jason as the hamster on the wheel inside his head was running overtime.

"Now that I think of it yeah, right before your initial meeting with Marty; I said you want to impress the new boss. Now we're not trying to impress him, but investigating things he might not want us to know. I think some fine aged booze is just what we need." Bryan knew he and Jason needed all the help they could get.

"Too bad smoking isn't allowed on this plane, I could really use a doobie right about now," Christina blurted out. She realized that helping her love find what he was looking for, would help them all find what they were looking for.

"Now that I think of it, my whole dad's side of the family is from Detroit and around Michigan. Well the guy I always thought of as my dad." Jason was trying to gather his thoughts, which made it confusing for everybody because he was thinking out loud. "There was a little bar that I'd always pass when I was younger. Obviously I wasn't old enough, but my uncle would always say he would go in there and watch whatever game was on. I think we should make it our first stop when we land. We could get a drink and mingle with the locals. The best way to start I think."

After what seemed like a ten hour flight but was really only three because of all the thoughts floating around, they saw their runway.

The tires touched down like any normal plane, but when things stopped being blurry from moving so fast, Jason realized that they weren't landing at any airport. This was another private airstrip tucked in between some trees, with a beautiful lake less than half a mile away.

"Here we go, from one private air strip to another. I am beyond ready to start this adventure," observed Bryan wanting to express his true feelings, but also because he pitched Jason a softball that he wouldn't be able to resist hitting out of the park.

"Isn't that what I said before I went over to your mom's last night?" Jason inquired without missing a beat.

"At least my mom requires a special membership card for admittance, your mom takes in anyone off the street," replied Bryan as they both started laughing. Jason and Bryan felt together once again. Now that they had Christina on their side, along with some hidden help from Jay, they knew they had a chance.

As the plane slowed to a stop, the bumps in the big grassy field made the twin engine plane bounce all over the place. This made Jason realize that if they were going to make some bumps of their own, they would have to shake things up. I mean people don't shoot missiles at you for no reason, right?

"That bird drone thing back in Cuba was weird right, I had no idea they disguised them that well," realized Jason as they exited the plane and walked towards the black Tahoe waiting for them.

"How are we ever supposed to see them coming, if we have to suspect every bird in the sky?" Bryan pondered, hoping the simple joy of enjoying nature wouldn't be taken from them.

"We have to be skeptical but not cynical, trust no one, and above all else, stick together," answered Christina who felt like Elmer's glue the way that she was helping them stick together. "Come on, let's go. That bar you mentioned sounds great."

The three of them walked toward the car, not even thinking about how they had been shot at recently. Right when Jason, Bryan and Christina were ten feet from the car, they heard three loud pops.

"Was that a gunshot, Is somebody shooting at us already?" questioned Jason as he, Bryan and Christina hurried to get in the car.

Just as they were about to touch the handle to open the door, the pops got louder. "Those gunshots are getting closer and closer, we better hurry up. They might be hunters, we are in a pretty wooded area. It's still kind of freaking me out though, let's scram," exclaimed Christina whose Elmer's talents were fading away.

Just as the three opened the doors of the car, the gunshots sounded like they were less than a hundred feet away. "Those aren't hunters, they're trying to get us," replied Bryan, as the three of them jumped in the Tahoe which sped off in such haste, that the dirt kicked up disguised the two men standing 10 feet away with 44 revolvers.

"Damn, this is going to be a rough ride," barked the driver as they sped down a road that led away from the airstrip. After about five or ten minutes of bouncing along, Christina had a question.

"Do you work for my dad, the Madman for Good?" Christina asked of the driver who was very calm and collective, considering they were driving away from a pretty violent situation.

"You must be Christina, he always talked about you. He said you were the apple of his eye," expressed the driver knowing how stereotypically nauseating it sounded, but he wasn't good with niceties. "He also said that you'd change the world if given the chance, because you were his daughter, his Honey Bear. What else could you do?"

Christina sat there for a minute before she spoke, things were happening so fast. She thought about how her dad could be dead back in Cuba with a missile in his chest, and they'd never have the chance to reconnect.

"He talked about me all the time huh, what else would he say?" Christina asked trying to fight back tears of anger and joy at the same time.

"He wished he could be part of your life, there was nothing he wanted more," replied the driver who seemed to be an expert at multitasking, considering he was having a conversation, while also dodging rocks and potholes trying to get them back to civilization.

"He could have picked up the phone at any time."

"He really wanted to, but after the people he was investigating caught wind, which you now know was Marty Jackson, he couldn't risk your life. That's when he escaped to Cuba, where he could spend his time with dissidents and activists trying to figure out the truth about Marty."

Jason and Bryan sat there silently, and wondered what it had to do with them, but also what it didn't have to do with them.

"You're a crappy shot Bill. You couldn't hit them with three drone strikes, or a 44 magnum when you're right there," shouted the man in jeans and a jacket with dust an inch thick on it.

"If you had just killed them before divulging our entire plan, not only would we not have ended up in jail, we wouldn't be on this God forsaken airstrip in the middle of nowhere, firing at two little piss ants that think they can bring down the entire system."

"I want to take them down too, for ruining my plans of selling influence. I was making lots of money before they arrived and messed everything up. I want to take the guy down that messed up the water park thing; you want to take down your brother for trying to mess you up."

"What's your point, do you have one? Do you ever have one? I'm tempted to take this gun and shoot you instead so you'll shut the hell up. You know from this distance, I would be sure not to miss."

"Okay okay, don't get all pissy. Let's just go back to the spot. We need to regroup, and if we know these people like we think we do, I'm sure they'll come looking for us sooner than later."

The Tahoe had been on the road for about ten miles, and Christina was starting to wonder when they'd get back to some kind of main road. "What's your name by the way and where are you taking us?" Christina asked the driver cautiously.

"My name is, well, probably better you don't know my real name, don't want more people to come after you. They call me Goose."

"Well Goose, nice to meet you. This is Bryan and Jason." Christina pointed to the two guys beside her, who were both wondering why she was saying anything.

"I know who you guys are. When Jay started looking into Marty, he came across you two. He was suspicious of both of you because you worked for Marty. Then he realized his daughter was involved with Jason here, and thought if she was good, than he must be as well," Goose explained as the Tahoe finally pulled onto a paved road.

"How does he know I'm good? Is his ego so big that he thought just because he helped create me, I would automatically be somebody he could be proud of?"

"He was always proud of you."

"Then why didn't he call, I missed him so much. Ever had your dad abandon you?"

"As a matter of fact I did."

"So you know how heart breaking it is."

"Of course I do, and that's why I have to protect you now. My security team will be your eyes and ears while you're in the Motor City."

Just as the words left Goose's mouth, three more Tahoes pulled out from side streets and surrounded the one they were riding in. "What's all this?" wondered Jason, scared that this much security was needed, but excited because if they were this much of a threat, they must be getting somewhere.

"This is what Jay thought you would need. He made a lot of enemies looking into Marty before he went into exile, but he also made a lot of friends. Since you're going to be taking up the fight he couldn't finish, he knew you'd need all the help you could get."

"Can you take us to this bar my uncle talked about when I was younger?" Jason inquired, trying to get back on track. He knew a good drink and a few laughs was always a good place to begin.

"You'll have to be more specific. With how many people work hard in this town, they like to drink," quipped Goose with the first thing that could be considered a smile since they left the airstrip. He knew that smiles were a rarity when you pick up people you don't know while being shot at.

"It's in downtown Detroit I know that," remembered Jason as his memory banks worked overtime. "I think it was called Mary's Alibi or something. Always seemed like a place that kids didn't belong. And now that I am not a kid, I'd love to check it out."

"Let me think, oh yeah, I know that place. It has gotten really run down over the years, but has been standing in the same place since the 1930s. I'll take you there." Goose was happy they had some kind of direction.

"Sweet."

The four Tahoe caravan cruised down the road lined with pine trees before getting on the highway.

"I feel like we're cruising in some kind of secret service thing. Four big black S.U.V.s' rolling down the road, says top secret government agent to me," blurted Jason thinking about all the action movies he had ever seen.

"Oh God, don't come up with one of those cheesy one-liners you think are the funniest things in the world," remarked Bryan, rolling his eyes.

"Oh come on man, I know a lot of shit has happened in the last couple days, but it's been years since I've seen you. I have to catch up for lost time."

"I guess so, I did miss my friend."

Christina was starting to smile because she never thought she would be the one to comment. "I never thought the lady with the lady parts would say let's stop this emotional outbreak before we all grow them, because then I would be in a car full of guys with boobs." All four of them starting laughing so hard the car was shaking, or maybe it was the roads that were falling apart due to lack of political will to rebuild infrastructure. When everybody can agree on something, but then refuse to act, they're not only hurting everybody around them, but they're hurting themselves as well.

Figuring out why Marty was buying up water systems was number one on the list of things to do. Was this how he supported Jason all those years he was underground? Was Democratic Republic magazine just a cover for his illegal dealing? Was it a magazine at all? All these questions and more were swirling around Jason's head as the city skyline came into view.

"We're approaching the Motor City. Next stop Mary's Alibi, where Mary isn't the only one to have an alibi," Goose sniped, trying to get in on the joking even though he hadn't had much practice.

"You should come in and drink with us, it might help with your comebacks," replied Christina trying to make Goose feel better because his joke fell flat as a pancake. "If you're going to be hanging around these jokers you'll need it. Don't worry, you'll get lots of practice."

"I'd love to, but I have a job to do. Besides once we get into the heart of the city, it's important that we stay vigilant. Since we were able to watch you, there's no telling who's watching us. With this water shortage, and so many people being shut off for failure to pay, everybody needs a buck; which means you can't trust anybody."

"How do we know we can trust you?" queried Bryan. "How do we know you weren't sent by my brother Bill to make us think we're being rescued?"

"Well that is a possibility because he and that Congressman you took down did get released from jail."

"Geez, now I really need a drink. Maybe some Pb and J's," expressed Bryan with a smile.

"You know what happened the last time we had Pb and J's, Ridell came in and threatened us," Jason recollected, nervous about their next move.

"Of course, which is why it's a great place to start."

The skyline got bigger and bigger until skyscrapers towered over their heads, they were about to get off the highway. "We only have a few more miles, the exit is right up there," stated Goose who was always on point, despite being just as human as everybody else. He wondered when he would find his Christina.

The four Tahoe caravan pulled off the highway and onto the downtown streets. The streets were lined with homeless people, run down businesses, apartments and abandoned buildings of all sorts. No matter how decrepit things looked, there was a positive energy that Jason felt immediately.

"It's great to be back here, it's been so long. Now that I'm an adult, I can experience so much more." Jason looked out the window and saw urban and moral decay, but at the same time a want for positive change. "This place is seething for somebody or something to come along and help them back to their glory days."

The caravan pulled up at Mary's Alibi at about 4pm. The parking lot was empty as the middle of the day drinkers were still there, and the after work crowd hadn't shown up yet.

"So my guys and I will be parked right out here. Here's a cell phone, it's untraceable of course. If you need anything, or when you're ready to go text me, and we'll be ready to take you where you need," relayed Goose in his best I got this one handled so you should relax voice.

"Sounds good to me, I think we could all use a drink after that ordeal getting out of Cuba," chuckled Bryan to Jason and Christina as they got out of the Tahoe. They waved at the man that seemed nice, almost too nice, like he was trying to win their approval.

As the three of them walked toward the front door, they saw what appeared to be graffiti on the side of the building. Since the writing was in red, and the building was an off tan whitish color, it showed up very easily.

"Viva Madman for Good. Do you think they know your dad?" pondered Jason knowing how obvious it sounded, but wanted to support Christina at the same time. They were on a quest to find out where they came from and who their parents were, then use that to stop privatization of natural resources so the average person could survive. Being from California and knowing all too well about their droughts, Jason and Christina knew that whatever happened would lead them to the next step, and then the next.

Christina knew water was the key to the future. Since 70% of the world was covered by water, she thought it was pretty ridiculous anybody was running low. She started thinking about how much of an impact her dad had acting on the same thought, when a lady about seventy-five came walking out of the bar towards the parking lot.

The older lady walked right up to them. "You must be Christina. Jay said you'd be back one day to continue his fight."

CHAPTER NINE

Thoughts were racing through Christina's head faster than a top fuel dragster making a pass at 330 miles an hour. She was having a hard time finding the words. "What?" Christina wondered very cautiously.

"Jay used to talk about you all the time. He said leaving you was the biggest mistake he ever made. He only hoped that you'd be a warrior for humanity and searcher for the ultimate truth," replied the old lady who seemed as passionate for this fight as anybody. "I saw many pictures from when you were younger, and some from right before Jay went into exile."

"I'm sorry, we've been through a lot in the last few days, getting shot at while leaving a foreign country we illegally entered was the icing on the cake," Christina expressed. She forcefully tried to crack a small smile. "What's your name by the way?"

"People call me Angie."

"Well Angie, want to come in and have a drink with my boyfriend and his partner? I'm sure we have a lot of things to talk about."

Bryan and Jason looked at Angie and then back at each other. They smiled at the fact they reunited with a purpose, and that they were partners again.

"I wish I could, but I have to pick up my grandkids from daycare. I was just having a beer until it was time. Your dad did want me to give you this if I ever came across you."

Angie handed Christina a piece of paper with numbers on it, which resembled the same numbers her dad whispered in her ear when they left Cuba. She knew this was no coincidence.

"When we left, my dad, Jay, whispered some numbers in my ear," revealed Christina who felt this was yet one more step in finding the answers they were looking for. She also thought the word dad was spoken rather easily, and she liked it; even though she knew their relationship needed a lot of work before it was where it should be. "We thought it was a phone number at first, but then we realized they were coordinates."

"He was investigating somebody before he left, which is actually what caused him to leave. I used to work for the guy he was investigating, and I know he had certain places he liked to hide things. I was thinking this might be one of those places," hypothesized Bryan who wanted to know if the guy he used to work for was really the evil mastermind he was starting to seem like.

"You must be Bryan," remarked Angie with a strange smile that said hi how you doing, but I'm not sure I should trust you. "We came across your name when we did that last investigation."

The group was getting a little nervous because everything was starting to fit together a little too snug. They knew it was something they had to finish. It could lead them to the truth about Marty, but also toward the six entities.

It was 5pm and people were starting to pull into the parking lot for after work refreshment. Jason, Bryan and Christina knew they shouldn't be talking too loud considering they didn't know who was listening.

"So what do you know about me?" asked Bryan very suspiciously.

"There isn't time I have got to go. The last time I was late picking up my grandkids, they almost banned me from bringing them back. Since they're the cheapest place in town, I can't lose them," Angie divulged nervously because she always felt like she was being watched since Jay left. A dark sedan pulled up fifty feet away. She couldn't quite make out who was in the driver's seat, but they seemed to be staring at her.

"Okay, okay no problem. Can you tell us anything about the numbers on that paper? Are they coordinates or directions, could you give us a hint?" wondered Jason who was aching to get a drink because they had been shot at two different times, but he also wanted to move things along. He knew this might be the tip of the iceberg because he felt something big around the corner.

"Yeah sorry. Those numbers are an address, and a locker combination." Angie pointed her pink press on nailed finger at the numbers on the ratty piece of paper that looked like she'd been carrying it around since the depression. "There's a bus station and some lockers about ten minutes from here. I think you'll find all you need. Good bye and good luck, and when you see Jay, tell him I'll always remember our weekend together."

Angie smiled as she walked away, not wanting to wave and draw more attention. She wanted to show how happy she was that the man she was once in love with, had his offspring come to Detroit to finish his work.

"How can we get a hold of you if we have any questions," Jason yelled but Angie couldn't hear him as she was hurrying for her car. How weird he thought for a 75 year old woman to have a few beers before she picked up her grandkids, but to each their own.

"Sounds like your dad was quite fond of the ladies," quipped Jason to Christina with a sly smile. "Sounds like she wasn't a jilted lover."

"Ha, ha, ha you're so funny Mister." Christina thought it was interesting her dad had lovers that weren't her mom. Her dad had been out of the picture for some time, and something was telling her that the mystery of her parents would be figured out soon enough. "I think we should go in for a drink, we all could use one or four. Besides we now have our next move," stated Christina who held up the piece of paper.

The dark sedan that made Angie nervous was still parked even after she pulled away. Since Jason, Christina and Bryan had drinks and bus station lockers on their minds, they didn't notice two men get out and follow them into the bar.

Mary's Alibi was something of a marvel. Well a marvel in the sense that it still stood after countless fights, cop interruptions and drunken idiots thinking they could get laid by anything that moved. Paintings lined the walls of animals playing poker, golf, football and all other sports that could be played by humans. People that liked drinking establishments for its surroundings and the crowds, this was not the place for them. If a person liked a bar that was a dank pit, this was their home away from home; a perfect dive bar for the dive bar patron in us all.

Christina, Bryan and Jason sauntered over to an empty table near the back, their feet sticking to dried up beer that didn't get mopped up the night before. Several guys in hard hats and overalls sat at the bar being their loud obnoxious selves they couldn't be on the jobsite, or when they went home to their wives.

"This reminds me of that place back in Arcata, remember where we liked the Bloody Marys?" Christina queried as they all sat down at the booth. "They'd get upset if you asked for a Bloody Mary with the works, acting like it was so much work for them to make. God forbid if you wanted a second one."

The three of them started laughing, knowing they needed all the good energy they could get because this was the calm before the storm. Just as Bryan tried to come up with a witty response, a very well-endowed waitress walked up to their table. She took a quick glance at Jason because she thought he was cute. Since he was sitting next to Christina who was giving her the evil eye, she decided to fix her gaze on Bryan.

"What can I get you folks today?" quipped the 26 year old waitress attempting to show Bryan as much cleavage as her 3 sizes too small bra would allow.

Bryan who looked like a deer in the head lights quite literally, took a minute to find his words because the huge boobs he was fixated on were a foot from his face. Then he gained his composure and spoke. "Can I get three jugs, I mean three Pb and J's?"

Christina and Jason snickered, but the waitress who didn't mind this reaction because it usually meant a good tip continued. "Sure, coming right up big boy." She looked at Bryan like pulling him into the bathroom would take too long, and pulling him behind the bar would be quicker.

"Wow, it's amazing how guys can be completely controlled by boobs. No matter what the messaging says, women really do control the world," joked Christina who laughed as she looked at Jason.

Jason chuckled, but then he spoke. "Hey Bryan, doesn't this all seem familiar, like déjà vu or something?"

"What're you talking about? I'm about to have some drinks with my friends and then hopefully have some boobies in my face before we leave," expressed Bryan who couldn't stop staring at the waitress whose blouse was being strained to its complete limits.

"I know you want boobs in your face, heck I do too," agreed Jason as he looked at Christina who glanced back like you are such a man. "What I mean is, doesn't this all seem like it's happened before?"

"Kind of, but refresh my memory. I've smoked a lot of good weed with Jay since I was last in an American bar. My memory is a little hazy."

"It was after the anti-immigration rally, when we met up with my old friend Aaron."

"I remember that, and?"

"We were all sitting around having Pb and J's, and this well-endowed waitress comes over with the same look in her eye as that waitress that just took our drink order. Doesn't that seem weird to you?"

"I think the only thing that's weird is you're jealous. This lady seems like she is either depraved or deprived I don't know which. Either way it could be lots of fun."

Just as Christina was giving them a glare etched with a smile, the waitress came back with their drinks. "Three shots of Jameson and three Pabst Blue Ribbons," exclaimed the waitress who was undressing Bryan with her eyes. Her boobs were now inches from Bryan's hands, trying to make it very obvious what she wanted. He thought she wanted to do him right under the table as she walked away and blew him a kiss.

"That's what I'm talking about, don't you remember this exact thing happening." Jason was trying to help Bryan think past the little brain in his pants.

"What, you don't think a woman would go for me?" asked Bryan as he flipped over his coaster to reveal a phone number. He showed Jason like see, she does want me.

"Of course a woman would go for you. Heck I didn't think a women would go for me until Christina showed up, but then she did," remarked Jason as he looked deep into Christina's eyes because she was everything he wanted. "Don't you remember what happened at the bar after the rally?"

Bryan tried to think, but it just wasn't coming to him. He took a drink of his beer to help jog his memory, but it wasn't working. "I remember we had some drinks."

"Yes we had some drinks, and the waitress that brought them was coming onto me just like she's coming onto you now." Jason started to wonder if Bryan's brain got perma-fried down in Cuba, or if it really been that long.

"Yeah, and?" inquired Bryan with a look that said I know it's been a while since we hung out or worked together, but please get to the point.

Christina was starting to wonder if the waitress did pull Jason into the bathroom. She didn't know where this story was going, and was just as eager as Bryan to find out.

"What's your point?" Christina quizzed impatiently.

"My point is the waitress kept trying to shove her boobs in my face every time she brought us new drinks. Heck she even gave me her number on the bottom of a coaster. But remember she did it because we looked like lonely guys getting drunk, and she knew she could make us do whatever she wanted," replied Jason as he took a big drink of beer because he was getting a sinking feeling something was about to happen.

While the three of them sat there drinking their beers trying to think of what's next, the well-endowed waitress walked behind the bar to make a call.

"They're here. They have a woman with them, which makes it harder to keep Jason here. His old partner is with him and he is the one that I have my triple f cup sized hooks into," stated the waitress very concise and to the point, everything a good agent should be.

"That's good, he'll be the one to make them stay because Jason has Christina," replied the confident voice on the other end who had planned these setups many times before. "Don't worry, Mark will be by to talk to them soon. Thanks Mary. Remember, my bedroom door is always open."

"You couldn't handle this. Anyway, as long as your money is good, I always need work."

Mary hung up the phone and pushed up her boobs so they were mere millimeters from popping out like all the ladies at the renaissance fair, then she walked back over to see what else she could find out.

The bar was filling up and the loud conversations reached a fever pitch. Jason, Christina and Bryan couldn't even begin to hear what Mary said on the phone. "When she comes back, you'll see what I mean. I know that many women want you, I just think she's trying to keep you here." Jason was trying very hard to jog Bryan's memory.

"Well here she comes, let's see," Bryan hurriedly finished his beer so he could order another one by the time she got to their table.

"Another round?" asked Mary, as she inched closer to Bryan, encouraging him to cop a feel

"Yes, I'd like another jug, I mean another drink. The same," Bryan answered as Mary walked away, but not before she lowered her shirt so Bryan could see the entirety of her cleavage. "Is that what you mean by her holding me here, I don't think so."

"Just wait till she comes back. Man you'll see," Jason persisted because he wanted his partner to see the importance of the situation.

Two minutes later Mary came back with Bryan's drink, set it on the table, and walked away without even giving him a glance. "See that's what I'm talking about, that's what I've been trying to tell you; the giant boobs in the face thing is just an act." Jason's feelers were now up because he knew what came next in the original story.

"That was weird, she didn't look at me at all that time," realized Bryan, who thought for a minute before he spoke again. "Something is coming back to me."

Just as Jason was about to lay down another I told you so, and Christina another comment about how men only thought about boobs, somebody tapped Jason on the shoulder.

"Hey Jason, fancy seeing you here; I'd say this isn't your usual watering hole, but I've said that before and I hate to repeat myself. Then again, why mess with a classic?" queried the confident man who made room for himself at their table by forcing Bryan to scoot to the edge of the booth.

"This has happened before," replied Bryan as things finally clicked.

"You think?" Jason immediately recognized the guy who once again sat at a table of his without being invited. "Nice to see you again Ridell; I heard you got out of jail, I hope not before plenty of good loving."

"Ahhh, I've missed your wit. Even though I only spent nine months inside, I'll never get that time back. You'll pay for what you did, I just have to figure out how." Ridell was trying to instill the same fear he inflicted when he was in the spotlight with his immigrations schemes.

"I figured you'd be out one day, people like you don't go to jail. The system is built to sweep things like that under the rug. I knew they wouldn't hold you for long, but I didn't think you'd beat it that quickly." Jason wasn't just going to sit there and be threatened.

"If you're here, I'm sure my brother isn't far behind," Bryan interjected, knowing that Bill had to be around the corner. Even though Ridell was the specific cause of his downfall, Bill cleaned things up, that's what he did. He knew Ridell would always need help, somebody to force him to be more careful.

"He is, in fact we've been following you for some time," Ridell expressed as calm and confident as any powerful ex-politician above the law would be. "To think, it all started with a postcard."

For Jason the picture was becoming clear. When he and Christina first arrived in Cuba, and went into that Paladar for Cubanos, they saw some postcards by the cash register very similar to what they'd been sent. When they inquired about them, the lady there said two guys had asked about them recently, and were very rude, just like stereotypical Americans.

"Was that you trying to kill us with the drone back in Cuba?" Christina demanded, starting to sweat not from fear, but anticipation.

"Bill wanted to target you guys with one of those because he was used to flying them, but I wanted to get you bastards also. We must make you pay for what you did, but first a toast." Ridell grabbed a shot of Jameson from the table and raised it. "Here's to the reunification of enemies. Without the other, we wouldn't have purpose."

Ridell downed his shot as Bryan piped up. "So if you couldn't kill us then, why have a drink with us now? You were shooting missiles at us and we escaped."

"I still want to kill you guys. Things were going so well and I was making so much money before the water park incident, before the rally, before all that crap. My life isn't close to where it used to be." Ridell's anger was building, but was still in check. "After Bill and I went down, the six entities abandoned us because we got tripped up by two nothings with no power. They thought what help could we be in implementing their final plan?"

"What would that final plan be, what do they have up their sleeves?" asked Bryan who didn't appreciate being put down by trash he took out a long time ago.

"I won't be making that mistake again. I told you the whole plan when I believed I had the upper hand. Bill said if I did that again he'd kill me himself."

"Sounds like you're still my brother's bitch."

"Yeah we will see who's still a little bitch, want to step outside?" Ridell yelled. He wasn't afraid to get in an old fashioned bar fight because he wasn't holding office anymore.

"Let's stop this pissing contest and get down to brass tacks." Christina was getting tired of the back and forth. She knew if Ridell still wanted to kill them, he would have when he walked in the door. "So if you just tried to kill us, why should we listen to anything you have to say?"

"Always the voice of reason, thank you Christina for mediating this very tense situation. I'm actually very glad you're here." Jason's face became beat red because this scumbag was talking about the love of his life, but Ridell continued. "After we got arrested, the six entities didn't have our backs anymore."

"You said that already. Get to the point shithead," Jason fumed. His rage was reaching the boiling point.

"Aww, I remember you saying that, classic. Anyway, once I stopped being supported, I got all these threats that I couldn't do anything about. I couldn't find anybody I could work with. The six entities put the fear of God into everyone that could help us. That's when I tracked down Bill because he'd also been released.

He suggested we go after you because you really did ruin our lives. Since he had access to all sorts of gadgets and machines from his time in government, we used a drone. We've been following you three ever since."

"So again, shithead, if you were trying to kill us not too long ago, why are you here and why aren't we dead in an alley somewhere?"

"I love that mouth on you, almost as much as I love your mom's," Ridell sniped causing Bryan to start laughing uncontrollably.

"Don't laugh at this jerk. Whose side are you on?" asked Jason like what the hell man.

"Sorry, but you must admit that was pretty funny," remarked Bryan trying to lighten the situation.

"So funny, get to it already," blurted Christina.

"There she is again, the voice of reason. Anyway, after I missed you with several shots as you left Cuba, I thought there had to be another way. Since the six entities were going to try taking me down, I realized I had to take them down first."

"You're going to take down a worldwide organization with immeasurable power just like that?"

"Yes Christina I am, because I know how they work and what they're trying to do. They are more of a threat than you because they can do infinitely more damage. You know the old saying, the enemy of my enemy is my friend."

"And shithead and?"

"You know if it wasn't for this sweet lady here, I'd slit your throat right now," Ridell explained to Jason. "I discovered this Marty Jackson guy was linked to them through a treasure trove of information he built up."

The bar was bustling like it always did at 5:30, which was good because it meant nobody was paying attention to this meeting, or so they thought.

"How is Marty involved with them?" Jason asked very eagerly.

"Oh so you can talk normal, good for you," answered Ridell who smiled at Jason. "I don't know if he is involved with them, linked to them or was just investigating them. All I know is that Marty had built up something that he was hiding."

Christina felt the note in her pocket and wondered if it had something to do with the bus locker. "And where do you think he was hiding all this stuff?"

"I think you know."

Christina looked at Jason and Bryan like should we really trust this guy, or was this just one more scheme because he couldn't kill them earlier that day.

"I can see you're mulling this over, never good to make a hasty decision," remarked Ridell as if he wasn't the guy who made a hasty decision to shoot their plane down with a missile, and ended up taking out a few trees instead.

"How do we know we can trust you?" Christina insisted with a death look that said don't fuck with me or I'll tear your eyes out and make you look at yourself before I kill you.

"You don't, and by now I'd think you'd know that's how the game is played."

Jason looked at Christina like should we tell him, she looked back with eyes that said only if you believe it'll lead somewhere we need to go. They both thought it was amazing that two people whose souls were authentically intertwined, could just read each other's thoughts. Bryan picked up on all the inner dialogue. Jason was the most trustworthy guy he ever met, and had never done him wrong. He looked at Jason and nodded.

"We know of this locker," Jason stated very cautiously. "We want to find out about Marty just as much as you."

"That must be his hiding spot." Ridell was glad they were finally getting somewhere. "What are we waiting for? If we don't find whatever Jay hid soon, there's no telling what the entities will do. They might shut off all the water. They might use the Emergency Powers Act."

Was Ridell aware of what Marty was investigating, or even that Jay found out and was pushing them to the same locker? Since he was never one to pass up a synchronicity, Jason decided they should let this play out as long as they were on their toes.

"Just to put you guys at ease, maybe we should smoke this first; I'm sure the three of you could use it." Ridell held up a joint so perfectly rolled, Christina would have been proud if it was one of hers.

"Now you're speaking my language. You didn't lace this with anything did you?" Jason joked, not clear about anything anymore.

"Haven't we been over this, if I wanted to kill you I would have already."

Ridell got up from the table which caused Jason, Christina and Bryan to look at each other. They all thought what the hell, so they followed him out the front door.

"You got a lighter man? I think Bill stole mine. Ha, ha, ha, ha," chuckled Ridell, trying to lighten the situation.

"He always had a tendency to do that." Bryan laughed as he produced a lighter from his pocket and handed it to Ridell.

"Thanks man." Ridell lit the joint and took a big puff. "Awwwww, that's much better. I haven't smoked in years."

Jason grabbed the joint next and took a big rip just to get the taste on his tongue. "That has a nice flavor, what is it?"

"Good green bud number five."

Bryan and Jason laughed because of their interaction with the two joints Bryan gave him when he first arrived in New York. That seemed so long ago, now they were smoking a joint with the very guy they brought down.

Jason handed the doobie to Christina who wanted to speak before she took a hit. "I know we have a common enemy, but again why should we trust you?"

Christina took such a big hit that when she exhaled, a big cloud of smoke surrounded them all.

"It has to do with your mother and how she might be the mastermind."

CHAPTER TEN

Christina never thought her dad would try to take down her mom like something out of a political conspiracy handbook. Who would think their parents were out to destroy everything, just to fix it? Maybe kids do think parents are out to ruin their lives. Then their thoughts, feelings and actions evolve as they gain more life experience.

"My mother? How could my mother have anything to do with this?" Christina asked so passionately and skeptically she almost forgot they were smoking a doobie with a former Congressman Jason helped to take down. "I know I lost touch with my mom after dad took off. She said she had to find her own way, but to find her pulling the strings of an evil organization meant to tear down the world, just to build it back up is almost too much to fathom."

"All I know is I heard some chatter about a lady running the organization now. Seems even a group bent on world domination through privatization of everything is an equal opportunity employer," Ridell added with a smile.

Was everything coming together like the last time Bryan and Jason put themselves in the right place at the right time? Was something bigger going on all together? They didn't have it figured out yet, but this was their first clue along the path.

"Even an extremely powerful group has to be on the side of women in power. I realize sexism and racism are still very much an issue, and minorities are marginalized before being allowed into certain positions only if they go along with the status quo," Christina blurted out all in one breath. "But, again, what does this have to do with my mom?"

Ridell still had Bill's threat of ending his life hanging over his head, and he wanted to prove to Christina that even if they didn't trust each other, they did have common goals. "I don't know for sure, when you're talking about the six entities, you can never be sure of anything. I did find something in your dad's papers from when he was investigating Marty. It said the only woman he ever loved might be the leader of his worst nightmare, and Marty would lead him there."

Jason looked at Bryan who was wondering if they were done exposing themselves to any of the hundreds of people that wanted to kill them. From the look on his face, he knew they needed to get the hell out of there. "So you're saying that Bryan's brother is threatening somebody we took down? He wants to find somebody that's going to help them take down his former boss who will lead them to my girlfriend's mother? This is all because her father said something in a secret paper after he was driven out of town by the person he was investigating?"

"If you were any more vague I might know what you're talking about," remarked Ridell who was just as weirded out by the whole thing. "That's what I'm saying. We just have to make sure we keep the same goals. I'm sure we all have leverage on each other, which will keep us honest until we accomplish our common goals."

Bryan wore a smirk because he knew that one of the reasons Riddell murdered his father, was to cash in his insurance policy. He was sure Riddell held something on him, he just didn't know what. "So my brother is threatening you if you divulge too much, but he's okay with you coming to us for help? Seems like he's lost a step in his old age. Why doesn't he just come out here and tell us himself?"

"You know your brother, he likes to stay in the shadows. He doesn't want to come out until the entities are done. He's prepared for the long haul," stated Riddell.

"Okay, as long as you don't get in the way when we have it out, because I'm sure he knows it's coming just as much as I do."

"He does."

The four of them eyed each other trying to see if they should trust each other. Who knows who might be watching or from what angle, or with what kind of camera or recording device? It seemed the technological world meant to connect every one, made the world grow further apart by making it suspicious of itself. Jason knew it was important to do their small part to put society back on the right path. Nothing in life was inevitable, it always came down to a choice.

"Follow us to the bus station and we'll figure out where to go from there," Jason exclaimed. While he loved to smoke doobies and bullshit all day, important work needed to be done, and he wanted to get moving. "We don't need to trust each other, we just need to have the same goals. If not, all bets are off."

"Agreed," Riddell replied with a smirk.

Jason, Christina and Bryan hopped into the Tahoe that was faithfully piloted by Goose. "You guys took long enough, over there," Goose blurted out. He was a little worried they may have been seen because the parking lot was full, and cameras could have been anywhere. "Christina, I know your dad told me to protect you, and by extension Jason and Bryan. That guy will try to screw you over the first chance he gets."

"That's why we have to use him before he uses us. We have to throw him out with the trash before he throws us out," Christina replied feeling the full confidence that comes when speaking truth from your soul.

Jason looked at her admiringly and thought this woman is amazing, I love her even more now. "I love you baby, I'd follow you anywhere."

"I know, and I you, but right now we have to keep our eyes and ears open because nothing is a sure thing."

"Truer words were never spoken," added Goose, happy to see the down to earth reasoning that made him follow Jay, was passed down to his daughter.

They pulled onto the street for what would have been a ten minute drive if there wasn't traffic, but that was practically impossible since it was right in the middle of rush hour.

The sun was fading away, and the remaining light reflected a yearning for a better society off of closed factory after closed factory that had moved overseas.

"I wish we could do something about this. The government gives tax breaks to companies who move their factories thousands of miles away, putting many Americans out of a job. Meanwhile the companies say they need these tax breaks because it gives them money to expand and create more jobs. They just fail to mention those jobs won't be in this country," Jason seethed. His face was getting red with anger the more they drove down the street.

"That is very true. We have to deal with rampant unemployment, which causes a drain on natural resources because the infrastructure that kept it affordable is gone. The companies say that If they took control of power and water systems, they could streamline its delivery to the people." Goose wanted to ensure that he was part of the conversation. Every kid they saw playing outside seemed to be wearing clothes and shoes that should have been thrown out years ago.

Goose joined up with Jay years back after convincing him that after years of investigation, Marty wasn't the great guy he made himself out to be. He continued to dig up information while the Madman for Good was in exile, as he waited for that right opportunity to make his dreams come true.

"Yes. They think of profit first when delivering water and power to the people. Since they're the only ones providing it, they can charge whatever they want. Working people can't afford to pay because the rates have been raised so much," quipped Christina. She looked at Jason because she was getting just as excited as he was since they were getting an opportunity to do some good.

"Maybe we need some kind of technology to save us. It's true that technology is partially responsible for the downfall of society by making everything impersonal, but we can also use it to our advantage. We can use technological breakthroughs to help advance society. Some people say the road to hell is paved with good intentions. Without good intentions however, a person will never know what the right course of action is. People get in trouble when they think that if their intentions are good, they don't have to take action," replied Bryan since he had just as much to gain or lose as anybody else. Would his brother really allow this to happen without it being just one more scheme?

"I agree. That's why the Madman for Good became the Madman for Good. Unrelenting positivity through the action of doing the right thing," expressed Goose, whose passion and hope grew from the energy building in the car. "He wanted to start as a catalyst for change, then transition into an agent of change. I'm not sure which one I am yet, but something tells me I'll soon find out."

As they meandered through the city, people were walking home from work, kids were playing in what little space they had, and homeless people hoped somebody would come along and be their agent of change. Was it possible for people to be their own agents and catalysts of change at the same time? Jason knew that if they were honest about who they were and what was in front of them, their authenticity would initiate positive results.

The north central downtown Detroit bus station was a sprawling facility that went on for several blocks. Jason and Christina were familiar with bus stations that had one pick up and drop off point, not 20. "How will we ever find the right locker?" wondered Jason as he followed Bryan and Christina who were getting out of the car. "You coming with us Goose?"

"Unfortunately I have a few people to meet with, but don't worry, they'll help us down the road," Goose answered with a wink and an authentic smile.

"What do you mean a few people that will help us down the road?" asked Christina, wondering if they should trust the guy supposedly protecting them.

"Just remember that if the early bird gets the worm, the hawk gets the bird."

"What? Think you could explain using a metaphor that actually makes sense in English?" quipped Christina with a fake laugh because she was feeling the stress of the situation.

"Even if things are dark and look like they'll never work out in a million years, if we have faith that they will, they will. It's when we close that door, that it stays shut. Never close that door."

"I'll try not to. I'm glad my dad was such a positive influence on you."

"I could say the same. He raised a daughter with a great head on her shoulders. Good luck, and if you need anything, here's another untraceable cell phone whose signal bounces from tower to tower so it can't be nailed down. Call me if you need anything."

Christina, Jason and Bryan waved at Goose who led the caravan of four black Tahoes as they disappeared back into city traffic.

"There are so many people here, any of them could be a spy," thought Jason, keeping his eyes peeled for anybody suspicious. Men and women alike were bustling around everywhere trying to get to their buses, while trying to have that last minute conversation before they went home to their family.

"Let's try going that way." Christina pointed toward the information booth. "Maybe they can tell us where the lockers are."

"Ooh and look, a Coney dog place right there," replied Jason as his mouth started to water. "I haven't been here in years but they were always so tasty. I mean it's no Cuban sandwich or anything, but there's something you can't beat about a bunch of chili on top of a great tasting wiener."

"Not that I want to get in between a couple of guys arguing over which wieners taste better," quipped Christina with a laugh that caused the guys to immediately have more respect for her because she could take a joke. "In fact, all wieners have different flavors."

"Excuse me?" inquired the mid-fifties man standing at the information booth. Jason, Christina and Bryan had been laughing so hard, they didn't notice they walked across the busy station right up to the booth. Most of the people were stuck looking at their phones, the rest were staring at them.

"I'm sorry sir, my boyfriend just made a joke." Christina lamented, trying to lighten the mood for the obviously offended booth man. "We're looking for some lockers we can put some things in while we ride around the city?"

As the guy in the booth looked down at a computer screen with a scowl because he had to deal with obnoxious jerks for crappy pay, Bryan whispered from behind them. "He looks familiar, like I've seen him somewhere before." Bryan seemed to be having a flashback, or maybe the ex-Congressman's weed was just that good. "It seems like he's helped us before, I just can't put my finger on when."

"Now that you mention it, he does look familiar," noticed Jason.

The guy in the booth leered at them suspiciously before he spoke. "You know I can hear every word you're saying, you aren't exactly being quiet you know. Trust me you've never seen me before. Don't say we all look alike so I must be the guy you ran into."

"The lockers?" inquired Christina trying to restore order.

"Yeah, at the far southwest corner of the station is a bank of lockers. There might still be a few available. You'll see a pay station with instructions there that should explain everything."

"Thank you," Christina responded graciously.

"No problem. Make sure your punk-ass friends don't talk trash at my booth again, or I'll have to come out and kick both their asses."

Christina led the boys away. She didn't want to draw any more attention to themselves, other than the people already watching them. "Why did that guy get defensive all of a sudden? We didn't even do anything," implied Bryan. "Somebody must have pissed in his cheerios."

"He only got upset when you said you'd seen him before," conveyed Christina, happy she was there to settle down the testosterone. "People only get that upset when you're speaking truth, and they have something to hide."

Jason was happy to see that the woman he loved was becoming more attractive as time went on. "I love you baby, you're right. We probably have met him somewhere, but where?"

Just as Bryan was following Christina and Jason to the lockers that were now only a couple hundred feet away, it dawned on him, were people following them? How were they able to move through this crowd without somebody jumping out and grabbing them? Were they being led into a trap? "What about Ridell? What about my brother for that matter? Weren't they going to help us out, where are they?"

"That's a very good question, but right now we just have to grab whatever is in that locker," suggested Jason because they were getting closer to what led them to Detroit.

"I pointed them to where Marty hid the information, should I take them down now?" inquired the guy in the booth who had picked up the phone.

"Not yet, just keep an eye on them. We need them to open the locker, grab whatever is in there and then we'll take it from them. After that, be creative. I know this isn't as exciting as being security at a rally, but you're doing your part to keep the American people strong," expressed the mysterious voice on the other end which had a strange tone to it, almost like it was healing from a face lift. "I know you're down for the cause, you helped us stop Aaron. Even though he was lost, we know you can still help the entities. Without them, the mongrels would take over."

"Understood sir. You might not be serving anymore, but you're still my Commander in Chief."

Christina and the boys walked up to the locker with combination in hand, not noticing the two men who had been following them 100 feet behind since the info booth.

"Now that I think about it, we have seen that guy before. He was security at the anti-immigrant rally in New York. He directed us towards Aaron," remembered Jason as Christina began to enter the numbers.

"You know I think you're right," stated Bryan whose brain moved from food back to the task at hand. "You think Riddell and my bro sent him?"

"Maybe, but they couldn't pull something like that off since the six entities don't support them anymore, or so they said. Then again who knows about anything at this point."

"Well if you guys are done babbling, do you want to see what Marty was hiding?" Christina interrupted as she opened the locker and found one simple manila folder inside.

"We came all this way for one stupid folder?" queried Jason as he reached out to pick it up. "Let me see what this thing says."

The folder had no markings on the outside, but the inside was filled with plenty of pertinent information.

"These look like blueprints, specs and financial reports for something called a water bio-analyzer. Geez, I hated science classes. How are we supposed to know what this means?" pondered Bryan, not knowing what to make of it.

"I didn't much care for science classes either, I had to hold study groups for months just to get a C," Jason chuckled, and realized he very much missed laughing with Bryan since he had been away. He had Christina and couldn't be happier, but sometimes he needed some friendly male interaction. He was just glad to have his friend back.

"How about you hand it to somebody with an actual science background," replied Christina with a smirk that said Geez, let a woman fix what men have messed up once again. "It's interesting when a woman has more book smarts than the guys. Let me see that stuff."

Jason handed Christina the folder with a loving look in his eye because he was so turned on when she intellectually took charge. He knew that love was behind it, she really was a Madwoman for Good.

"Oh man, this is, oh my God. I didn't even think this was possible. No wonder dad was after Marty, and who knows why Marty had it, or even if he was trying to hide it from somebody else. This could change the world," exclaimed Christina whose eyes were bulging out of her head.

"Really, then what is it? I thought I was the only one who liked to beat around the bush," Jason sniped with a dirty smile.

"I'm not touching that one. Well maybe I'll touch it after we figure this out and get some alone time. These are blueprints for a revolutionary new way to desalinate and purify water. From the pictures, it looks like they pipe the water in from the ocean or feed in snow, and put it through this bio-analyzer which cleans it quick enough, so when it comes out of a kitchen sink, you can drink it. This could change the world."

Just as Jason pondered the right response, a hand tapped him on the shoulder. "Remember me, I told you guys to stop looking because you'll never take us down."

Jason turned around and looked into the eyes of seventy year old Terrance Shipley, who had five of the biggest armed body guards he'd ever seen around him in a defensive formation.

"I remember you, but where is that Australian shepherd, it was so cute. Way better looking than your ugly mug," remarked Jason, not wanting to cede an inch.

"Ahhh, there's that wit, that angst to fight. That's why we knew we should follow you. We knew you'd eventually lead us right to these plans your former boss so gracefully stole from us. He thought he'd cut us out of the deal. Little does he know…." the old man quipped.

Just as Christina was about to defend Jason and Bryan verbally once again, the old man stopped her before she opened her mouth. "Before you say it, let me say it for you. We knew your dad was following Marty, and we knew he discovered where Marty hid the blueprints. Now we have them and don't try to stop us."

"What makes you say that you son of a bitch," asserted Christina accusingly as she lunged to punch the old man before one of his body guards pushed her to the ground.

"You're such a big man you like to hit women," Jason fired back, defending his lady.

"If you would have just stayed away from the water park that day, none of this would have happened. Why couldn't you have just gone to get anesthetized in an air conditioned movie theater like the rest of the population?" questioned one of the bodyguards menacingly.

"Okay enough," interjected the old man who was starting to feel inconvenienced, but nowhere near threatened. "This is how it's going to work. I'm going to take these blue prints and you aren't going to follow us."

"After all we've been through, what makes you think we won't?" Jason stalled, trying to play along so they could get as much information as they could. "Continue. What are you threatening us with so we don't come after you? Who did you kidnap?"

The old man was stunned that Jason had already jumped two steps ahead, and wondered what Jason was insinuating. For now, the threat was the plan. "When this country lost the most powerful man in the world they trusted to carry them to a brighter day, I asked myself what purpose could that serve? We could make it look like the people triumphed over evil, giving the bad guys time to regroup and attack even harder next time."

"You going to get to it, or are you just going to talk big about things we already know, like the President faking his death after you made him resign?"

"I always respected your ability to cut through the bullshit Jason. If the cards were different, you could have helped me and the six entities carry out the master plan."

"What master plan?"

"Do I look like Riddell? Do I look like I'm going to tell you just because you asked me? While we're on the subject, have you seen Riddell or that guy Bill who always told him what to do?"

Jason chuckled under his breath before he answered. "We haven't seen him, and we're actually telling you the truth this time. I'm not telling you because I want to screw you over like a used car salesman, I want you to tell us who the hell you kidnapped, so we can get on with the rescue. I really want to eat one of those Coney dogs over there."

"Okay, not being one to get in-between a man and his food," joked the old man, wondering if Jason was actually hungry or was attempting some sort of diversion. "We tracked down Christina's father in Cuba, and asked him where Marty hid the blueprints. He said somebody was on their way to grab them and re-hide them. Naturally once we said we had an eye on you guys, and that we'd kill him if he didn't talk, he told us."

"You're telling me my dad cracked, just like that?" Christina queried suspiciously.

"He said he didn't want to let you down like he had before. After he told us you were headed to some bus station locker in Detroit, we decided we'd hold onto him for insurance until we received the blueprints."

"Well now that you have them, are you going to let him go? Where are you hiding him?" questioned Jason, hoping the old man would let something slip.

"Once we feel that you have backed off, we'll let you know when and where we're letting him go. You don't want to start receiving his limbs one by one in the mail, do you?"

"Not really, I wanted to spend some more time with my entire dad, not just parts of him. Don't hurt him. How do we know he's still alive?"

As the old man walked away holding the manila folder, followed by his monster bodyguards, Jason looked down at a vibrating burner phone Goose said couldn't be traced. Somehow the old man sent him a video message.

Jason opened it to find the Madman for Good tied up with a copy of the Detroit free press in his hands to show what day it was. "Sorry Christina, I tried. I just didn't want to see you hurt. These guys mean business. Don't question their authority because they won't put up with it. I love you."

The video cut out and the screen went black.

"So we have to find him, right?" inquired Christina as she frantically looked at Jason and Bryan like why haven't we started looking yet.

Just as Bryan was about to open his mouth a familiar voice spoke up. "What did we miss?"

Jason turned around to see Ridell standing there like he was out of breath from running. "You're a little late to the party. We found what Marty was hiding, but the entities came and scooped it up before we could leave. They also kidnapped my father and said if we followed them, they'd send us his body parts one at a time," Christina exploded two inches from Riddell's face. She had an expression that said tell me what I want to know, or I'll rip your balls off and shove them down your throat. "I suggest you tell us everything you know about the six entities or so help me God, I'll rip your heart out and send it to your father. Oh sorry, I can't do that because you killed him. Talk asshole or I'll think of somebody else to send it to."

Jason backed up five feet from Christina because he never saw her so mad before. He decided it was better to get out of her way because he knew you don't get in the way of a woman and her dad.

"Okay, hold on. You'd think I was the one that took him."

"How do we know you're not?"

"So we're going to play this game again?"

"Just talk, NOW!"

"Remind me to never piss you off again. Without your mother, the six entities would have never gotten off the ground. She was the architect."

CHAPTER ELEVEN

"So my father investigated Jason's father for investigating my mother?" asked Christina in disbelief of the words that spilled from her lips.

"Pretty much," replied Riddell, who knew how unlikely an alliance this could be. "I want to help you guys because the enemy of my enemy is always my friend."

"You said that before," Bryan piped up, remembering how many times Riddell had done him wrong in the past. "Not that I trust you, because I don't. How exactly are you going to help us?"

Riddell chose his next words carefully, "I want to bring these guys down just as much as you do, and the less time we sit here jawing, the more time we'll have to track down her mom. Like I said, she is the key."

Jason needed to fill his stomach because it was growling like Tony the Tiger. "Can we finish this conversation over at that Coney dog place? I'm starving and I don't want to start this fight on an empty stomach."

After staring each other down for what seemed like an eternity, Jason, Bryan, Christina and Riddell all realized that if they kept standing there staring at each other somebody would notice them. Without talking, they walked through the noisy bus depot and across the street to Bull's Coney Dog.

The place was fairly busy when the four of them walked in. The smell of chili and hot dogs beaconed across their nostrils and permeated the room. After a long wait in line, they hoped it was worth it. "What kind of wiener are you going to get? Something puny and un-flavorful that makes you sick when it goes down," Jason bantered with Riddell, trying to get a rise out of him, and to see if he could take a joke.

"Isn't that what your mom said last night Jason?" Ridell quipped. Bryan laughed at the surprisingly funny joke his former and future enemy came up with. "Let me buy this round and purchase some good faith."

Christina and the guys agreed so Riddell ordered four Coney dogs with the works, and a few baskets of fries because he knew it would be plenty to share. As they walked over to an empty booth and sat down, Riddell spoke, "about your mom, she's been at this for a long time, getting close to her won't be easy."

"If anybody could get close to her, I could. I'll play the long lost daughter who wants to reunite with her mother, which in a way I am." Christina barely believed that in the span of a few weeks, she found out her father was alive, met up with him while he was exiled in Cuba; and then discovered her mother at the helm of a worldwide conspiracy bent on world domination, It was something right out of a movie.

Jason sat next to Christina on one side of the booth, and Bryan sat uncomfortably next to Riddell on the other side. "Ladies first," Bryan chuckled, motioning for Ridell to scoot down so he could sit on the end.

"I thought it was age before beauty. Wait, I meant you," replied Riddell, badly messing up the joke. Bryan laughed anyway because the attempt was there. Ridell's plan of getting close to the people that took him down was almost complete.

"Ok, let's get off moms, I got off yours," Jason shot back, who wanted one more dig because he couldn't help himself.

"Ha, ha, ha Mr. Jason. Bill always said you were the brains behind taking us down, but from the lack of quality in your jokes I'd have to disagree." Riddell didn't like this set up either, but he knew it was necessary.

"What do you have for us? What about the blue prints for the bio-analyzer? Did my mom invent it or did the six entities steal it from her?" Christina blurted out. She wanted to start this mission as fast as possible, because she couldn't sit next to Ridell much longer. "What's the next step? How do we get the blueprints back?"

"It all goes back to the President faking his death, or should I say your mom faking his death. She knew the entities would hemorrhage major cash, if he was held accountable; as would the system designed to slowly chip away at the working class till there's nothing left. Why do you think unions have declined since the eighties?" asked Riddell who wanted to prove himself.

The air of bullshit was thick in the air, so Bryan tried to cut through it. "Okay, we know unions and workers have been downplayed for years. That's nothing new. We want to know how Christina's mother is involved."

Christina's eyes said thank you for getting things back on track. "Yeah what about my mom, and how do you know she's my biological mom?" Christina queried, wondering how both her parents got involved in this. Her parents always told her growing up that she'd have to find her own path. She'd have to be her own agent of change, and not wait for somebody else. She lost track of her mom when her dad left. Little did she know what was going on behind the scenes.

"Your mom had a science background like you," Riddell interjected, trying to appeal to Christina's intellect. He needed her help most of all. "She came up with the idea of the bio-analyzer all by herself. She knew it would be extremely useful as the entire world goes through drought after drought. She showed her ideas to a guy she met in school who had government contacts. It was your dad Jason, Marty Jackson."

Jason was stunned. "So my dad was working with Christina's mom?"

"Yes. They were childhood friends who grew apart as they got older as many tend to do. Anyway, she showed Marty the blueprints because she trusted him, and thought he could get it to the right people."

"So what happened next?" wondered Christina with baited breath.

"Once Marty realized the importance of what he was being shown, he showed them to his other old friend from school. You know him as the former President. He went behind Marty's back and offered your mom a job and a boatload of money for the blueprints. He of course wasn't the President yet, but he knew the bio-analyzer could make him billions. Your mom wanted to share the technology with the masses and make good money at the same time. She came up with plans to not only use the bio analyzer to fix the environment, but also plans to fix the military, the health care industry, the chemical industry, the financial industry, and the government itself. Then to top it off, she wanted these six separate parts to work together to help the world, while making huge profit."

"So the six entities came from my mom, so she could have her hands in all the areas she'd need to control the world? Was this the master plan that you were talking about?" Christina fired back with an inferno in her belly she hadn't felt in a very long time. She wasn't bitter anymore about leaving Shane Corp., just another stepping stone toward her dream. She knew once you're on the path toward your dream, it will take you places you never thought you'd go.

"You're mom wanted to change the world, one area, one entity at a time. Which brings us to the master plan," responded Riddell, wanting to divulge just enough to get the gang's juices flowing, because he knew they would screw him over the first chance they got. He just had to make sure he screwed them over first.

Just as Christina was about to ask another pointed question the food arrived steaming hot. If heaven had a smell, Jason surmised it would be something like this. "Man I've waited for this a long time," Jason recalled, remembering when he was a kid and would visit his family.

His dad grew up in the area and told many crazy stories about the sixties. He was always in the picture, but his real dad wasn't. What was the story with Marty? Jason needed to find out soon, but he knew Christina's journey would have to come first. He thought it was interesting that once he was traveling his path, it led back to her. Little did he know, it was now driving them both back toward their parents.

A million thoughts were steamrolling through Jason's head, but an amazing chili dog was sitting in front of him, so he took a big bite. "Mmmmmmmmmmm, this is good."

"I've had chili dogs before, but this is good," exclaimed Bryan happy to be back with his good friend. He knew the road ahead wouldn't always be rosy, so he decided to just enjoy the moment.

"Should we look for Marty? Christina's mom? Christina's dad? Who will lead us to what we're looking for?" Bryan theorized as he took another monster bite. He was in ecstasy just as much as Jason. "I think we need to locate Christina's dad first. Ridell, you must know where they're holding him?"

Ridell was enjoying his Coney dog with such gusto, chili was dripping down his face. He had to wipe his chin before he was able to get his words out, "yes."

"Yes, is that all you can say?" replied Jason who was lulled into relaxation by the delicious food in front of him, but not so much that his brain went to sleep. "What's the next step?"

"Tell us, where are they hiding my dad?" Christina gasped, starting to get anxious.

"Ok ok, don't get your panties in a bunch. When I was still in their good graces I visited an abandoned factory they used as their secret headquarters."

"Whose secret headquarters? My mom's? The entities, whose? So help me, if you tell me one more time not to get my panties in a bunch, I'll make you choke on that Coney dog you're shoving in your mouth," Christina shot back because she was tired of playing games.

"It's across town. Let me walk in there and see what I can see. I'll find out what I can."

"Didn't you just say they were after you too?" queried Christina. She wanted to make sure everybody was on the same page. "How are you just going to walk in there?"

Not wanting to give up his leverage right away, Ridell knew he'd have to give them just enough to keep their beaks wet. "They do want to see me go down. That much is true. If I tell them I can bring you to them, while helping you find them, it will be a win win."

"Then what, we're just supposed to stroll up there because you say it's cool?" Bryan fumed because he didn't trust Ridell anymore than he could throw him.

"Look man, you don't have to trust me, hell none of you do. We all want the same thing, and the sooner you realize that, the better off we'll all be. Basically I'll go there, tell them I know where you're at, and that you're looking for Christina's dad," offered Ridell.

"After the old man showed up at the bus station and told us they're holding Christina's dad, I'm pretty sure he's expecting us to go after him," remarked Jason trying to see where this was going.

"He probably is expecting that. I'll say I'm sorry for what I did, and I'll help take you guys down just to show them I can be trusted again. Then when they tell me where he is, I'll simply send you a message. You then swoop in and rescue him," Ridell suggested.

"Just swoop in huh, and how in the hell are we supposed to do that?" quizzed Jason angrily.

"I don't know, you'll figure it out. Hell, you took me and Bryan's brother down by using your wits. Which at this point, is the only thing you can trust," Ridell retorted.

Bryan began to ponder everything he had been through with Ridell. All the years he tried to bring him down after discovering what he was truly about, then actually taking him down, and now having him come back to help was unbelievable. Bryan was still confident though because he had leverage on the former Congressman.

"Go ahead and do it. You have something on us, we have something on you. We don't have to trust each other. We just have to remember either one of us could end the whole game. That will keep us both honest. Jason and Christina want to change the world for the better and so do I, especially since our families are somehow involved. What do you have to gain?" Bryan cross-examined, wanting to know Ridell's motivation before they were off to the races.

"What makes you think I don't want a better world too? You know I did at some point in the past. I realize we're in different places now, but that kind of thing never goes away," pondered Ridell, remembering days gone by.

"I'm still not sure if I believe you, but at this point we just have to see what happens," Jason answered confidently.

This was the only way to get the truth they were all seeking.

"That's the voice of reason I was searching for," Ridell remarked, trying to hide an evil smile, but which Jason picked up on immediately.

"What was that smile for, you planning to screw us over?" Jason snapped back. He had to hold his nose because the stench of bullshit was just too much.

"Not any more than you're planning to screw me over," Ridell volleyed in return.

Not wanting this thing to get into a stalemate because of a measuring contest, Christina spoke up. "Go talk to them and get back to us. Since we don't trust each other anyway, we don't have anything to lose."

"I know I don't," Ridell snarked with an even more deceitful smile than before, which made the guys trust him even less. "You've got a good woman here Jason. You don't want to lose her over this. Don't let her kill herself trying to outdo her mother by starting the twelve entities or something."

"Why did you have to say that, don't you know when to shut your stupid mouth?" uttered Jason whose anger was boiling over. He was very passionate about making positive change, and about the amazing woman that was sitting to his right. He also knew his purpose was to uncover what was swept under the rug so the world could see it, rise up and institute the changes that needed to be instituted.

"Since I know the next words out of your mouth are going to be shithead, I'll be on my way," Ridell remarked smugly with a cool confidence that made Jason want to punch him. "I'll message you when I have something. Just remember to always look over your shoulder, you never know who is watching." Ridell got up from the table and walked toward the door, right behind him, he was followed a man in blue jeans, a black hoodie and dark sneakers.

"See you later man, don't screw us over. That goes for you too bro," Bryan conveyed to Ridell, and the guy who followed him out the door he knew was Bill.

"What do we do now? We know we can't trust that guy. Marty could probably help us find where Jay is because of the information he found," Jason exclaimed. He was trying to wrap his head around the situation because it was a crazy truth. "Marty was tracking the entities so he could find Christina's mom, all the while holding onto to technology he knew they'd love to get back. I think we should start there."

Jason hoped Christina could handle this thing they were about to get into, but he knew she could; that's one of the reasons he loved her so much. She was just as much down for the cause as he was.

"Sounds like a plan. Let's go ask Goose if my dad had any contacts in the city that could lead us to Marty," Christina demanded. She was getting riled up because a deep passion for justice was rushing through her veins.

The three of them finished up their food, and walked out to the car. "I know I just ate a bunch of chili, but don't worry I won't fart too much," Jason joked, trying to lighten the mood.

"Hey, I ate just as much you did buddy. I'll stink you both out," Christina fired back with a laugh that made both Bryan and Jason smile.

"Two people turning each other on by describing their farts, I don't think I've been grossed out more in my entire life," Bryan added.

Goose had been patiently waiting by the Tahoe that was in the same place as when they left. "You came back?" asked Jason, surprised Goose parked in the same spot.

"I couldn't leave you guys, not until this fight is done. I'm a Navy Seal, it was ingrained in us to never leave a brother behind, and see the mission through to the end," answered Goose with as much conviction as his soul could exude. "Besides, I'd do anything for Jay, he saved my life."

"With everything that's happened so far I totally want to hear that story, but for right now we have to find Marty. My dad must have discovered something about where he could be," Christina expressed anxiously.

Goose got a twinkle in his eye because Christina truly was the daughter of the Madman for Good. "I think he did. When he was looking into Marty, he found out Marty was looking into the entities, which is how he found out about you."

"We know all this," Christina stated. "Tell us something we don't know."

While Goose was trying to come up with a witty response, a call came over the police scanner attached to the dashboard. "Officer down over at the corner of 86th and Hunter St. requesting ambulance and all units in the area for backup."

"That sounds like a hairy situation," exclaimed Jason who was a little nervous, but glad because they had a battle hardened Navy Seal on their side.

"It definitely does, especially since Jay had tracked Marty to that location some years back. I think we should take a ride over and check it out," replied Goose instinctively. He looked and sounded like he was going into battle, because he knew he was.

Goose pulled the car out of the parking lot and headed down the road toward the address. The streets were filled with angst because of all the traffic. Driving down the road in downtown Detroit, must be like driving down any downtown street in America Jason thought; poor people struggling to survive outside of skyscrapers filled with jerks laughing in front of computer screens while counting their billions of dollars. Jason felt like finding Marty was the next step in stopping them, and to rescue his girlfriend's dad of course.

They pulled up at a warehouse which had already been cordoned off with crime scene tape, and had a bunch of cops trying to keep the crowd at bay. "Great, how do we get in there now?" queried Jason, wondering what trick Goose might have up his fully tattooed sleeve.

"Judging by this crowd I don't think we are, but I see a guy I used to serve with," noticed Goose as he parked the Tahoe a block away and walked towards the scene.

"Let's follow him, especially if it leads us to my dad and eventually my mom." Christina jumped out of the car so fast, Jason and Bryan were barely able to keep up.

Within five minutes, Goose found his way to the front of the tape and was talking to one of the uniformed officers. "Hey Goose long time no see," expressed the late-fifties officer who looked like he had seen better days, but still had much work to do before he could retire. "How are you, how's Jay?"

"He's been better, the entities took him," remarked Goose with both sadness and rage in his eyes thinking of what he was going to do to the people who took him. "I'm actually here with his daughter trying to find him."

Goose turned around to introduce Christina because she was nipping at his heels. "So you knew my dad also?"

Christina asked as she went to shake the hand of yet another person that worked with her dad.

"You could say that. Goose and I go way back, we were both Seals. He went into private security, I obviously went this way," the officer explained pointing at his badge. "But my passion for being one of the Mad People for Good has never dimmed. What can I do for you?"

"We know Jay had been tracking a guy named Marty Jackson years ago, and this was one of the places he tracked him to; we figured it was a good place to start. We just didn't figure we'd come across a dead body in the process," Goose stated inquisitively. He wanted to find his leader. Jay was more than a mentor to him. He was a man that re-instilled hope within his soul.

"It's funny you bring up Marty. He was just here, but then he split," the officer wondered.

"Why?" asked Goose.

"He heard his hiding spot had been located, and the entities were coming to get him. They sent in one of their henchman, but I guess Marty got to him first. The kicker of the whole thing, was that the guy they sent in was disguised as a federal agent, some guy named Bill something."

Bryan stood there stunned. "They sent my brother in, and Marty shot him, is that what you're saying?"

"You want to keep your voice down?" whispered the officer who knew anybody could be listening. "You must be Bryan, I heard Jay talk about you, nice to meet you. Anyway, Marty found out they were onto him, this guy Bill goes in to do the deed, but Marty got to him first."

"Marty what, killed him and escaped?" Goose chimed in, not wanting to lose track of the mission.

"Pretty much. After I arrived on scene, the uniforms, suits and lab geeks were roaming around trying to find whatever evidence they could. I saw a little scrap of paper hanging out of a crack in the wall. Since nobody was around me at the time, I picked it up and started reading."

"Well, well? What did it say?" demanded Christina who was just as impatient as she was excited.

"The note was addressed to followers of the Madman for Good. It was some kind of coded message I was never able to figure out," deciphered the officer who really was confused, but happy he ran into some friendly faces that could help. He wanted to fight the same good fight that the Madman for Good instilled in him.

"Do you still have it, let me see it," Christina insisted. She held out her hand and the officer put a dirty scrap of paper in it.

"Beside the fact this thing looks like somebody wiped their ass with it, I think it might be the answer we're looking for," observed Christina who knew that to get at the heart of a situation, you had to keep things light. "It's addressed to all Mad People for Good. It says I had to do what I had to do, Honey Bear knows the answer. The location is beyond Pooh's forest where honey no longer exists. Find Marty if you d-aver."

"This message was obviously meant for me, or for somebody else to find and give to me. I have no idea what d-aver means though," explained Christina as she got a tingling feeling they were onto something really big.

"When I worked with Jay, he was building up his movement as he was investigating Marty and the entities. He held neighborhood meetings all over the place but listed them secretly. He would give a random street name to throw people off, but the last letter was the key. When he said D-aver, he didn't mean it's on D street, he meant it's on R street," expressed Goose who even though he was one of the toughest guys anywhere, he was happy that people with unrelenting positivity were on his side and would also see the mission through. "Jay must have stashed the note, who knows if Marty even knew it was there while he was hiding out."

"It sounds like he was trying to make the clues just hard enough, but not so hard that nobody would figure them out," Jason wondered out loud.

"He was, but he wasn't. He was building a movement to take down the people who hold the real power behind the scenes, the entities in the shadows so to speak."

"So this place is on R Street or something then?" responded Christina.

"Not exactly. You put the R in front of the word ave. and you get the word rave. Since he hoped people would be ravenous for change, he thought having a meeting on a street called ravenous would be a great place to start. It's a quiet, discreet office park about ten minutes from here."

"Well let's go," Jason demanded, eager to find out about Christina's dad, but also about his own. Meanwhile Bryan was still trying to process the fact that his brother was dead. Ridell must have told him what they were up to. He told Bill to drive over, kill Marty who was at the safe-house they were in front of right now; but Marty got to him first. Bryan expected his brother to get killed one day, but Bill was still his brother and that would never change.

"Nice to meet you Christina. When you find your dad and I know you will, tell him that I owe him so much and would follow him anywhere. I'll gather the troops at a moment's notice, he only has to say the word. There are many people like me and Goose ready to take these bastards on. We all want to do anything we can," stated the officer who stuck out his hand so Christina could shake it.

"I will, and thanks so much for your help."

As they walked back to the car, Jason realized that the waterpark, the Congressman, the President, hell everything they'd been through led to this point. Even though it was scary to delve into the unknown, this time was more exciting because he knew they were directly helping the world to evolve.

The Golden Meadows office park looked the same as any of the million office parks people pass as they drive down a busy street. It was the perfect meeting place to set up the downfall of a secret organization.

The parking lot was half full as Goose pulled the car into a spot. "Okay, this is the place. I remember going to a few meetings here before your dad went into exile."

"He really must have meant something to you for you to risk so much for him," related Christina.

"He did and he does. Like I said before, he saved my life, and when we have more time I'll tell you the whole story. For now, all you need to know is that you're looking for suite 5d. It's the one down there in the far corner," Goose explained as he pointed at the small brown door. Even though it looked like any run of the mill door, he knew that behind it was their collective next step. "Why don't you go down there, I'm going to stay back and have a smoke."

Christina nodded at Goose in agreement, while she, Jason and Bryan got out of the car and walked toward the far end of the parking lot. Each step they took was another step forward in a journey with an unknown outcome. They might not know their destination, but they were traveling their correct path.

Before they could think of anything to say to each other, the door that read suite 5-d was staring them in the face.

"Should we go in?" Bryan reluctantly inquired like he didn't already know the answer.

"No I think we should go home, smoke weed and watch Seinfeld reruns. Of course we should go in, but that whole weed and Seinfeld thing sounds good. Maybe we could afterward," babbled Jason to himself, not noticing if Bryan or Christina were listening; he was just trying to make himself feel better. He turned the knob on the door and they walked in.

There was a familiar looking secretary at the desk, knowing he'd seen her somewhere before, Jason walked up.

"We're here to see, wait a minute, Barbara?" inquired Jason with a dumbfounded look on his face.

"Go right in, he's expecting you."

The office door behind Barbara was big and made of a beautiful stained oak, which seemed odd for a discreet office, but Jason knew they had more important fish to fry.

The door opened to a man sitting behind a desk, who was trying to hide in the shadows. "I've been expecting you, how you doing son?"

CHAPTER TWELVE

Jason considered himself a pretty open minded person, but the idea of meeting his biological father who lured him to New York for God knows what, was almost too much to take.

"I don't know if I'm ready to call you dad, there are so many things I want to ask you," Jason spoke a million miles a minute, a habit when he was nervous.

Marty motioned for Jason, Bryan and Christina to sit down because he knew this was a meeting none of them would soon forget. Jason pondered how the six entities were six different parts of an organization put together for the purposes of controlling every aspect of the world. He knew this was the next step in taking down the first entity, whether it was his father or not.

"So I'm sure you're wondering what the hell is going on," chuckled Marty with a half-cocked smile meant to convey his happiness, and uneasiness about his truth coming to light.

"I worked for you for years, I had no idea you were part of some cover-up. How do I even know you're on the side of the good guys?" queried Bryan because he had just as much invested in the truth about Marty as anybody else, even though he knew this was Jason and Marty's moment.

"Remember that feeling you had when you first walked into my office," Marty reminisced looking right into Jason's soul. He realized it might also have the same meaning for Bryan because their relationship started much the same.

"Of course, how could I forget? I had never been to New York and was being offered the opportunity of a lifetime to take down some corrupt politicians," answered Jason as he immediately flashed back to his beginnings. Thoughts about insider trading, immigration, the water park and more zoomed through Jason's head all at the same time. The one thing that could always bring clarity though, was the calming and down to earth words of the love of his life, Christina.

"Were you investigating my mother? That Congressman said she designed the six entities, that she put them together?" interjected Christina who wasn't trying to upset the awkward family reunion, but wanted to get down to business. Her reunion with her dad was a little more peaceful because it took place in a foreign country while he was in exile. Marty however was under the radar in his own country with all sorts of people out looking for him.

"This is the famous Christina? Jason told me a lot about you, thanks for allowing him to come to New York," Marty sniped.

"It wasn't so much allowing him, but more loving him enough to push him toward his dream even if that meant leaving me. Once we were both firmly traveling our respective paths we reunited. Through the simple act of following synchronicities, we took down the most powerful man in the world. Which of course leads us back to you," stated Christina who was letting her energy flow, because she knew the more honest she was with herself, the more truth she would find.

"Good job on that by the way. We didn't talk after that happened," Marty inferred because he knew they all had secrets.

"We met this old man on a beach, who said he was roommates with you, and the President in college; he actually helped to take the President down. Then he disappeared for a while, until he threatened us on the phone," recalled Jason, curious what Marty was really up to. "Since he knew you from back in the day, we weren't sure if you were just drinking buddies, or if you helped him with the cover-up. Now that they have the blueprints of this bio-analyzer thing..."

"They have the blue prints, how did they get their hands on them?"

"Christina's dad was investigating you for a while, he thought it was weird that you had all this money, but never had any obvious investments. It made more sense when he found out you had this technology at your fingertips."

Marty wondered why this was all tying together now. The way things went in the past however, he knew they'd reveal themselves soon enough. "Sounds like you guys have been busy."

"That's all you can say, it sounds like we've been busy," fumed Jason as the rage was building within him. "We take down the most powerful man in the world who knew you from college. Then we're threatened by the guy who helped us do it, who was also your friend in college. Considering all of that, all you can say is, sounds like we've been busy? What kind of person are you to give false hope to someone with dreams, and make them think something you know not to be true?"

"What did I make you believe that wasn't true? I brought you to New York and set you up in style so you could take down corrupt politicians. Which is exactly what you did," retorted Marty.

"We discovered you've been making money for a long time off of a secret water technology, which is probably how you sent me money all those years," Jason shot back as if he was in a counseling session.

"I don't want to interrupt this family reunion, but I'd like to have another one of my own," Christina insisted. She was past niceties, and wanted to get down to the nitty-gritty. "My dad was taken hostage because he'd been investigating you and this bio-analyzer. They scooped him up because he had knowledge of the whole thing."

"Yeah, what about that? Jay was really nice to me and took me in after Jason and I took down Ridell. I was lost and wandering until I discovered the Madman for Good was more than a catchy name, but of a way of life," Bryan shouted, because he had to get his own portion of shit off his chest.

"You seem to know all the power players, how do we get my dad back?" Christina demanded as she saw right through Marty. She knew a possible way to locate her dad was to first find the blueprints, and take down this leg of the entities.

"I don't know where they took him, I'm not in the inner circle," replied Marty who didn't look them in the eyes because he knew it wasn't 100% true.

"That's bullshit. A guy you went to school with is one of the top dogs controlling things. The old guy we met on the beach that helped take down the President, threatened us by saying they have my dad, and if we don't back off, they'll send us his body parts one at a time. So I'll ask again, where do we start looking?" Christina fumed as she pictured her dad being proud of her in this exact moment.

"Okey dokey. I know I haven't been completely truthful with any of you, and you have no reason to trust me," Marty expressed, hoping there was a shred of humanity left in the three people sitting in front of him. He knew the fight ahead was for the future of the country's natural resources.

"And???" Jason added, hoping Marty was leading somewhere.

"I can tell you the whole story right now if that will make you feel better, but I don't think it will."

"So why don't you just tell us what we need to know."

Just as Marty was about to open his mouth, the phone rang. "Thanks Barbara."

"What is it?" Jason, Christina and Bryan asked in unison.

"It seems I've just been threatened. Now that the entities have the blueprints for the bio analyzer, they want to shut everybody up who knows anything. That's why I originally held onto the technology, I had to find the right way to release it."

"And make yourself a ton of money in the process. That thing has to be worth billions of dollars," Bryan sniped very skeptically. He understood that the disappearance of his dirty joking mind made room for critical thinking.

"I'd be compensated for sure, but not compared to the importance it brings to the collective evolution of humanity. I only want to help the world," Marty quipped, trying to sound authentic. How did he know Jason and Bryan weren't spies, or that Christina's dad sent her to take him down since he'd been investigating him so long?

"We have to take them down before they take us down," raged Christina, ready to get after it.

"That is the only way to really beat them. If hiding out worked Christina, your dad and I wouldn't be in the positions we presently find ourselves in."

"Enough jawing, can you help us or not?" Bryan questioned. He was growing testy because this meeting wasn't going anywhere.

"Okay okay. I know a guy, he works at the UN. Let me make some calls and see what I can find out. In the meantime, why don't you guys chill out and relax. Seems like we all could use it."

"I'll rest when my dad is safe. You expect us to do nothing while we wait for you to call us? What Jason did before, led us here to you," Christina remarked with a fiery passion. "My dad has many people behind him who are willing to do the hard work necessary to bring positive change. Now that we are on the cusp, it seems like we aren't getting anywhere. Come on guys let's get out of here, this guy is no help; Goose can rally some troops. I'm sure some of them have heard something."

"Did you say Goose?" Marty asked with surprise.

"Yeah why? He was one of my dad's best men."

"Because I know he's only out for his own best interests."

"How do you know that, he brought us here and to you?"

"Because people aren't always what they seem, I'm living proof of that. He's probably outside smoking right now, I told him he should have quit years ago, but he never listens to anything. Go ask him about the Grand Charade?"

"The what?"

"Go ask him about it, I'm sure it'll lead you in the direction you'd like to go. I'll call my guy at the UN and see what I can find out, I'll let you know."

Jason, Christina and Bryan walked out of Marty's office a little clearer than when they went in, but also more confused. Was Marty saying that he could be trusted and that Christina's dad couldn't? Or was he saying that just Goose couldn't be trusted? What was this Grand Charade thing? Was he talking about life, or a particular scheme he pulled? What was certain, there was no turning back.

The three of them approached the Tahoe and Goose who was leaning against the hood, standing over a pile of cigarette butts. "Smoke much?" Jason casually asked because he wanted to ease into it.

"Just a bit," answered Goose with a laugh. "How'd it go in there?"

"Marty said we should ask you about the Grand Charade?" Christina blurted out, hoping she could trust her dad's right hand man. Even though her dad abandoned her when she needed him the most, he always did what he thought was right for the betterment of the world. "He also said he knew you?"

"I should have told you, Marty and I served together in the Marines before he went to college. I was a lowly corporal and he was my CO. We caught wind of the schemes that corrupt regimes in the Middle East and Africa were pulling. Or should I say the schemes that corrupt regimes were pulling with western backing," Goose admitted like he was in confession.

When Jason heard the words Western backing, his ears perked up immediately. "Was this Grand Charade a means of creating crisis, so private money would flood in to help? Then when the real emergency hit, they had sole control of the relief effort, making them and their friends even more money?"

"Pretty much," responded Goose who was stunned Jason figured it out so quickly. He was happy the daughter of the man he looked up to found somebody equally on her level. "Not that the bio-analyzer alone wouldn't have made billions of dollars anyway, because it would have. If they produce fake crisis after fake crisis, they would be sole possessors of something that helps sustain life, drinking water and the ability to grow crops. If you want to control a society, you have to control the essentials."

The sun was beaming directly over their heads, and was starting to make them all sweaty and anxious. "I thought this far north was supposed to be cooler. What about all the frozen lakes I've heard so much about?" Bryan interjected, trying to lighten the mood.

"That's it, frozen lakes," Goose replied as a light bulb went off in his head.

"What does something I did when I was seven have to do with anything?" Jason asked curiously, but with a smile of the happy memory; because if it helped Goose lead them somewhere, that's all that mattered.

"Don't you get it, solid ice?"

"What, as opposed to melted ice? Don't they call that water?" Jason replied, trying to sound like a smart ass so Goose would get to the point.

"I'm trying to say melted snow and ice is the key. All the snow they got back east was more than they knew what do with right?"

"Yeah and?"

"Since they had nowhere to put it, they just dumped it in the ocean. If they built a pipeline that melted snow into water, and piped it and ocean water across the country, purified and desalinated it, would we even be thinking drought?"

"Are you saying this because you're remembering something you didn't tell us before, or because your smokes had some wacky tobaccky in them?" Jason joked as all of them had a good laugh.

"I wish they did, Jay always knew how to grow the best stuff." Goose remembered how red his eyes were when the Madman for Good was still in the picture.

"He definitely knows what he's doing," agreed Bryan, who smiled because he knew exactly what Goose was talking about.

"While I was growing up, who would have thought that my dad would end up secretly leading a band of followers against corruption, while simultaneously growing some of the best weed around?" quipped Christina, who laughed at the happy memories of her dad. She was a little sad she might not be able to make any new ones, but was determined to not let that happen. "Not that I mind this stroll down memory lane, but what about this pipeline?"

"Years ago when your dad was investigating Marty and the bio-analyzer, we discovered a pipeline that the entities were ready to build. Not only would it provide people with much needed sustenance for themselves and their crops, but was an opportunity to privatize and pillage along the way. They'd do whatever they could to get the eminent domain right of way to build this thing.

They could say it was for the public good, so they deserved the property the pipeline crossed. That way they would hardly have to pay anything for it, and make themselves even more money. When you're greedy, you don't give a shit who you step on."

"Wouldn't they have to pass something like that through Congress?" wondered Jason, knowing under normal circumstances that might be true, but when you take down a President for massive corruption, the rule book gets thrown out the window. He was starting to realize that the rule book might have always been an illusion, and might have never existed in the first place.

"They would have to pass a bill, and normally it would have been a bitter partisan fight pitting everybody against each other. The entities wanted control of the entire population so they'd continue their role as worker bees. They also knew they had to give them at least the illusion of security. So they funded campaigns to get friendly people to champion their cause and get them elected. Once that happened they pushed the approval through with no problems."

"If that passed years ago, I haven't heard of it being built yet," stated Bryan, wondering if Goose was telling them stories that led in the exact opposite direction they needed to go.

"It did happen years ago, but even with backroom deals, it still takes years for the pertinent government agencies to fall in line, and all the right wheels to be greased."

"Or is that just what they said? Now that they have their hands on the blueprints, they can desalinate ocean water and purify melted snow. By the time it's piped to the west coast, people could drink it, water their farms and fields, hell even golf courses in the desert wouldn't be hurting."

"So what do we do with this, and how will it lead to my dad?" Christina asked urgently because she felt like they were finally getting somewhere.

"Jay and I took the pipeline seriously after we heard the bio-analyzer was needed to make it work. We discovered the middle point of the pipeline, where the device needed to be connected to initiate the filtration process. The snow would slowly melt as it and the ocean water traveled through the pipeline. Then when it got halfway, the bio-analyzer filtered it; which became fresh water by the time it traveled the other half of the pipeline. The site is actually not too far from here."

Goose waved for them all to get in the car because he was worried about them talking out in the open. Everything seemed calm as he looked around, nobody even milling about, so he started the Tahoe and pulled away.

"Did they take the bait?"

"I don't know, I told them I'd call a friend at the UN and tell him what happened to Christina's dad, but I don't know if they believed me."

"We have to make sure they aren't coming straight for the pipeline. I haven't been funneling you money for years for you to screw up. Find out where they're going, or so help me I'll kill your kid. I don't care if I'm the most recognizable

person in the world or not. I care about making this pipeline go through. Your son took me down, luckily the entities still saw me as useful because I got the surgery and made this pipeline thing happen."

"It'll happen don't worry. One way or the other we'll still make billions of dollars, and if we can do something for humanity in the process, why not?"

"You still care about doing good for people?"

"You don't? Isn't that why you went into politics, and why you were so upset you got taken down by my son?"

"Your son might have helped take my bully pulpit away, but when you took the bio-analyzer from us because you wanted a bigger cut, I had to gain some leverage."

"What leverage?"

"A little something called disappearing your son. If you try stopping the construction because of some wussy heart feelings, then so help me God I'll make you wish we never met in college."

The United States had many pipelines, oil, natural gas, pretty much anything and everything that could be sucked out of the ground for profit. They even built massive reservoirs to transport water from areas with abundant water to places that had little. A combination snow to water and desalinization pipeline was something so revolutionary, Jason was glad he was a part of it.

"I was just thinking," stated Jason who always prefaced his words when he thought he had something important to say.

"You know that's dangerous," Bryan joked, causing them all to laugh because they knew how true it was.

The Tahoe was barreling towards memory-lane Goose remembered from his days with Jay. "Not much farther, I'd say another five minutes."

"I know we want to rescue Jay of course, but do we want to necessarily stop this pipeline? I mean the technology could literally save the planet?" inquired Jason whose brain was in full truth mode.

"That's why rescuing Jay is all the more important, because he can help wrestle control of something that could make a few people more money than they can imagine. Jay trained me well, but I'm nothing like the original Madman for Good."

They pulled up to a locked gate with a guard shack next to it. Goose got out and went to talk to a guy who was holding at the ready one of the biggest guns Jason or Christina ever saw.

"What do you think they're saying? Do you think we should trust Goose? How do we know he isn't leading us into a trap?" pondered Christina as she dug her nails into Jason with apprehension.

"Oww babe, damn," Jason reacted as he felt Christina's nails breaking the skin. "Relax, let's see how this plays out. I realize everything hasn't been smooth up until now, but the more rationally minded we stay, the better."

Just as Christina was about to give Jason a kiss that defined the depth of their love, Goose walked up and got back in.

"What was that about, what is this place?" Christina questioned rudely because she was interrupted.

The guy Goose talked too had signaled the guard tower to open the gate. It took a minute, but then the gate creaked open to what looked like a military training ground.

"Welcome to the para-military wing of the Six Entities. A secretive organization bent on world domination has to have a secret army protecting it, don't you think?" bellowed Goose incredulously, with a no shit look on his face.

"I expected them to have that. I just didn't expect us to drive into the middle of it. Would you mind telling us just what the hell we're doing?" Christina shouted as she went into full protective mode.

Goose pulled up to a barracks, the same type that could have been found on any military base around the country. He parked and shut off the engine. "You know how I told you Jay saved my life?"

"Yeah, I'm still wondering about that," Christina shot back. She wanted that particular blank filled in she just didn't know it would be coming this soon.

"Well I actually saved his life. Like I said earlier, I met Marty in the marines. Once he saw that I could be trusted as the impressionable young soul that I was, he told me about private security options I could look into when I wasn't serving anymore. I'd be doing the same job, but making ten times the money. Being in my twenties, how could I not want to make a ton of money, so I took the job."

"So how did this lead you to my Dad?" Christina wondered as the guys in the back seat noticed their bullshit detectors were also going off.

"Well once Marty felt I could be trusted and that I loved money, he brought me on board. My first assignment was to watch this guy who had been threatening the power of the people he worked for."

"Are you telling me Marty worked for the Six Entities?"

"He didn't call them that. Hell, I don't think they called themselves that; kind of like how the mob doesn't call themselves the mob. They're just a bunch of guys doing evil deeds. Anyway, my first assignment was to help him keep an eye on this one place twenty four hours a day. When you spend that much time with somebody, you get to know them whether you want to or not.

We'd get into these deep conversations about the nature of humanity, privatization and how people with all the money sustained that money by always increasing their power. He told me he was starting to have second thoughts about his employers. After a while, he started to convince me that the path I had chosen wasn't the best. He said Jay had a lot of people on his side that knew about the corruption, and were ready to bring the struggle to the people who deserved it," the group was enthralled as Goose continued.

"Marty and I would drive down this crazy dirt road, that I swear had Deliverance banjo music playing from the trees. He found out where Jay's people were being held, and that they were planning an escape by way of spreading food poisoning. The entities camp only had one kitchen where they could bring in the poisoned food. Long story short, he needed my help to make it happen for Jay. So I did, and I've been by Jay's side ever since."

It was starting to click for Jason, and from the look on Christina's face, he could tell she also understood. "I think I want to solve the puzzle Pat," Jason quipped, knowing that a crappy gameshow reference might be just what they needed.

"Go for it man, let me see what that brain of yours can do," Goose replied, hoping Jason would impress him.

"Judging by the ease with which we drove in here, that guy and everybody else here sees you as a friendly, that's also why nobody has been staring at us just sitting here."

"Go on," stated Goose who was becoming intrigued more and more by the words coming out of Jason's mouth.

"You said Jay's people were going to escape by poisoning everybody in the camp with food they brought in. I'm guessing they did that, and since Jay saw that you had an in with the people he'd been investigating, that you should remain as his man on the inside. You could feed him information so the entities could be broken up bit by bit."

Goose just smiled as Jason went on. "Which brings us to this place and the pipeline. I'm guessing that the interchange of the pipeline where the bio analyzer needs to be hooked up isn't too far from here. What I can't figure out is exactly why we're here now. We can't get out of this car without being seen, good thing we have tinted windows." Jason looked outside to see platoons of troops marching, doing drills, and heard the pop, pop, pop of a gun range that couldn't have been too far away.

"I'll tell you about that, and how I started working for Jay instead of Marty after we leave. I just have to run inside and grab something, I'll be right back."

Jason looked around not sure what to think. During the search for Christina's dad, they somehow ended up in the heart of the beast. They had no guns, and were being protected by a guy who was a double agent for one of the scariest groups on the planet. He thought about how easy it would be to make somebody disappear out here. While thinking of all the horrible things that could happen, he saw Goose walk out of the building leading somebody to the Tahoe. The figure wore an orange jumpsuit, had a hood over his head with headphones on to completely cut off his sensory perception.

"Just what the hell is that, does he have a prisoner? What the hell is he doing? He's bringing that guy right toward us. I think Goose is going to put him in here, what should we do?" Jason spouted to Christina because the most beautiful woman in his world always calmed him down, even though she was presently pretty riled up herself.

Just when Christina was about to answer, Goose opened up the back hatch of the Tahoe and pushed the guy in; he then got back in the driver's seat and pulled away toward the front gate.

"You going to tell me who this is and why you're bringing some guy we don't even know with us. I knew we shouldn't have trusted you. The entities probably told you to grab him, and take him out to the woods and kill him with the rest of us. I'm sure they need to tie up loose ends so they can get the pipeline built, and that looks like exactly what's going on," exclaimed Christina without taking a breath. She wanted to get her dad back more than life itself, but it seemed like all her hope was drifting away.

Goose looked back and winked at Christina in the rearview mirror which she thought was evil, but nothing compared to being threatened by powerful people who felt threatened.

The Tahoe finally pulled up to the gate of the compound, and Goose waved at the guys standing guard out front. "See you guys later, next time I'm in town we have to get some beers and catch up," shouted Goose as the heavily armed and extremely confident men opened the gate and let the Tahoe pull through.

The ride was silent until ten minutes down the road when Christina couldn't take it anymore. "Who the hell is that, and just what the hell is going on?"

"We're clear," Goose yelled to the curled up prisoner in the back who sat up, took off his headphones and hood to reveal his true identity.

"Hi honey bear," Jay stated as Christina started crying.

"Dad, but how, how did this happen?" Christina was so stunned that she spit out random words because she couldn't convey the million emotions coursing through her.

"There's plenty of time to explain later, right now we have more pressing matters. Thanks Goose. I owe you, another one," expressed Jay happy to see his most trusted guy come through once again.

"My pleasure boss, whatever I can do to help," Goose replied with an admiration only reserved for the most respected people in society.

"I'm glad you said that, rally the troops. We have some pipeline construction to seize control of."

CHAPTER THIRTEEN

The Mad people for Good have been Jay's brain child ever since he realized the status quo wasn't sustainable, and was actually detrimental to humanity's collective evolution.

"So what's the next move?" Jason asked anxiously as they sped down the road to their destiny.

"Maybe we should chill for a couple days. Dad just got kidnapped and must have gone through quite an ordeal. He probably needs a few days to rest," Christina expressed with a warm feeling toward her dad she thought would never return.

"It's okay Honey Bear. We need to do this now while it's still fresh in our minds. The only way we can beat these guys is to go on the offensive and beat them to the punch," remarked Jay with as much passion as he could muster. "Besides, I've been waiting a very long time to fight for truth with my only daughter."

Goose and Bryan nodded in agreement as they saw the familial interaction going on. The day was just as sunny in the sky as it was in their hearts. Now that the gang was back together, the real work could begin.

"Goose you know where to go right, you kept the place up while I was gone?" wondered Jay, hoping his most trusted confidant had kept the Mad People for Good ready while he was away.

"Of course, I knew you'd be back one day. I just didn't know that it would be with your daughter. If she has half as much heart as you, I'd say we're well on our way to defeating humanity's enemy," Goose stated with a smile below his trademark black sunglasses.

The drive to the secret base of the Madman was long, and caused Jason to fall asleep. "He must be relaxed, I don't know how anybody could sleep at a time like this?" asked Jay of Christina.

"I think he is, but at the same time the passion for peace and justice that burns within him is so strong that when he gets it moving in the right direction, there's nothing that can stop him. It's one of the things that attracted me to him in the first place. So tell me more about this pipeline," Christina replied, trying to get her mind to grab onto something real so it didn't go spinning out of control.

"First of all, I think we all have to be careful about this Marty guy. He'll act like he wants to fight corruption, then at the last second he'll pull the rug out, and make off with something that only benefits himself. I've seen him be two-faced on too many occasions."

Thought bubbles swirled around the Tahoe as they pulled up to the gate at yet another cult like compound.

"It's good to see you Goose. I didn't think you'd make it back after that last mission," quipped the guy in the guard shack whose smile was obvious on his mustachioed faced.

"I wasn't so sure either, but then I realized ugly chicks need loving too. I did what I had to do and got out of there," chuckled Goose. Christina wondered if all her dad's guys were after some sexual conquest or were just lonely. She had asked herself that same question about her own experiences in the past.

"What a trooper. Man, thanks. After I went home with her friend, we really connected."

"That must be where that little stuffed animal by your computer came from. Aww, how cute is that; a stuffed chipmunk with your name on it. Do you have the matching skirt to go with it?"

"Ha, ha, ha, ha Captain funny man, I seem to remember you saving your fair share of gifts from women who meant something to you. You don't want your secret identity to ruin your street cred, do you?"

"Not that this isn't entertaining, but we have a mission to plan," Jay interjected. He was happy to see his guys joking around, but wanted to get back on point. "Besides, I'm the king of doing what I need to do to make myself happy."

The guy in the guard shack immediately changed his demeanor into one of instant readiness because he recognized the voice of the Madman for Good. "Sorry sir, you've been gone so long, we didn't know if you'd return; come on in."

"Let us get settled and then we'll continue this," replied Goose who was happy to see some friendly faces that were always on the right side of history.

"Sounds good to me," spoke the guy in the shack. He pushed a button to open the electronic gate, which opened to a private road that stretched back a few miles.

Jason had barely opened his eyes before he looked around, and started to wonder if they'd been turned around. "Where are we, what is this place?"

"Welcome to my playground," exclaimed Jay very proudly as he looked out the window and saw that his men had kept the property up very well in his absence. While he always wanted to take the fight to people who deserved it, he came to the conclusion that weapons were needed only as a last resort; they were good to have just in case.

"Your playground, this is how you play? Usually if I want to play, I'll bust out some scrabble," Jason bantered whose habit of trying to lighten the moment was a coping mechanism. He wondered how a rag tag militia would fair against those who controlled the U.S. government with nuclear weapons at their disposal.

"I work hard and I play hard. I organized this place to bring like-minded people together, and instill in them the power to make positive change," replied Jay very confidently. He was a little defensive because he felt like his motivations were being questioned.

"Then what are all these guns for? If you want to make positive change, why do you need heavy weapons?" inquired Bryan very curiously as they drove further down the dusty dirt road and saw small open fields on either side with targets set up. Chants and "ooh rahs" came from people marching together in small units that reminded Bryan of an authentic military base. "Are you trying to build a movement so you can take over the government?"

"Not take over the government per say, just show them we mean business. Words only get you so far, but some people only listen when they're staring down the barrel of a gun," Jay blurted out. His passion was mixed with anger because he knew his methods spawned from an authentic desire for truth, and justice.

"But dad, that's not how Jason and I do things. We took down the President because we put ourselves in the right place and the right time without knowing it was the right place and the right time. How do you know something like that can't happen again?"

"Poor, naïve Honey Bear. Do you think for one minute the old guy you met on the beach wasn't there purposely? You think it was just a coincidence? The six entities are into everybody and everything as they try to succeed in their ultimate goal of world domination. We must be ready to stop them."

"After we stop them, then what? It seems like we take one person down just to have another one pop up. How do I know going after the entities isn't just an excuse for you to take down mom for going behind your back?"

"Okay guys, calm down, we can't lose focus," Goose chimed in, trying to hold everyone together; just like he did with the Mad People for Good while their leader was in exile. "Here we are."

After a twenty minute drive down a heavily forested road, they arrived at a big brick building that looked like something right out of a fable.

"She's a brick, house," Bryan joked, trying to break the tension.

"That she is, but she is also a metaphor. When the big bad wolf came to blow down the house of the three little pigs, he couldn't blow down the one made of bricks; which is how he was defeated. All I'm trying to do is stop the six entities when they come after us, as they have done numerous times," Jay explained as the fire in his eyes raged for doing what must be done. "Let's go in and see what we can come up with."

Goose, Bryan, Jason and Christina exited the Tahoe, but Jay took a little longer to get out because he was wedged in the back where Goose had tossed him.

"Hey man, can I have a little help?"

"Seems like I've heard you say that before," whispered Goose with a laugh as he unfolded Jay's legs from the awkward position he landed in, and helped him out of the Tahoe. "Marty was supposed to call his friend at the U.N. to help us investigate corporate takeovers of water systems. I wonder if he got a hold of him yet."

"I don't think we should trust him," Jay expressed, whose stare pierced through Jason's soul. "I know he's your biological father, but after investigating him all these years, I can tell you his only motivation is preservation of his own best interest. I don't know if he has the capacity to feel remorse."

"I could say the same about you when you left Christina," Jason fumed with anger because of the insult hurled at his father. "How do we know your number one priority isn't your own best interest?"

"Let's not start this again," remarked Goose who was growing tired refereeing these unplanned family reunions. If they were going to hand the pipeline construction to conscientious people who weren't only out for their self-interest, he knew they must hold it together. "We have a difficult mission ahead, and we must stay strong; falling apart is exactly what the entities want."

"He's right, we have to remember what the real issue is," Bryan added because he felt Goose's passion wash over him. He knew that if they focused on what needed to be focused on, they'd all make it through.

The gang walked up three very wide steps and onto the front porch of the brick house which had chairs set up under a canopy to block the rain. They all sat down as Jay went inside.

"If the people are so thirsty for water, that they're willing to pay dramatically higher rates that put them in the poorhouse, the entities will have another leg of control for the entire plan," Jason argued. He was so tired that he was getting comfortable in the plastic chair that really wasn't all that comfortable.

"We all need water to live. The environment needs it to resupply itself because it's the lifeblood of nature. If agriculture becomes controlled by a single entity, food prices, fuel prices and everything else will go up in kind," replied Bryan, happy to see his partner's mind was back in the swing of things. "Remember how we took down Ridell? We came up with a plan, and then we executed it."

"Of course, that's what started us down this rabbit hole," Jason remembered with a nervous smile because he didn't know what was around the corner.

"I am trying to process my dad being a militia leader, it's all just too much," Christina thought out loud. "I think once we find where the entities are hiding the blueprints, we can snatch away their control."

"It's not so much about finding the blueprints, as much as taking over the pipeline," mentioned Jay, as he exited the house with a laptop and a small wooden box he set on a TV tray next to the only empty seat left on the porch.

"So we know where the intersection of the pipeline is, which tells us where the device is going to turn up," surmised Bryan whose mind was chugging along. "Maybe Marty's friend can bring in the cavalry and take control of the pipeline."

"Didn't we wait for the cavalry to bust in the last time we up-ended somebody?" asked Jason whose trust in Bryan never waned; but he knew that if he didn't ask questions, he wasn't an authentic seeker of truth. "This is going to take more than suits with listening devices built in."

"That's probably true, but it doesn't mean we should go in with guns blazing, we have to think about the next step."

Christina was listening to the back and forth and wondered why none of them came right out and said it. "I think my dad is right. We have to take control of the pipeline out of the entities hands, so it can benefit all of humanity like it was designed for; basically mom's original idea for it before she became what she became."

"Okay honey bear, how do you suggest we do that?" queried Jay, delighted to see Christina taking control like he always hoped she would. He wanted to pass his legacy down to her and felt like she was finally ready. He was anxious to hear what she had in mind.

"This technology can help curb the severe drought conditions in the west. We've been under historic drought conditions for several years now, and the legal battles over the little bit of water that remains have only just begun. If we get this thing up and running before the summer hits, we can avoid the problems that will be much worse than last year," exclaimed Christina to Jason's delight because the love of his life was becoming more attractive as the days and years went by.

"I agree, but how do we do that?" inquired Goose who wanted Christina to get to the point.

"We do that by feeding into what they already think. We make them keep their illusion going that they're really in control, and let them build the pipeline. Once the water is flowing, we show how corrupt the people are that built it. Hopefully the government, the news and mass groups of people take notice, and show the shell company they set up for the sham it is."

"Not bad honey bear, not bad. But, once they're discredited who'll control it when they aren't anymore?"

"What about Marty?"

Bryan and Jason both wondered if the man they trusted for so long, would do the right thing after being so deceptive in the past. Marty hadn't always been truthful about his actions, but he always seemed to look out for them, and to Jason maybe that was enough.

"Maybe Marty can...." Just as Jason was about to articulate his latest stroke of genius, or what he thought was his latest stroke of genius, a phone rang.

"Is that a phone? I didn't think you could get coverage out here," asked Christina who wondered where the call was coming from.

"That's the funny thing, we don't. I have a satellite phone, but nobody has the number," remarked Jay who was starting to get weirded out because nobody was supposed to know where they were. "Looks like I found the culprit."

Jay looked down to see the satellite phone sitting on the chair next to him was ringing. "I didn't put this here, did you?" Jay asked Goose.

"No, I mean I used it while you were gone sure, I had to stay in touch with the ladies somehow. Maybe one of the other guys moved it," Goose explained, trying to defend himself because he was also curious about the phone.

"Are you going to answer before they hang up?" Jason asked very directly.

"Of course, It's just I've never received incoming calls on this phone because nobody has the number. It doesn't even have a real number. It has a random password that changes every three minutes, it needs to be punched in every time you want to reach it," Jay blurted at a million miles an hour. "Somebody must've hacked it."

Jay was stalling to answer the phone by explaining its technicalities, which were important. With everything that's happened to this point, he knew random and unexpected things always seemed to push him in the right direction.

Jason grabbed the phone out of Jay's hand and answered it. "Hello?"

"Aww Jason, I wasn't expecting to hear you, how are you?" Marty inquired in a friendly voice, as if nothing was strange about him tracing an untraceable phone.

"Marty is that you?" replied Jason, who immediately knew it was Marty, but out of pure instinct he blurted it out anyway. "How'd you get this number, this phone was supposed to be untraceable?"

"Nothing is completely untraceable, and besides it was the only way I could get a hold of you," remarked Marty. He didn't want to divulge anything for fear of making the entities kill everybody around Jason, instead of just Jason himself. "I talked to my friend at the U.N. He said they've known about the bio-analyzer for some time, and would love to help us gain control of it from the entities."

"How can we trust you? How do we know you haven't been working for them the whole time," questioned Jason as his rage was building. Jay just looked at him and smiled. He wanted to take the phone and deal with Marty, but he saw Jason had everything under control. "They seem to have their fingers in every pie, and probably traced this call too."

Christina looked at Jason with just as much admiration as her father. Every day she discovered more and more how much she wanted to fight alongside the man she loved in the battle for truth.

"You have no reason to trust me after all the deception," explained Marty who sounded like he was authentically trying to do the right thing. "My guy said all the environmental reviews have been completed, and pipeline construction is going to start very soon because the entire route has finally been approved."

"How exactly is he going to help us take control of this thing?" insisted Jason whose patience was wearing thin.

"He discovered the bio-analyzer is going to be at the intersection of the pipeline."

"Tell us something we don't know."

"Do you know why it has to be placed there?"

"It's half-way across the country. The snow melts on its way there so when it gets to the analyzer, it's water. It and the ocean water are then purified and desalinated before it arrives out west as clean drinkable water."

"So you know that too huh," Marty mentioned as he choked on his words. The ex-President told him to lure Jason somewhere away from the intersection point so when the pipeline started flowing, there would be no way to stop it. All he had to do was steer Jason and his friends away from the truth. As long as their bottom line wasn't hurt, the entities didn't care about anything, just like any major corporation.

"What are you trying to say?" Jason inferred because Marty was being of no help.

"The only way I can earn your trust is if you meet me at a spot I have set up for this sort of thing."

"What sort of thing?"

"I can't say on the phone. Meet me back at the office where you met me the first time, I'll explain everything," Marty conveyed as he teared up for leading Jason away from his dream, when he had spent so much time driving him toward it.

"Explain what to us?"

"Just meet me back there, and everything will become clear."

Jason hung up the phone just as puzzled as when he answered it.

"Not that I mind you grabbing my phone when somebody has secretly hacked into it, but what the hell man?" Jay queried, a little miffed that Jason grabbed his phone. Jay was also intrigued because he sensed that Jason was the type of person who always had a plan, and was always a few chess moves ahead of everyone else.

"It was Marty. His friend at the U.N. told him we have to wait for the pipeline to start flowing, and then he'll send in some people to take control of it from the entities. He wasn't real clear," explained Jason who was even more perplexed now. "He said he couldn't be detailed over the phone, and we should meet him back at the office where we met him before. He said only then everything will become clear."

"Sounds like a trap," interjected Bryan who never shied away from looking out for his buddy. "How do we know he can be trusted? He seems to have proven himself otherwise so far."

"He might be and he might not be. All I know is this gives us the next step that we're looking for. If I've learned anything from investigating people, it's that there are no coincidences. When things come out of the blue we must pay attention to them. That doesn't mean I don't have a plan."

"So what is it, prove to me why my daughter loves you?" Jay sniped with a smart ass look on his face.

"Not that I don't want to go in there with guns blazing because I do, but if it's a trap, I think I should be the only one to go in. That way if they take me or kill me, you guys can still stop them from taking control of the pipeline," Jason retorted.

"Is that why they want the thing to flow as soon as possible, because once people are benefiting from it, they won't care who is controlling it?" wondered Jay, curious wondered where this was leading.

Jason and his friends wanted the pipeline to go through, and the six entities also wanted the pipeline to go through. If they wanted to control the pipeline just as much or more than the entities, did that make them just as greedy? What would they do with the billions of dollars that would be made from it once they had control?

"What if we had the pipeline setup in some kind of co-op situation where it's owned by the public? The users themselves would be shareholders, so they'd be the ones to see the profit. That way they get the fresh water they need, and get some of the income that's been syphoned from them over the years," expressed Jason whose mind was flowing like it hadn't in a long time. "The real reason the entities don't want to lose control is they're afraid they'll miss out on billions and maybe even trillions of dollars that will be extrapolated in the future. The bread and circuses they've been force-feeding the population will be replaced by actual living wages, which will help people evolve out of the survival mode they put them in so their control stays absolute."

"How do we put it in the hands of the public?" wondered Christina, hoping Jason had an answer to the burning question before them.

"I'm not sure. If the entities have found their way into every branch of government, we can't trust anybody," surmised Jason who was stumped on what to do next.

"What about me and my guys?" asked Jay who wanted to help Jason because they both knew the pipeline would help every generation to come. "Maybe the answer is Marty? He seems to be the only one with connections to pull something like this off."

"How do we know he wouldn't just keep all the money for himself, or become some kind of seventh entity or something?" Jason queried, wondering what Jay had in mind.

"That's where my guys could help keep Marty on the straight and narrow. I investigated him for years, I know how he ticks. He might only be out for his own self-interest, but he also loves you very much. He always tried to accumulate as much money and power as he could, but all to benefit you."

"He wanted me to become just as greedy as him?"

"No. He wanted you to see how corrupt the world really is, and that once you take down somebody in power, it just goes deeper and deeper. He wanted to make sure you had the backing to go as deep as the mission called for."

"I'll go talk to him and see what he says. I'd like to believe he's out for my best interest, but I'm not so sure," replied Jason.

"Trust me man, he is. He wants no harm to come to you. Go meet him. We'll hang back in case it goes south."

Jason reluctantly agreed even though he was nervous as a 12 year old boy asking a girl to dance at the junior high winter formal. He didn't know where this was leading, but he knew he had to see it through. If Marty was as deceptive as Jay said, he had to have something else up his sleeve.

Goose piled the gang into the Tahoe and drove them back to the office park. "It's nice to not have you bound and gagged in the back, but sitting beside me," Christina quipped, who was ecstatic to work alongside her dad, but was also worried for Jason. "Thanks so much for your help. I'm only sorry that it took us this long to work together. There's so much to catch up on."

"That's true Honey Bear, but something tells me we have many adventures ahead of us," remarked Jay who smiled because he felt like he could be open for the first time in his life. "I started being the Madman for Good because I wanted the world to see how unrelenting positivity can save it."

"Would you consider the use of heavy weapons against your enemy's unrelenting positivity?" Jason chimed in, breaking up the family bonding session.

"It's not for offense, it's for defense. If somebody comes up and punches you in the playground, are you going to sit there and let them pummel you? Or are you going to fight back?" Jay fumed like Jason was questioning his fortitude.

"I don't want to start a holy war and tear down the whole system. I just want the system to actually work for the people. We don't have to destroy everything to rebuild it how we think it should be. That's what the entities are trying to do."

"Are you saying the entities and I are in league with each other?"

"All I'm saying is that you and the entities seem to have some of the same goals."

"Well let me prove to you how that's false."

Goose pulled up to the office park and tried to get them focused back on their mission. "Jason, go in there and see what Marty couldn't say over the phone. If something goes south, we'll carry on the mission."

"And save him too right?" chattered Christina who became frightened about Jason's prospects for success.

"Of course, I just want him to understand the risk."

"I understand the risk just fine, let me go in there and just get this over with," stated Jason who could see everybody was restless because they'd been talking for too long with no action. Meeting up with Marty was the action that would move them all forward.

"I'll give you fifteen minutes, after that we're coming in to get you," remarked Goose who felt good when he was in control. He watched over and built up the Mad People for Good when Jay was in exile, and liked controlling their direction. Now that Jay was back in the picture, his job was to keep everything flowing in the right direction; but whose right direction?

Jason started walking toward the office door. There were a few random looking Hondas and Toyotas in the parking lot that you'd see anywhere. He knew what people did to stay low key, he had to stay vigilant. He opened the same door of the same suite he came to the first time.

"Hey Barbara, what's up?" Jason asked of Marty's long time secretary. "Is something wrong, you look like your cat just died after pissing in your cheerios?"

"Marty will see you now," replied Barbara with tears streaming down her face because she knew what was coming. "I've always liked you."

Jason almost knew what to expect when he walked into Marty's secret office, but almost only counts in horseshoes and hand grenades. He opened the door to see Marty standing in the back of the room, and a shadowy figure in the corner with his hat pulled way down low.

"Marty what's up, what couldn't you say on the phone? Jason inquired very nervously.

"Wouldn't you like to know?" snickered the shadowy figure who walked out of the corner and pulled up his hat so Jason could see who he was.

"Mr. President???"

CHAPTER FOURTEEN

Charles Bowman always has and always will be hell bent on power. Whenever he feels threatened, he takes action. When people are stuck in survival mode they only serve their most primal needs, and will do whatever is necessary to ensure their survival.

"You just don't know when to quit do you," remarked the ex-President who looked a little different after the surgeries. His teeth and other various parts were switched out so he would look similar to the President everybody thought died in a plane crash, but wouldn't match him forensically.

"Quitting is not in my blood, but is in yours," Jason retorted, trying to stick up for himself. He was nervous having never talked to the leader of a nation before, let alone the most powerful one on earth.

"Ha, ha, ha, we got us a comedian here. Why don't you come over here and put these on," the ex-President joked as he handed Jason some handcuffs, prompting him to put them on.

"I'm sorry man, I've spent my whole life trying to protect you, and now look where we're at," Marty expressed a sadness that touched every part of his soul.

"Aww, what a sweet family moment, let me go get a box of tissues," the President quipped in the most smart ass tone he knew. "Let's get down to brass tacks."

"I hope he's okay in there," exclaimed Bryan, concerned for his friend. "What do you think Marty is telling him?"

"Who knows, maybe he has a secret plan," Christina wondered, knowing how cliché it sounded. "Sorry, that sounded like something out of a bad spy movie didn't it?"

"A little," remarked Jay who rolled his worried eyes because Jason was in the thick of it now. The Madman for Good had seen many battles. Many times he expected one thing to happen, and because some faceless entity was after him, something completely different happened. Handling those types of situations is what made him the Madman for Good.

"Boss you got nothing to worry about, Jason will be just fine in there," Goose interjected with a confidence he was laying on pretty thick.

"How are you so sure?" asked Jay. "You don't know Jason any more than I do. Besides, aren't the entities out looking for you by now because you never arrived at the arranged destination? Since your cover has been blown, hasn't your information stream from them stopped?"

"Yes, I'm all in with you now. Years ago when you first came up with the idea that I go undercover with them, I wasn't sure what to think. After being around there for a while, I began to see how they think. Their aims are the same as yours, just greedier and motivated by profit. The sickening thing is how two-faced they are. They want alternative energy sources and new water technologies to be used, because they know it is needed in the coming decades with dwindling natural resources."

"What's taking so long in there?" Christina blurted out because she couldn't stop thinking about the man she loved more than anybody. They had a lot more truth finding to do. "What on earth is Marty's plan, I wonder if he hid another blueprint of the thing?"

Jason put on the handcuffs that were so cold they felt like they'd been kept in the freezer to make them as uncomfortable as possible. "Why are these things so cold?" inquired Jason.

"I put them in that mini fridge over there, but I had to take out Marty's candy bars first," jeered the ex-President.

"I could really go for a snickers bar right now," stammered Jason who had the munchies, but was mostly just nervous. He thought that if Charles Bowman the ex-President was keeping him there after Marty lured him, could they have been in cahoots the whole time? Could the pounding in his chest be from the fact that he might die in the next minute?

"You must be hungry from all that weed you smoked?" Bowman inferred in full dickhead tone. "You're probably wondering why I had Marty lure you here."

"Yeah dad, what's up," queried Jason, surprised the word dad came out so naturally; considering he hadn't given much thought to the fact Marty was indeed his father.

Maybe Jason was trying to suppress it, which only proved he was human.

"How sweet, dad. Why don't you call him pop, sit on his lap and tell him about your bad day?" Bowman asked, trying to get a rise out of Jason.

"Just because you had a father that touched you down there, doesn't mean I did," replied Jason trying to get a rise out of the President right back, not actually knowing what happened to the former Commander in Chief when he was a kid. However when Marty looked at Jason after the words left his tongue, he knew he wasn't too far from the truth.

"There's that fighting spirit, that's what I was waiting for," Bowman fired back.

"Dad what's up? Why did this shithead have you lure me down here? He must have something on you."

"He does son, you."

"In that case wouldn't you be the one in chains and not me?"

Bowman sat back and enjoyed watching the scene unfold in front of him. The entities might have cut his workload in half since being forced out of the oval, but with this mission he was going to prove that he was useful and could still accomplish their goals.

"Shut up, I don't have time for this. Marty here knows where another set of the bio-analyzer blue prints are."

"Didn't the old man take them from us? Don't the entities have them already, what would you want them for?" Jason asked the ex-President a direct question from the bottom of his gut, knowing his passion would protect him.

The room was dimly lit, but just bright enough to see that Marty was allowing the ex-President to speak a little more than he should.

"He did take them, but they've tasked me with finding Marty and any other copies of the blueprint so nobody else gets their grimy mits on them. What that bitch doesn't know is that I'm going to build the device myself with Marty's help. We're going to make all the money from it, and there will be nothing the entities will be able to do. They think I'm going to give it right to them, ha. I suffered immensely when they made me resign. Now I'm going to make them suffer by taking away a major part of their business."

"Aren't you afraid they'll come after you If you take away one of their major income streams?" Jason wondered, trying to lead Bowman on.

"That's true, and they will. They might have an army, but I have a private army of my own. If they come at me, I'll show them what real power is."

The ex-President droned on about how much better he was than Jason and his friends, and how they were little girls that couldn't put up a fight. Jason spoke because he knew he was on the right path, just like when Ridell had him cuffed next to Aaron. "So, shithead."

"There is that word again, your language is so edumacated. What intellectual metaphor are you going to come up with next? You going to call me a pee pee face?" Bowman shot back, trying to enrage Jason because he could.

Marty was quietly listening to Jason and Bowman go back and forth. His plans were also starting to fall into line. He would wait for the right moment to strike, and then move forward, because wasn't that what evolution was about?

"You're here by yourself with no guns or body guards. You must feel like actually getting your hands dirty," Jason commented, trying to find out exactly what he was up against.

"What makes you think I don't have guns?" Bowman quipped as he took off his suit coat to reveal an Uzi on a shoulder strap that was now firmly aimed at Jason's forehead. "Is that better?"

"Not really, but closer to what I was expecting," replied Jason. "Are you going to fight the entities because they controlled you? You partnered here with Marty and had him lure me here to what, kill me? Do you really think this will end with me? There are others who know I'm here and will continue fighting long after I'm gone. I just want to take it that next step. Whatever the people who come after me decide to do, it will be their call. All I know is that I'm going to do what good I can while I'm here."

Marty cracked a quick smile at the boy who had indeed come from his loins. All the support and intellectual nurturing paid off. He was looking at a great human being who knows about his priorities. Maybe that was what the world needed, somebody to tell them like it is because they genuinely care.

"You going to say something over there, you've been mighty quiet." Bowman questioned Marty who he could see was deep in thought. "If you don't slowdown that brain of yours, you'll pop a gasket."

"I was just thinking of what I want to do with all the money we're going to make. I'm going to buy boats, houses and a trophy wife. Maybe I'll even get elected President like you?" Marty sniped. He looked at Jason with a laugh, but also a wink that Jason spotted, if only for a split second.

"That was so funny, I forgot to laugh. Anyway, let's do this so we can continue with our plans," Bowman construed as he took the shoulder strap off his shoulder, and slid his finger over the Uzi trigger very nervously; he never actually killed anyone before. He had a talent for facing people in public, and bullying them to do whatever he wanted; which is probably why the entities installed him as President. Then a little guy named Jason had to come along and ruin everything. "Here, why don't you do it, it will prove your loyalty."

Bowman handed Marty the gun, which made a bead of sweat slowly drip down Jason's forehead. The thought that he might one day get shot in the head by his father, never entered his mind. Then he remembered that wink of Marty's, he must have something up his sleeve.

Marty grabbed the gun and pointed it at Jason. "Is this what you want?"

"That's what I said. Are you going to pull the trigger already, we don't have all day," yelled Bowman who was growing very impatient.

"After we kill him, then what, build the device with my extra blueprint, and then control the pipeline with an iron fist? How exactly do you propose to control an entire pipeline? It's like 3000 miles long, you don't have the manpower for that," replied Marty trying to see if Bowman really had a plan, or was just trying to get back on the entities good graces.

"Do I look like Ridell? Do you think I'm going to divulge my whole plan?"

"If you want me to kill my son you will," Marty fearfully shouted as a chill ran down his spine. He knew how far from his truth those words actually were.

Jason looked at Marty and hoped he had a plan, as he was getting extremely nervous because the ex-President was growing increasingly agitated.

"What did you think was going to happen? We kill him, get your blueprint, build the thing, and then sell the finished product for a ton of money? There is truth in what you said. The two of us would never be able to control an entire pipeline, which is why we must control its construction. What we're going to do now is stop talking, and put my plan into motion," Bowman demanded as he made a gun with his hand, put it to his head and acted like he was pulling a trigger.

"You know you're right, we should put my plan into action," remarked Marty with an evil smile. Before the ex-President could even consider what those words meant, Marty took the gun out of Jason's face and pointed it at Bowman.

"What exactly do you think you're doing? You going to shoot a President?" asked Bowman. He was trying to intimidate Marty, but fouled up once again because he was too much in the moment. He forgot that to accomplish your goals and dreams, you have to think ten steps ahead.

"You're not mine or anyone's President anymore, you always were and always will be the biggest puppet of all the puppets," Marty stated as he pressed the barrel against Bowman's head. "Tell me why I shouldn't pull this trigger right now and blow your brains out. It would give me a couple of huge advantages, my enemy would be gone and the entities would be pissed-off because you failed them again."

If Jason's hands weren't handcuffed behind his back, he surely would have given his dad a standing ovation. He always knew his parents loved him, and wanted great things for him; he just never thought he'd be helping them push the world to consciously evolve. Murder wasn't exactly helping the world evolve, but how else could you get past enemies that won't concede defeat.

"You shouldn't pull the trigger because I have a lot to offer you. Remember when we were back in college, all the fun we had at parties and just hanging out? We had some good times back then," Bowman reminisced trying to stall Marty, because he wanted to relive some happy memories if he really was going to die.

"We did, remember the panty raids? Remember the party ten thousand people showed up at? It took three weeks to clean up, the yard was destroyed," recalled Marty while having a good laugh with an old friend. He remembered you must never sweat the small stuff, but remember the happy memories when you can because they make life worth living.

"So you guys were good friends?" Jason inquired. He didn't know when he'd get another opportunity to have his real dad, and his dad's old friend the ex-President in the same room together.

"Very good friends, even if I had to serve so I could go to school and he didn't. After we graduated I went into the media and he went into politics; we just kind of lost touch until now," Marty blurted out. He was trying to get the words out as quickly as possible because he didn't want Bowman to say anything.

"Out of touch until now, what about for the last few years………" divulged Bowman right before Marty pulled the Uzi's trigger and shot him in the head, splattering the ex-President's brains all over the back wall.

"Holy shit man, why???" wondered Jason who knew that Marty had now killed two people, but also because Bowman had begun to contradict Marty. It made him wonder if Marty shot Bowman because he didn't want Jason to know his real plans, or because he wanted to catch him off guard. These thoughts and more zoomed through Jason's head like a bullet train in the span of two seconds. He knew the next few minutes were going to move very quickly.

"I was tired of his yammering. He doesn't know when to shut up. At least he's shut up for good now, and we don't have to worry about him coming after us," Marty exclaimed in the most caring tone he could produce, even though Jason just witnessed one power player taking out another power player because he felt threatened.

Jason thought of all the times he'd been helped by Marty. The money, the influence, the backing, was it all because Marty bullied what he wanted out of people? Then if they didn't do what he wanted, he got rid of them? How many people have you killed he thought. Just when he was going to ask those very words, Marty spoke.

"I don't know what you expect to come out of all this," stated Marty, trying to expel any thoughts of betrayal. "I did this for us. I want to show you I'm completely behind you, and am willing to do anything to help you move forward."

Considering splattered brains and blood formed a painting behind him any serial killer would be proud of, Jason didn't know what to think of his "killer father." Killer father, sounded like a crappy horror movie. "You going to un-cuff me? You aren't going to shoot me too, are you?" uttered Jason, nervous as the day he was born.

"Why would I do that when you're the person I've spent all my time trying to protect? I might have made some bucks along the way, but I always had my eye on making your life easier and more prosperous," Marty fired back as he grabbed the handcuff keys out of Bowman's blood soaked pocket.

After Marty unlocked Jason, he took the cuffs off and felt around his wrists. They weren't on very tight, but it was a common instinct when handcuffs get removed. Jason noticed a little speck of blood somehow made it under the cuffs while they were still on.

"Wow, I sure do make a mess," Marty joked with a demonic laugh that made Jason nervous about where he came from. Just as he started thinking of what Marty could be up to, Goose busted in.

"What the fuck happened here?" Goose yelled as he saw blood pooling around a dead body on the ground, and a Jackson Pollack of blood all over the back wall. "Jason are you okay? It had been fifteen minutes and I wanted to make sure you were alright, we were worried about you."

"We?" wondered Marty, very puzzled.

"Yes Marty, we," replied Goose, feeling confident because he and Jay looked into Marty for a long time and knew all his moves, or so they thought.

Marty was going to open his mouth and say what the hell, when Jay, Bryan and Christina entered the scene.

"Marty, long time no see," Jay exclaimed. He glared right at Marty because he seemingly proved once more that he was out for his own interests. "Somebody get in your way again?"

"Ha,ha,ha,ha," Marty chuckled as he gave Jay a half smile, because he knew their kids were together. Once Marty discovered Jay had been looking into him while Jay was building up the Mad people for Good, Marty started looking into Jay as well. "Let's not turn this into another ping pong match." Bryan and Christina walked up to Jason as Marty, Jay and Goose kept jawing at each other.

"Are you okay baby?" wondered Christina who was concerned because of all the blood, but rejuvenated because her love and inspiration for moving forward was still alive.

"I'm a little freaked out that my dad who I didn't know was my dad, just shot and killed the former Commander-in-Chief that you and I helped to take down. Other than that I'm totally peachy," Jason spouted very sarcastically. He was happy to see them, but very confused as to what was going on. "So what now?"

"I'll tell you one thing, we need to get out of here," interjected Marty who was anxious because he didn't want to get caught. He knew the key to a great escape was speed, that's what he remembered after killing Bill anyway. "I'll call my clean-up team. They'll get rid of the body, and make the place look like nobody was ever here."

"Marty, it's getting late. Mind if I, oh my God," remarked Barbara as she walked in and saw all the blood. She was freaked out, but not nearly as much as Jason thought she should be. "Do I always have to fix these problems of yours?"

"No, not always, just some of the time," Marty joked as he gave Barbara an evil smirk, causing the rest of the group to immediately question Marty's sanity. "Can you call the clean-up team to take care of this? This is priority number one right now. The entities sent Bowman to kill me and Jason. I'll bet they'll come looking when they don't hear back from him, which I've planned for."

Did Marty have some secret plan he'd been devising this whole time? Considering that he'd been making millions upon millions for years without anybody knowing, Jason wouldn't be surprised.

"You're right Marty let's get out of here, we still have a lot to talk about though," Jay barked. He felt his power come back, and remembered why he started investigating Marty in the first place. "Goose bring the car close, I know where we all need to go."

"Sounds good boss," Goose answered like the loyal soldier he had always been because his priorities were clear. He knew that when you see yourself more important than somebody else, things go downhill quick.

Goose walked out of the office to pull the car around, while Jay was trying to help the rest of them stay rational before panic set in.

"I'll call the guys to take care of this. You better get out of here," Barbara ordered like the loyal servant she was. She always felt her job was to take care of people. It's funny that even when the scenery of life changes, what you're meant to do never does.

"Thanks for all your help. I'll make sure you get a huge bonus this year," replied Marty as he looked more adoringly at Barbara more than a boss should. He seemed to not care about her looks in the past few years. "Have the team be here in ten minutes. We'll be gone by then."

Jay stared at Marty because they both had a lot to deal with, but it had to be put on hold. Jason walked up to Christina and gave her a kiss that not only filled up her soul with badly needed energy, but his as well. "Can't you two get a room, and don't worry I won't come knocking," Bryan commented, trying to make Jason laugh.

"You told me to leave one liners alone, but I see you couldn't resist," Jason remarked, happy to see his inner circle still intact. "Before the entities' men come and clear us out, we need to clear ourselves out."

Jason grabbed Christina's hand, and followed Jay and Marty out the door, with Bryan bringing up the rear. "Thank you for everything Barbara," expressed Jason, knowing she wasn't just a secretary to Marty, but the grease that kept his machine running at full steam.

Barbara nodded and they all walked out the door where Goose was waiting by the car. "Hurry up and get in, my scanner just said cops are on their way because somebody reported shots fired," Goose bellowed. He always looked out for Jay, knowing that being a right hand man was better than being a no man.

"That's impossible, there's nobody else in this entire business park right now. No witnesses could have heard the shot through those soundproof walls and doors," exclaimed Marty, starting to worry he might actually get caught this time.

"Don't you get it man? It's the entities. They have their hands in everything and everybody: cops, firemen, county, city, state and federal government. They have their hands in it all," Jay declared while looking right at Jason, but also making sure Marty heard him loud and clear. He might be the dad of the guy his daughter is in love with, but after countless investigations, Jay didn't trust Marty any farther than he could toss him.

"So you think you're smarter than me. Who made a ton of money, and who went into exile? Who succeeded and who got caught?" questioned Marty not backing down from a challenge.

"I didn't get caught. I left because I didn't want any harm to come to my daughter, who is totally fine and better than I could've ever hoped. You made a deal with the enemy to make even more money than you already have, while putting your son directly in harm's way. What the hell is wrong with you?" Jay fumed, letting it all hang out.

"Seriously, another pissing contest? Besides, I'd lose. I don't have a nozzle, and I just can't get the distance," Christina interrupted so quickly and directly that it made Jay and Marty bust out in full laughter; so much so that

Bryan started looking around to see if anybody heard them.

"See, you guys do have stuff in common. You might have different methods, but your end goals are the same. Besides, you have some pretty great kids," expressed Jason who played mediator just as well as Christina, just with much less grace.

"You guys done fighting and making up now? We need to move," ordered Goose who was always on task; one of the reasons Jay kept him around.

"You're right, take us to that hiding spot behind the lake," replied Jay, because he knew it could describe almost anywhere.

"No, my hiding spot it better, it's behind the rocks," Marty fired back trying to outdo Jay, but in a friendly banter sort of way.

They all packed into the Tahoe that seemed to make it through anything and go anywhere. Just as Goose was about to pull away, a car raced up behind them and they all heard a pop, pop, pop.

"What is this guy's problem?" Jason yelled out as a bullet whizzed through the front windshield, narrowly missing them all by mere millimeters. "Step on it." Goose didn't need to be told twice as he peeled out of the parking lot, with a late model Honda Civic quick on their heels.

"The entities couldn't have gotten here that quick, could they?" Christina wondered. She knew anybody could be shooting at them, but the entities were the most likely suspects.

"I don't know, but I don't want to find out" answered Goose who was a race car driver in his youth. He knew how to evade anybody when he needed to, which is why he was usually the wheelman.

The Tahoe raced down an industrial road passing mostly shuttered factories and raggedy buildings. It wouldn't be long before the ones that weren't were so raggedy and run down looking, would be. So many people were out of work Jason thought. What could he possibly do for them, how could he help? He knew it was a weird thought to have while being chased down the road being fired upon, but that's how the cookie crumbles sometimes.

The V-8 of the Tahoe might have been more powerful than the four cylinder of the Honda, but the smaller car could weave in and out of traffic more quickly. "Whoever is after us can really drive. I'm trying all my best moves, and I still can't shake him," blurted Goose who would have been happy to have the driving competition, if it weren't for all the flying bullets.

"Wait a minute, I know a shortcut," Marty interjected, as he told Goose to turn left at the road coming up.

"How do we know we can trust you?" asked Jay who liked the fact that he and Marty both had the same enemies and could laugh and joke together, but wasn't sure he could trust him yet.

"Let me prove it to you," replied Marty. When Goose turned down the road Marty mentioned, he saw a deep pothole ahead that the Tahoe would have no problem getting through, but not the Honda.

The Tahoe was moving very fast down the dirt road with the Honda close on it's heels. More shots rang out, one hitting the rear view mirror, causing it to fly off and shatter in a million pieces.

Just as Bryan was going to say something, they hit the pothole so hard, it made it him bite his tongue to the point that it bled. "Oww, fuck."

"You alright man, you get hit?" asked Jason, concerned for his friend.

"Even worse, I bit my tongue," expressed Bryan not caring about how wussy he sounded because it hurt a lot.

"Poor baby, you need a band aid?" Jason quipped, razzing his friend.

If he didn't look out the back window at that exact second, Bryan wouldn't have seen the Honda go airborne, and flip over resting on its roof next to a giant oak tree.

"I don't need a band aid, but that guy might," exclaimed Bryan as he looked back to see somebody get out of the car. "Looks like somebody is climbing out, I wonder who the hell that is."

Jason looked to see what Bryan was talking about. He was barely able to make out a figure who was getting smaller and smaller as they got further away. "I can't see him very clearly, oh wait a minute I think I know who that is," remarked Jason. He was just as surprised as the rest of the group that somebody could have survived a wreck like that, but even more so because he recognized who it was.

The man stumbled out of the car, and started walking toward the Tahoe that was quickly driving away. How he was able to flip his car onto its roof, and climb out still holding his gun, nobody knows. As the man raised his gun to shoot, the fire that started in the Honda spread to the gas tank and caused it to explode.

The loud bang caused everybody riding along the bumpy dirt road to think that they could undergo the same fate at any moment. The arduous journey they were on would be long, but would be worth it if they could make the bio-analyzer help all of society. They knew they'd be up against many obstacles, and being shot at was one of them.

"Jesus, that was nuts," surmised Goose who had been through some crazy stuff before, but explosions always got his adrenaline going. "Anybody get a look at that guy before he went kablooey?"

"I think it was Ridell," Jason remarked. He knew Ridell could be after any one of them, they had all messed with him in one way or another over the years.

"He's probably pissed because I killed his fixer," replied Marty. He looked at Jay and the rest of them to see if they agreed. "Talk about a way to earn a vendetta."

"I would say, so what do we do now?" Jay asked, looking at Marty like how are you going to get us out of this one.

"Goose, keep driving down this road, I know a place about ten more miles in," explained Marty as they drove along the completely natural manicured environment surrounding them. This must be what nature looks like before you mess with it he thought.

Just as Jason was going to start questioning his father, they pulled up to a cabin built into the hillside.

"What is this place?" wondered Jason, questioning what the hell this place was; just like everybody else in the car wanted to do. It looked like a crazy underground government bunker, very similar to the one that Bryan had. Jason remembered all the planning they did for Ridell, so it made sense that Marty had a similar hideout. Just as he was about to open his mouth, Marty beat him to it.

"This is the place we plan the next revolution, I hope all of you are ready."

CHAPTER FIFTEEN

The concept of the next revolution pounded in Jason's skull constantly. The difference this time was that Marty might have sinister motives, and might be using Jason's thought process to play right into his hands.

"Why aren't there any armed guards out here? My place has them, the kids could attest to that," surmised Jay, thinking Marty was either careless, or just not as militant as him. "Aren't you afraid somebody's going to find this place or you for that matter?"

Marty thought about his next words very carefully. Did he want the guy who had been investigating him for years to know what this place really was? Or was he tired from just having killed somebody? "It might not look like I have people out there, and that's the point. Trust me, if we were threatened, my guys would come out of their foxholes and swarm this place," Marty explained confidently.

They all walked into what would be their home away from home until a specific plan was in place. Jason didn't know what to think, all his preconceived notions flew out the window. He knew if he really wanted to accomplish what burned within him, he needed to be calculated. "So how can we get this bio-analyzer up and running? Society needs it, like yesterday."

"I realize your passion is high and your love for humanity is deep. To truly give this technology to the people however, we need to roll it out carefully," remarked Marty who was still intrigued by the young man he brought to New York all those years ago. Nurturing Jason's passion was how he made up for being absent. "I know I wasn't there for you when I should have been, but let me show you what's possible when great minds come together. I'm going to make up for all that time we lost."

The inside of Marty's secret lair as he liked to call it, was set up much like Bryan's when they conceived the Ridell plan; which made Jason think that's where Bryan got the idea.

"This place looks like my hideaway, when we planned to catch Ridell on tape by using all those secret cameras," Bryan explained, taking the thoughts right out of Jason's head. "Except this time it'll take more than just egotistical people divulging their plan. It will take sustained pressure."

"Which is where the Madman for Good comes in," Jay added, wanting to be part of the conversation. In all the years he investigated Marty, he found profit was made off of many things that benefited humanity. In that way he and Marty were a lot alike, they both wanted to move collective evolution forward, Marty just wanted to make a buck along the way. In a capitalist system, Jay thought that maybe the key was having the right kind of capitalist on your side.

"How can I help, dad?" asked Christina realizing the word dad came out lovingly, considering it wouldn't even have been a thought in her head a few months ago.

"You can help by keeping your mind and your body in synch. Feeding your body with the right things helps to feed your mind with the right things," replied Jay. He wondered what Marty had up his sleeve, not to mention what Goose learned from being undercover with the entities for so long.

Marty and Goose had spent time together before, but Goose ended up working for Jay because profits weren't his main motivation. He also discovered that to make changes on the scale the world needed, somebody would end up making a profit; which is why this renewed partnership was necessary.

It wasn't so much the ends justifying the means for Jason, but adjusting the means when the reality of life throws you a curveball. "It's strange being in the same room with you all together. Something tells me this is the beginning of something big, if we can keep our eyes on the prize, we can bring the people a technology they should have had a long time ago," Marty dispatched.

"I agree, when I investigated Marty here, I learned a lot about him. Hell, that's how I found you," stated Jay. He had to pay attention to the signs life threw at him because if he didn't, he'd miss something. "If Marty hadn't been investigating Christina's mom and the bio-analyzer, I might not have been able to do any of the things I did."

"You would've done a lot. Your passion runs so deep that you would've found an outlet for it. If it wasn't for this cause, it would have been something else," answered Marty, starting to feel a real connection with Jay. "I only want to make the world a better place. It is what I love to do. As the old saying goes, if you can make a living doing what you love, it's like being on vacation every day."

"That's why I came to New York, to make a living at what I'm passionate about," Jason proclaimed. He felt like the people sitting around this ancient redwood table, were the core group he'd been looking for to make the changes he's always dreamed of. "I think we need a safety meeting, I don't know if we're quite safe enough."

"I couldn't agree with you more," interjected Goose who was sitting on the edge of the circle because he knew his role as security and enforcer; even though Marty was the only one to have used deadly force. "I've been saving this for a very special occasion."

Goose pulled a small pill bottle out of his pocket and opened it to reveal some of the most perfect doobies he ever rolled. "Man, am I the only one that can't roll something good? Mine are always lumpy and bumpy, but they are functional," remarked Jason who admired Goose's rolling skills. "Kind of like my path to the truth."

"Kind of like all our paths to the truth," Goose shot back as he nodded at Jason, knowing the more insightful they were about what was ahead of them, the better. "I grew this stuff on the entities' base when I was there. Since I was running Jay's operation while he was away, and undercover with the group that we're presently going after, I figured a personal garden wouldn't be a big deal."

"How'd you hide it from them, weren't you afraid of getting caught? My mind would've been driving me nuts," wondered Christina. She knew she had a habit of over-analyzing, but sometimes it was advantageous because none of this would be happening, if she hadn't deciphered what the postcard really meant.

"When you work for a secretive organization controlled by the most powerful people in the world, a little weed on the side isn't any big deal. Hell, they have places set up all over the world where people high up in government and business do whatever they want without judgement, or fear of prying eyes." Goose knew that Bohemian Grove wasn't the only place of its kind around, there was a whole network the public didn't know about.

"Well let's light that work of art and see what thoughts appear," replied Jason, eager to get the show on the road. He didn't want to end up being shot at numerous times for nothing.

Goose grabbed a gold zippo from his pocket, and lit the joint. The marine he received the lighter from might have been killed defending people who couldn't defend themselves, but not before he gave the lighter to Goose. He told Goose that the most important things in life were being honest with yourself, loving your fellow man and doing what good you can in the short time you have on the earth.

"This is some good stuff. Jay did give me some good growing tips," remarked Goose as he took a hit that produced a cloud big enough that it fogged over the whole table.

"Looks like what we're going through right now," surmised Jason as he grabbed the joint through the smoke cloud to take a monster hit of his own. "The goal of the entities is to mask what they're really doing, so nobody knows what's actually going on. We have to be the ones to clear the fog so we all can see."

Christina grabbed the joint from Jason because she knew he had a habit of holding onto it when he started talking, and she needed the safety meeting as much as anybody. "We can clear the fog, but we have to figure out what's underneath first, before we tell everybody else."

Marty sat back and observed the scene. He knew he had a copy of the blueprint hidden away, waiting for the right time to build a prototype. It was crazy, he thought; that all this uproar was about something that hadn't even been built yet, let alone tested.

"The only thing I couldn't figure out was how you got the blueprints in the first place," inquired Jay, who was happy they were all together, but knew Marty always had his own agenda.

"Well that's an interesting story. It all started in a land far, far away," Marty quipped, making Jay think he was just as bad as the politicians he tried taking down.

"Will you get on with it already? How do we know you aren't in cahoots with the entities? Goose didn't know or didn't say, but how'd you become number one on their hit list?" Jay commanded with unrelenting passion for getting to the truth. This is what made him the Madman for Good.

"If I was in partnership with them, do you really think I would have killed former President Bowman?" asked Marty as if his worthiness was being tested.

"How do we know the old man didn't make you take him out after Bowman went into hiding? How many people have you killed anyway?" queried Jay, whose anger was starting to build. Safety meetings usually calmed his nerves, but this one was having the opposite effect.

"If you got something to say, just say it."

"How do we know you didn't bring us all here to get rid of us like you did Bowman? How do we know you're really on our side?"

Marty looked around the table and saw that Jason and Bryan were nodding in agreement. They both had been under Marty's wing for a long time under false pretenses. They were both waiting for the other shoe to drop.

"So now you all don't trust me? I got rid of somebody who threatened people I care about." Marty knew he cared for Jason just as much as Bryan, that's why he helped him escape the bad situation with his parents years before. "I don't know why I have to keep proving myself, but fine. I know in my heart this is the right course of action because I can feel it from the bottom of my soul. So let me prove it to you, once again."

Marty got up from the table and walked down the very brightly lit hallway and away from the group. "Where do you think he's going? Something is off about him I just can't put my finger on it. Why wouldn't he tell us how he got the blueprint, even though it might be a moot point?" theorized Christina who might have been the voice of reason, but that didn't mean she didn't have her concerns. "Let's see what he returns with."

"Okay, I can wait a little bit. I just didn't know I was coming to work for somebody in New York who kills to get their way. How do we know he won't kill us if we get in his way?" thought Jason who was still trying to comprehend that the man he looked up to for so long, just killed the 47th President of the United States.

After what seemed like an eternity of waiting and smoking, Marty finally emerged from the hallway with a folder in his hand. "You look like you're all finally relaxed enough for me to tell you what I need to tell you," interjected Marty, noticing everybody's eyes were droopy like Snoopy with the slight tint of firetruck.

"So what is it, you plan to kill your way to the top?" Bryan blurted out because his filter was completely gone.

"Is that what you think of me after all I've done for you?" Marty asked a little surprised at Bryan. He knew his first protégé would be one of the hardest people to convince, so Marty handed the folder marked top secret to Jason.

"Do you have to label this thing like you're part of some secret agency?" insinuated Jason, curious about the theatrics. Even though he had much more of a creative mind than scientific, Jason knew blueprints when he saw them. The man he always knew as his father had drawn them up for years for his construction business, which is why his dad's handwriting was always so neat.

"So these are them huh?" inquired Jason knowing the answer, but wanting Marty to say the words.

"Yes they are, I've been waiting for the right opportunity to show the right people," replied Marty who authentically wanted to make positive change as much as the rest of the group. He knew he had to purify himself of all the deception he wrought.

"If these are the blueprints for the device, what did the old man steal from that locker?" inquired Jason, with a hankering for this particular piece to the puzzle.

"They stole the blueprints that day it's true, but they weren't complete," answered Marty who hoped deception aimed at the right people for the right reasons would be okay with the rest of the group. "Once I found myself in possession of these, I created a copy. The one that the entities took is missing a few key components they will only discover when they're almost done building the device. By then, it would be too late."

"So you took these from my mom, the leader of the six entities?" Christina questioned. She tried her hardest to stay on track, even though her mom might have been running a secret world-wide conspiracy her entire life. "She's the one that came up with them. You don't have a science background, how did you know what parts to delete from the blueprint?"

"I had a guy for that."

"You had a guy for that, that's all you're willing to say?"

"Oh I'm willing to say more, it's just I haven't made it this far by revealing everything to everybody. I've been covering my tracks for years to protect myself and the people I care about, and the entities might still end up coming after me."

"So did they notice the elements missing from the blueprints, or were they coming after you because you knew something you shouldn't? If you created a fake blueprint, you had to expect them to come after you at some point."

"I did."

"So you were using your son as bait, so you could use your old friend who switched loyalties?"

Marty felt like he was under the spotlight, and needed to change the subject before they really lobbed their threats at him.

"I don't mind if you all gang up on me. I deserve it to a certain degree, but do you want me to tell you what I've been planning or not?" Marty knew he had to give them just enough information to keep them off his trail.

"No, we want you to keep us in the dark some more," Bryan fired back sarcastically as his anger began to build.

"Okay okay. I'd been dating Christina's mom a while back before she met Jay," Marty divulged. He was trying to tread lightly, because he knew Jay wasn't going to receive this story well.

"Wait, you dated her and you didn't know what she was up to?" asked Jay whose own anger started to rage.

"You were married to her for years and had no idea about any of this. Taking her down is the key to improving the whole world. Each leg of the entities gives them strength, and to take her out, we have to take the legs out one by one."

Jay was still weirded out, not to mention the look Jason and Christina gave each other because they could have been brother and sister. "I'm just glad this isn't some sort of Star Wars movie, where we find out we're brother and sister after we've kissed," Jason sniped as the rest of the group exploded with laughter.

"Now that we're on a little lighter footing, I'll confide I dated Christina's mom for a bit and discovered she had a very scientific mind. She told me about a device she invented that could stop all the devastating droughts and save humanity."

"So you what, got her drunk and she told you all this stuff?" Jay queried, remembering how he fell in love with the same woman. "Because that's how I did it. Well actually, we'd have a couple drinks and would turn each other on by attempting to outdo each other intellectually. The more we got outdone, the more we were turned on."

"Yeah, that's pretty much how it went," agreed Marty who was smiling at Jay, which Jason and Christina knew was a good thing; but strange because Marty and Jay were smiling at how they turned on Christina's mother. It's like walking in on your parents doing it with two different people at the same time they thought.

"We would tell each other how we thought society could be better. We would go back and forth like that until we pretty much ripped each other's clothes off."

"Eeewwwww, bad visual. I don't need the gory details," interjected Christina who was now definitely feeling awkward.

"All right, all right; one time she tried outdoing me by telling me about a device she designed that would change the world. She explained all the ins and outs, even about how without a few key components needed at the end of construction, it would never work. It was some kind of failsafe if the technology ever fell into the wrong hands."

"Just interesting how her hands ended up being the ones the blueprints need to avoid. So you what, got her drunk and stole the blue prints after she explained them. Don't you think that sounds too cut and dry?" suspected Bryan, whose feeling about Marty was so low he thought this was just one more scheme.

"I'll admit it does sound like that. Haven't you heard the old saying that the best place to hide something is in plain sight? It's the same with this. Sometimes we think that because life is so complex, the most difficult explanation has to be the correct one; when that isn't always the case."

Was Marty telling the truth? Did it even matter at this point because their goals were all to help the world consciously evolve and to provide safe water to the people? Wasn't that what Jason had been trying to prove not only with the words he put on paper, but the actions he took every single day. "So she only had the one copy?" inquired Jason.

"Yeah, it was before the internet was main stream. It was a lot smaller, but even then people were worried about being hacked and having their information stolen, so she never made a digital copy of it." Marty was trying to relate to Jay because they were in the same age range. He knew that he couldn't fully win any of them over until he did something meaningful, and not just kill somebody who was after them. "I took her to see The Net, with Sandra Bullock. The internet was pretty new, and it freaked everybody out."

"So you think that's what made her decide to only keep one copy?" asked Christina who felt empowered because she was working her passion right alongside the man she loved. From the way Jason looked at her, she knew he felt the same way.

"Maybe, I don't know anything at this point."

"Get your story straight. Do you know something or don't you?"

"You're not upset because this is about your mom?"

"Maybe."

Marty was glaring at Christina, while the rest of them were glaring at Marty trying to figure out if they could trust him. They all found themselves at a crossroads. If a solution was laid out, would they go after it?

"So that story about your friend at the UN wasn't true?" demanded Jason of Marty remembering what led to him being held at gunpoint. "How are you going to prove this isn't just a bunch of hot air?" Jason took a breath. "Don't use your kid as bait again."

Jason's statement crushed Marty, even though he knew it was partially true. "I can tell you that I went after the entities for quite some time. They will come after me for getting rid of somebody without their permission," Marty explained. "Jay, I need your help undoing the monopoly they have on this pipeline construction. See if you can get some of your men stationed at the main construction sites to delay things, and see if they can find out about or ask questions about the funding for the project."

"I'll have them there day in and day out making sure this thing doesn't get built by the entities," Jay replied. "We don't want them to build because then they'll control the water that flows through it. Then they will charge astronomical prices, and won't fix the real problem. So after we make them stop building it, who will? You?"

Marty knew that if he revealed his zest for making the billions that would be showered upon whoever constructed this thing, then they definitely wouldn't trust him. Then he thought they already didn't trust him, and maybe by telling them the whole truth was how he could get them to trust him. It was worth a shot.

"Yes, me. I would construct it. Well not me personally, but all the contacts I have in the industry. You investigated me for all those years, so I'm sure you found out water systems are how I made my money," revealed Marty.

"Which is why I'm nervous to put my faith and support behind you now. How do I know you're any different from the entities on this? You both want control so you can make a ton of money," theorized Jay whose inner fire was now well lit.

"That's true we both want to make a buck, well many bucks. We know this pipeline needs to be built to stave off environmental devastation. For the last time, I'm not working for a secret organization trying to take over the world one resource at a time," replied Marty. In a different context he could have been best of friends with Jay because both of their passions ran deep for things they believed in. "Would you rather have me do this or someone else?"

"I'd want you, more than them," remarked Jason who felt like Marty was at least partly on the right side of history. "So Jay sends his men to various sites along the route of the pipeline to halt construction, what about the rest of us? What do the rest of us do?"

"Prepare for the backlash that will rain down upon us once the entities find out what we're up to. They won't stop. They have police, government officials, not to mention countless staffers and paper shufflers on Capitol Hill who will come out of the woodwork as we move forward."

Jason looked at Christina, then at Bryan and they seemed to be nodding in agreement, saying without words that this was worth a try. What other choice did they have? They wanted to see this technology built and used, and they knew Marty was an asshole, but he was their asshole.

Just as Jay was going to ask Marty where he should initially send his men, a knock sounded at the door.

Marty jumped up like he was surprised somebody would be knocking, but also like he was half expecting it to happen. "Who could that be, nobody knows where I live," wondered Marty in an authentically surprised voice, even though his eyes didn't match his words. "Hold on. Goose can you cover me, it will be like old times."

Goose nodded at Marty, and then walked behind him until they got to the door when they heard the pounding again. "Damn, somebody knows their cop knock," sniped Jason trying to lighten the mood, even though the situation was still unfolding.

Marty opened the door to see four police officers with their guns drawn in a defensive formation. "Marty Jackson, you're under arrest for murder in the first degree," bellowed the 33 year old officer that looked too dirty to be a veteran on the force. Who wears Nikes under their uniform Jason wondered. "Come with us sir and there will be no incident. We're taking you in because you killed the former President Charles Bowman. The rest of you stay back, we don't want to haul you in too. If you attempt to follow us or find where we're taking him, we will come back and disappear you as well. Come after us if you dare, but remember we are everywhere."

What an odd thing to say Jason thought as the officers cuffed Marty and led him to the waiting police cruiser. Marty hit his head as he was thrown in the car, while the rest of them could only watch. The other officers had their guns squarely aimed at the gang's heads, and they did so until they got Marty loaded up and hauled away. They peeled out as they left, spitting up rocks and dirt from the driveway before Jason could even get a word out.

"What the fuck just happened? One minute Marty is telling us how he not only happened upon the blueprints, but how he planned to put his ideas into motion, and then the next minute he's being hauled away by the police?" Jason blurted out what they were all thinking.

"It was rather suspicious," Jay replied. He picked up on a few things the officer said that a normal cop would never say. He wanted to know if anybody else picked up on it.

"I know what you mean," expressed Christina as she looked at her dad, who smiled back because he knew the girl he abandoned all those years ago was about to make him proud. "The way he said don't follow us, don't come after us, was something you never hear an arresting officer say. It was almost as if he was threatening us, like we were getting close to something."

"I see what you're getting at," surmised Jason as he smiled at the beautiful intelligent woman standing beside him, because he was thinking the same thing.

"I think they work for the entities. It's too perfect that Marty tells us they're in every form of authority this country has, and then seconds later four run of the mill officers come to take him away," Christina added.

"Could be a coincidence," interjected Bryan who was on board with the threat, but wasn't able to put things together fast enough.

"It could be, but has everything been a big coincidence up until this point? Jason and I came to Cuba to look for you Bryan, and found out that our long lost parents weren't who they said they were, would you call that a coincidence? I like to refer to these events more as synchronicities," replied Christina with a gleam in her eye she hadn't felt since she got the job at Shane Corp. Leaving was hard for her, but the more she discovered her mother came up with a device that could save the world, the more intrigued she became.

The fact they were going to fix one of the biggest threats facing the entire planet was something Christina would have to think seriously about if the group was going to keep following synchronicities. "Marty wasn't telling us the whole story, but I also remember something you said dad. Marty might have too much of a profit motive sometimes, but since keeping Jason's best interests at heart was one of his stated goals, we should give him the benefit of the doubt."

The police caravan that arrived at Marty's not so secret hideout had been high tailing it down the dirt road for ten minutes before a voice came over the radio.

"Do you have him, is he safe?" snapped the demanding female voice of authority. "You guys didn't fuck it up again did you?"

"No ma'am, he's right in the back seat," answered the officer who had the professional cop knock. He wanted to prove he and his Nikes were dirty because he wasn't afraid to do the dirty work. "Where should we bring him?"

"Take him to a lockup where we have people we trust. If we're going to take these people down, we have to be smart about it. They have the Madman for Good on their side. God, I don't know what I ever saw in him."

"What was that ma'am?" responded the officer who thought the comment was weird, but knew not to question or he'd find himself in the same deep dark hole he'd placed so many others.

"Nothing. Just call back when you're in a secure location."

The female voice was breaking up on the radio, as the caravan made a bee line for the lockup.

"What was that about, she didn't know what she ever saw in him?" wondered the officer in the passenger seat who was older than the guy giving the orders, but had survived this long because he knew his place. He also knew when things didn't make sense.

"Maybe this will help," remarked the arresting officer as he reached back and took off the hood he placed on Marty when they tossed him in the car. "Sorry about the rough treatment sir, you okay?"

"I'm fine, I know you had to sell it. That group needs to think I've been caught so they'll still have faith in the justice system. If they catch a whiff the entities are behind this, let's just say I don't want to commit genocide to get rid of our enemies," surmised Marty like his manhood was being challenged.

"Wait a minute, we're taking our orders from this guy?" asked the older junior officer in the passenger seat.

"He is the enforcer for the lady we take orders from," stated the arresting younger senior officer who was getting just as tired of all the questions as Marty was.

"Can you guys just shut up so I can think?" shouted Marty, trying to determine what to say to these guys. He knew they were privy to part of the story, but didn't know everything (neither did the lady running things, or the gang back at the hideout). If his plan was to work, he had to play all sides. Considering there were endless variables to every situation, Marty knew he couldn't let on to what he was planning until after everything was over. Until then, he had to give everybody just enough to wet their beaks without getting them soaking wet. "Just take me to the war room, or the lockup, whatever she said over the radio to make it sound official. We need to get this pipeline built. I have lots of money to make."

CHAPTER SIXTEEN

The Mad People for Good used to be just a concept. An idea inside the head of a person with more than one screw loose. Now the ideas would have to be proven in reality. Protesting, talking back and being a general pain in the ass was one thing, but Jay knew that if the 6 entities were to be stopped, then the blueprints they were holding was the way to do it.

"What are we supposed to do with these now, and how do we even know it's the only copy?" deciphered Jay speaking a million miles an hour. "I spent a long time trying to find this thing and now that I have it, I have no idea what to do with it."

Jason didn't know what to do with a lot of things, but having know-how and a need to act towards the betterment of humanity he knew were two totally different concepts. Then he remembered he had a beautiful scientific mind right next to him, itching to do something meaningful. "What do you think Christina?" Jason inquired, hoping he could get her hamster running on its wheel. "Any ideas rolling around in that beautiful head of yours?"

"Now that you mention it, my mom did come up with this thing, so it seems poetic if I'm the one that makes it work," Christina replied feeling grateful that she was in this moment right now. "First things first, we need a different place to plan. The 6 entities obviously know where we are now, they could be back."

"Any idea where we should go?" queried Jay with a smile watching his daughter work. "I think we need to start looking into the entities funding streams."

"How do we do that if they have their hands into everything?" surmised Bryan who thought it was a legitimate question. If this organizations influence was seemingly everywhere, what chance did they have? He then remembered the fire he had when he went after Ridell, and what made him push on. "We can't forget the reason we're doing this, is to bring water to the people; to stop a powerful corporate entity pardon my French, from controlling the water a huge majority of the population uses. This summer is going to be hotter than last."

"That's true. Maybe the entities are like a snake, if we cut off the head, the rest will wither and die," Goose calculated, remembering some of the missions he conducted over the years.

"That sounds good. Why don't you do some recon on where she might be located. Keep your eye on the intersection point. They'll be headed there at some juncture. We can't let them control this thing, do what you have to do," barked Jay, knowing that Goose could be leaned on when the going got tough. He ran his operations for years, now would be the proof that Goose had what it took during the most important mission of his life.

"Sounds good boss, I might have to stay behind the scenes somewhat because my cover was blown with the entities when I picked you up. Either way, I'll find where this bitch is and put her down," Goose fumed like he was going after Bin Laden.

"Watch yourself, that's my mother you're talking about," Christina shot back, very surprised she rose up to her mother's defense. "We don't want you to put her down. We just want to find out where she is, then maybe we can talk to her."

"You're going to just walk in and talk to the most dangerous person on the planet and what, give her those puppy dog eyes and say "please mom, don't"," Goose quipped as he wasn't sure Christina had what it took.

The anger was boiling inside of Christina, her face was as red as a firetruck. "You got something against women, or are you just stupid?" Christina retorted ready to fight.

"Settle down you two," Jay chimed in, as he saw Goose and Christina getting closer and closer to punching each other, so he stepped in-between them. "Goose, why don't you just take off for a little bit, you're not helping things right now. You have your mission. Gather some troops and get it done."

"You think you can just tell me what to do? Maybe I'll just refuse and say no," remarked Goose as he backed off and slowly inched towards the door. "Maybe I'll just take the troops and go somewhere else."

Jay looked like somebody just landed a sucker punch on his chin. At no point had somebody close to him flip flopped their support so quickly. He stared at Goose who just stared back. This went on for about five minutes before Goose turned around and started for the door. "You think you can just come back and tell me how things should be when I've been running them for so long? The troops believe in me because I was here," yelled Goose as he walked out the door, slamming it behind him.

Jason watched the whole scene. He didn't step in for Christina because he knew she could hold her own, what he didn't like was her power being taken away. "Screw that guy. We can do this by ourselves just the four of us. I think we should start with Marty," replied Jason as he felt the bitterness escape to be replaced by a thick sense of hope. "We don't know what side Marty is on, but right now we might have to trust him to do the right thing."

Christina's skeptical look led to the cynical words that came out of her mouth. "How can we trust him or anybody for that matter? They all seem to have their own agendas."

"That's true, but so do we," expressed Jason while looking into Christina's eyes with the full passion and fire that burned within his soul. "Ours just needs some fine tuning."

The four of them sat at the table and thought for a long minute that seemed like hours. If most of their time had been spent taking down the powerful who deserved it, what would they build in its place? What would be the replacement for the system they all agreed needed major change?

"I need some air. Jay, do you know a spot by the water around here where we could just go and think?" wondered Jason who needed some peace and quiet to figure out their next move. The sounds of nature always brought him inspiration, and with it grand ideas to save the world all around him.

"I know a spot like that not too far from the base. I used to go there quite often. Sitting there listening to the sounds of the earth always brought me answers," Jay responded. He was very intrigued that the guy his daughter chose to love, was basically following in his footsteps. Jay never had a son, but a future son-in-law who was down for the betterment of humanity would definitely do.

"Not that I don't have deep thoughts, it's just not what usually drives me, like the hard facts," interjected Bryan who wasn't sure how to handle all the flowery language being thrown about. Since he was sitting with some of the most authentically down to earth people he ever had the pleasure to associate with, he thought he'd give language a try. "Where to partner? I'd drive us like I did in New York, but Goose left with the only vehicle."

Jason, Christina, Bryan and Jay had been standing on the front porch jawing ever since the 6 entities posing as cops took Marty away, so they didn't notice the carport neatly tucked away on the side of the house that Marty called his secret lair. He didn't really call it his secret lair, even though Jason kind of hoped he did.

Jason turned around and was starting to walk up the stairs on the front porch, when he heard a bird fly overhead. He wasn't really sure what kind it was, but it sure was loud. Since he couldn't see it, he kept looking around the skies for where it is coming from.

"You okay man? You look like you could use a joint to calm your nerves," mentioned Bryan, remembering how Jason always seemed to settle down enough to let his true thoughts flow once he was relaxed.

"I'm fine man, just thought I heard a screeching bird," wondered Jason, starting to feel like he was crazy because nobody else seemed to hear it. He kept turning around to see if he could spot it. This was making him a little dizzy.

"Why don't you sit down baby, you're making my head spin by making your head spin," quipped Christina not sure what was rolling around in Jason's head. After having been through as much as they had together, she knew it was only a build up to the truly great things that awaited all of them now that their true working group came together.

Jason sat on the porch and closed his eyes for a minute trying to listen. After he didn't hear it anymore, he opened his eyes and spotted the carport. "What is that over there?" Jason asked as if he didn't already suspect what it was.

"Looks like one of those really cheap things people erect to keep rain off their car, instead of building a garage," replied Bryan knowing that some people couldn't afford all the things that came with suburban living, but he was always one for a wisecrack. "We should go check it out."

The four of them walked over to the carport, which was four metal poles with some sheet metal looking stuff spread in-between. It could have been part of a corrugated roof for all they knew. Even if their trust of Marty was up in the air at the moment, they could never fault him for being resourceful.

"Looks like a car under there," Jason stated knowing how obvious he sounded, and knew Bryan would have a retort. He hoped he did, as it would lighten their mood.

"Thank you Commander obvious, what gave that away? The fact that we can see the license plate through that little plastic window down there, or maybe because it's the same shape and size of a car?"

"Maybe you're the one that needs to smoke that joint, you're getting a little snarky."

"All this Marty stuff is just a little hard to handle," explained Bryan, wondering what would come of the man who was practically a father to him. He felt that traveling with the guy who was his actual son was a good place to start.

Christina and Jay stood there and watched Jason and Bryan's back and forth exchange. "You guys sound like brothers the way you bicker, I'm surprised neither of you have said "your momma"," sniped Christina who always loved Jason's sense of humor and everything that came with it; but sometimes, she just had to have the last laugh.

"I'd say "your momma" to you pretty girl, but we might be after her soon enough," chuckled Jason with a chortle because he knew he was matched with the only person who filled out his deficiencies so perfectly.

"Just take the car cover off. Enough with the suspense," Christina remarked with a sexy smile that always drove Jason wild.

"You keep looking at me like that, we might have to borrow the back seat of whatever is under here and tell Bryan and Jay to go take a walk," Jason shot back hoping that Jay would get in on the fun.

"You have some balls to say right in front of me that you're going to bone my daughter, but anybody who has such passion for the mission ahead of us, how could I say no? Bone away," bantered Jay, which caught them all off guard and they burst out laughing.

"Nice try dad. While I very much appreciate the effort, your delivery needs some work," expressed Christina who put her arm around her dad and gave him a big hug. She missed out on so much with him, but she would be damned if she would miss any more. Besides, she knew her dad just needed more practice. "Hang out with these guys for a little while longer, and you'll see how quick you can get."

"I thought you didn't like it when I was quick," Jason remarked, trying to keep the laugh-fest going. "I thought you like when I take my time."

"I do, but just like your pancakes and your joints, you need a little help," Christina replied as she gave Jason a kiss that filled up his soul with an energy transfer so strong that Jay and Bryan saw what was going on.

"We could all use some of that good energy. I only hope that one day I can find what you've found man," admitted Bryan, who truly felt Jason was the best friend he'd always been looking for. "So let's take this cover off and see what's underneath."

Bryan started to pull the cover off a car that seemed to be huge, but once it was off, Jason knew exactly what it was.

"How did Marty get, how did, how?" Jason stammered as he kept thinking in half sentences. His thoughts were flying through his head so fast, that he couldn't complete a thought before the next one came rushing in.

Sitting under this non-descript carport in this non-descript place Marty possibly called his secret lair, was the 61 Lincoln Jason and Bryan had become so familiar with.

The way Jason was looking at the car, Christina knew the exact thoughts pounding in his brain.

"This must be the famous Lincoln you and Bryan drove around the streets of New York City, unseating evil-doers wherever they sat," boomed Christina like a voice announcing an old batman episode.

"It's not like we drove it through Gotham or anything," quipped Jason, kind of wishing they had. The batman analogy led him to think about all the money Marty had made. "I wonder why Marty kept this, or how he even got it here to Michigan?"

"I have no idea. When we parted ways and I took off, I thought you had it," theorized Bryan, throwing the ball back in Jason's court.

"I did, it's what I drove to California in. It's what I was driving when I met back up with Christina. Heck it's what we drove to the rally when we heard from the old man he could take down the President," pondered Jason who was thinking out loud now, and not noticing the things around him. His blinders were on, but that's why having such a loving, caring and motivating inner circle around him made such a difference.

"Yes that's true," agreed Christina, whose memory banks were starting to regenerate. "Then we drove it up the Pacific Coast Highway and just enjoyed the scenery. In fact, that's where we heard on the radio that the

President's plane went down and everything was missing from it, including any wreckage or bodies."

"So what happened after that?" Bryan questioned, who was intrigued by the evolution of the black Lincoln he called home in the Big Apple.

"We drove it back to Arcata and parked it outside of our house," added Jason, who was trying to put pieces together. "Then when we got the Cuban sandwich postcard from you guys, we came down to Cuba to find you; and after that, I don't know. We didn't drive the Lincoln around town. Everything there was close enough to walk to. We left it at the house, I have no idea how it got here."

"So how did this beautiful piece of machinery from northern California get all the way out here then?" inquired Jay who was trying to keep their eyes on the prize. What that prize happened to be, none of them knew. What kept them going was the journey, and the realization that the synchronicities never end.

"Do you think Marty moved it? He did say he'd been keeping an eye on it for me," surmised Jason who was trying to think what could have happened. "He knew how special this car was to me. Maybe he thought I'd meet up with him one day and be re-united. Of course he did lead me on, by not telling me he was my dad and all. Maybe that's it, maybe he kept this car because he knew he wouldn't be back for a long time, and that taking care of one of your sons dream cars was a way to take care of your son; or at least a piece of him."

"That's very poetic," replied Bryan who heard this soapbox from Jason before, and knew it always led to some great thought to steer their upcoming mission.

Jason opened the door and looked inside. The seats were clean and the carpet vacuumed, the outside had even been washed and waxed recently. "Looks like Marty knew we'd find this soon, he had it detailed," mentioned Jason, about to hop in the driver seat.

"Oh no sir, allow me, let me drive you like old times," quipped Bryan as he gently pushed Jason away and slid into the driver seat. "This leather is just as comfortable as I remember. Something about leather being worn in for years through lots of ass heat makes it so soft."

"So articulate, you have to go to English class to think that one up?" Jason shot back knowing the respect between them had never been higher. "Not that I don't want to keep joking and carrying on about your ass heat, but let's go to that place Jay knew about. I'd still like a spot to go to, just to think for a bit."

"And smoke right?" queried Jay as he held two of his finest joints. "I've been saving these."

"Looks like you had a great teacher Christina, I see where you get your rolling skills from," chuckled Jason with a smile.

"Yes I did," recalled Christina. She remembered an old beer commercial, and since the others started laughing, she knew they got the reference as well.

Jason smiled as he sauntered over to the passenger side and got in. Bryan slid behind the wheel, wanting to fire up the engine. "Hope this baby still purrs."

Bryan looked under the visor and found a key. He stuck it in the ignition and the over 60 year old beast roared to life. "Sounds like he kept everything oiled and lubed," quipped Jason, knowing that he threw Bryan a softball down the middle.

"You always have to keep things lubricated and slippery. It helps them slide in much easier and with less effort," replied Bryan. This made Jason laugh out loud as Christina and Jay got into the back seat, and started to wonder what was so funny. Since Christina knew Jason like the back of her hand, and Bryan was his right hand man, she knew it had to be something childish.

"Okay okay, I know you're happy to be back in this car, but we have to stay focused on the road ahead. We have to put away the ten year old sense of humor for a little while," Christina interjected as she slipped into the comfortable leather backseat that could hold five people.

"Christina's right, we should get going," remarked Bryan as he put the car into drive and they pulled away.

"So this is one of your dream cars, huh?" Jay chimed in, always curious to find out what made the guy his daughter loved tick.

"It is. I always loved convertibles. I had a few growing up. This Lincoln is one of the only four door convertibles I know of. It's a sixty one and jet black. It looks bad ass, I must say," explained Jason with his lip curled up, and nodding in approval. He was happy to have his chariot back.

Bryan pulled onto the road and back toward the highway. There was nobody following that he could see, but that's what they thought when Ridell was shooting missiles from a drone as they tried to escape Cuba.

"Just out of curiosity, you said this was one of your favorite cars, what's another?" asked Jay. He was always mindful to the language and the words people used to express their thoughts. This came in handy when investigating Marty, but also when he wanted to truly know the person who was in love with his daughter.

"That's an easy one. A silver 1967 corvette convertible with side pipes," replied Jason thinking how cool it would be to ride in one, let alone drive one.

"Good to know," Jay thought out loud with a sly wink. Christina might not have been reunited with her dad for long, but she felt he had something up his sleeve.

Deep thoughts swirled around the Lincoln as they drove ten minutes along the dirt road away from Marty's place to the highway. "Which way Jay, I don't care anyway," wondered Bryan, knowing how cheesy it sounded.

"Do you always rhyme when you talk, or just when you're playing chauffeur?" Jay expressed with a laugh from the bottom of his soul which was respectful banter between truth seekers.

"Ha, ha, ha, you're so funny," chuckled Bryan, not sure what to say, but glad Jay joined in on the good natured ribbing. "Hey, hey, hey by the way; over the bay, is maybe where I'll lay."

"That's it I know a spot by this little bay. Well it's not really a bay, more of an inlet. I think it should serve our purpose," surmised Jay realizing that because Bryan continued with the banter, it led him to the next step, which is what the rest of them had been waiting for. "Go up another ten miles or so, make a left at Old Find Road, and go about ten more minutes. It winds through some farm land and some private property. Anyway, it's the perfect spot."

Bryan nodded in agreement because he loved to joke as much as the next person. He also knew when to turn it off, at least most of the time.

The Lincoln pulled into the little dirt parking lot at Old Find State Park at 4:30 in the afternoon. There were a few other cars parked, and a few more were pulling in; as this was a popular place to watch the sunset. After Bryan parked the car, they all exited and walked towards a picnic bench near the water.

A lot of birds had gathered around the edges of the shore, as the tides were such that it gave them much needed food. Migratory birds picked through the mud and the shallow water for some buggy treats.

"This reminds me of a place back home that I used to go to three or four times a week. I'd go there after work or after my day was over and relax, read, write and do an open eyes kind of meditation," recalled Jason. He remembered what life was like at the marsh, his refuge, his own personal Walden Pond. "This place is perfect."

Christina and the others followed Jason to the picnic table where they sat down and looked out at the water. It wasn't the lowest tide of the day in fact it looked like it was coming up. Many birds were playing around in the shallow water as they had plenty to eat, and no fear of predators.

"So now that we're here, want to tell me what we're doing?" Jay inquired, wondering where this was leading. He knew all too well what it meant to fall into an existential trap.

"Remember those two joints you broke out earlier, let's start with those," replied Jason who knew a safety meeting was just what they needed.

"Now you're speaking my language," Jay grabbed a joint from the pocket of his flannel shirt and lit it up. "You're right, that's much better."

"See I told you," Jason remarked as Jay handed him the joint and he took a big puff, letting out a cloud of smoke that covered his entire face.

"Did you even inhale?" asked Christina, who took her first hit off the amazing dad rolled joint. "So?"

"Yeah. What?" Jason inquired, wondering what was on Christina's mind.

"So when's the inspiration going to come? What are we waiting for? We have a million things to do, and not nearly enough time to do it in. We need to put a plan in motion like yesterday," blurted Christina who was relaxed, but very antsy about the unknown.

"Come on baby, you know you can't force inspiration," added Jason as he stared at the birds picking in the mud with their beaks; making a sound he had never heard before. "Do you guys hear that, it sounds like bees flying through watery mud?"

Jason pointed down at the birds he was staring at, trying to get the rest of them to look. "Those things are pretty cool looking," remarked Christina who thought it was special to see some birds, but didn't get Jason's fascination. "What's the point? What are we going to do? When are we going to go get Marty?"

Jason thought for a minute, but no concrete ideas flowed in. There were a few other people milling around on the partly sunny afternoon that was blindingly average. Just then Jason saw something that he couldn't ignore. "Hold on, I'll be right back." He got up from the table and started walking towards a man sitting about a hundred yards away that looked familiar.

"I guess he's on a mission. We should let him be, or call out the funny farm I'm not sure which. Since we don't know where to go or what to do next, let's allow this to play out," expressed Bryan because he had faith in the partner that never steered him wrong.

Jason got closer to the man sitting on a rock overlooking the water. He still wasn't sure who it was, the guy's overcoat and side profile looked so familiar, he just couldn't put his finger on it. The gang back at the picnic table was mesmerized by somebody who was truly letting go and following a feeling. They didn't know what to think, except Jay who had a few ideas.

"Oh shit man, is that you?" wondered Jason who was now about ten feet from where the guy was sitting.

"I'm me that's for sure, but is that you, that's the real question," the man replied knowing it was the expected response.

"Of course it is, Tim put it there," Jason answered, in shock that he spotted a friend randomly after twenty years, in a place he never thought he'd be.

Jason held out his hand for a shake, but that wasn't good enough for Tim. "What is this handshake bullshit, give me a hug brother," quipped Tim who always felt a strong connection to Jason, and was curious what happened over the past twenty years since they'd seen each other.

"What the hell have you been up to? I haven't seen you in forever," inquired Jason very curiously, but confident this was the next synchronicity he was supposed to follow.

"Not much man, I was a firefighter for a while. It was good and I had fun. I felt great that I was able to help people when they needed it most," Tim remembered how much he loved his former life, but also why he came out east.

"I heard about that, why the change?" asked Jason who always knew the true sign of friendship was when two people who haven't seen each other for years, come back together and it's like no time had passed.

"I needed a change of scenery. All the lakes around here are great. The weather is cold and they get actual snow. Hell you can surf on the lake," Tim joked, thinking of how crazy that sounded.

"It sure is nuts. Waterskiing on the lake back home was fun. I loved going on the boat," pondered Jason. They both laughed remembering simpler times when beer was cheaper, it got them drunker and women seemed prettier. Of course, that was how they felt when they last met, not how they felt now.

"We did have lots of good times. I guess that's what I am doing out here, I'm trying to recreate some of those good times," responded Tim to the puzzlement of Jason because his previous question still hadn't been answered.

"You're trying to recreate good times?" Jason asked because he needed a little more clarification. "My friends and I over there have been tracking this guy named Marty. He works for this crazy secret organization that pretty much controls everything in government financial markets around the world. From what we can find, they want to broaden their influence by privatizing everything they can. We came out here today because we weren't sure where to go next. Marty escaped and screwed us over, so we're not sure if we should go after him or the main structure of the organization."

It was difficult for Tim to find the right words. "I know, the six entities have been a thorn in my side ever since I started the Anti-entities," explained Tim. He wasn't worried even a little bit that Jason couldn't be trusted, because he knew from the bottom of his heart that he could.

"The what?" Jason asked, thinking it sounded like a bad spoof movie.

"The Anti-entities. A group I started that goes after the entities of course, but we go after their environmental leg, their business leg, their pharmaceutical leg, their military leg, and of course the most powerful of them all, their political leg. It ties them together and gives them power," blurted Tim whose mind was on fire with all the things he and Jason could accomplish.

Jason was stunned that Tim was looking into the same people as he, Christina, Jay and Bryan. He had already taken the next step and started an organization to attack the supports of the 6 entities control structure.

"I'm not sure what to say, other than would you like some help?" Jason inquired, almost too excited to speak understandable words. He had to contain it for this moment because he knew it would give him direction. "I've wanted to do something like that for a while, take down the parts of the government and the world elite that mess up things so badly on a daily basis. What I've been thinking lately is when all the corrupt people are thrown out of office along with their businesses, what do we replace them with?"

Tim had been thinking about an answer to that question for a very long time, and hadn't come close to anything that would be considered a real answer. Maybe it took being next to an old friend to help him remember. "That's it, we just replace it with the same thing, but the difference this time is real accountability and real humanism. Basically, we help this country live up to its ideals that I could argue have never been fully realized, no matter how many people have tried. I just want to try, that's all."

"I want to help you try, and so do my friends," expressed Jason with unimaginable happiness as he waved back at the gang who were still wondering just what the hell Jason was doing. "We've been trying to get this pipeline out from under the thumb of the entities, and into the hands of somebody who will truly give it to the people; and not raise their rates dramatically just for the privilege."

"That's funny, I'm on the same page. That is the big part of the environmental leg of the entities. If you control the water, you control the farms, the fields, the produce, basically the entire structure of humanity. Somebody is going to make money off of this thing that's a given. We just have to make sure the money is going to the right people."

"I agree, and who are the right people?"

"Somebody with the infrastructure and the know-how. We don't want to stop it from being built, the bio-analyzer will help all of humanity. We just have to make sure the entities don't control it, and make sure that people know a company intended to make billions off it just to line their pockets. We need to give it to the people for free. They will love having plenty of clean water and of course no bill. Once the entities see they can't make any money off it, they'll shift their focus to the next leg. That's what we must do, force them to that next leg; then we can work on taking that one down."

Jason didn't know what to say, but when he opened his mouth it all became clear. "Tim, you have to meet my friends. We're working on the same thing. They say one person can't change the world, but enough people working together can, and we've got five right here."

Jason led Tim back to the picnic table to introduce his oldest friend, to the newest members of his inner circle. "This is my old buddy, Tim. I knew him from school back a million years ago," Jason quipped sarcastically because they'd been through a lot together, and were getting older. "He's going to help us."

"With what, his group called the Anti-entities or something?" theorized Bryan because it was the first thing that popped into his head.

"Well actually yes, that's exactly what he's going to do."

CHAPTER SEVENTEEN

Marty Jackson was a complex man, becoming less complex as he became less mysterious. His actions had been covered up for so long sometimes even he didn't know where his loyalties lie.

"What did you find out," inquired the mysterious female voice over the loud speaker in the dank and dirty room where the officers brought Marty.

"They know about the pipeline, the bio-analyzer and the intersection point," stated Marty whose honesty was becoming a liability. He didn't want to take chances anymore with calling somebody's bluff. "I showed them a blueprint I did a rough sketch of, right after I took it from you."

The officers in the room went white with fear because they wouldn't dream of talking back to the thunderous female voice none of them had ever met. The young senior officer felt an immediate respect for Marty, even though he knew he couldn't show it because cameras were hidden everywhere.

"That's right. You stole it from me, never forget that," as her voice got angrier and louder. "How do I know I can trust you? How can I believe anything you say? You played upon the drunken musings of a vulnerable woman. You know how that plays out in the greater part of society."

Marty knew what she was getting at, but didn't see its significance because it was so long ago. Stealing the blueprints was important, because he wanted to make lots of money; which is how he supported his long lost son. He wanted to help society and change the world for the better. He just wanted to be financially compensated as he was doing it.

"That might be true, but that was years ago. I'm a different person now. I'd never take advantage of a woman unless she asked me to," Marty quipped. He winked at the young officer who didn't wink back, but was cheering for Marty on the inside. "I've been earning my way back into your good graces ever since. I got rid of your enemies who wanted to throw a monkey wrench into your aspirations, and aspirations of the 6 entities."

"You think you can just freely use that phrase, and anybody will believe you? You, Marty Jackson? You think I haven't had complete control of you the whole time?" insinuated the voice that was beginning to calm down, as she realized Marty was trying to get her upset; that was exactly what she didn't want to happen. She didn't fend off countless insurrections within the entities just to let some do-gooder mess everything up. "Thank you for taking out Bill, and the President for that matter. Having a guy to get rid of liabilities is something a person like me will always need. What I don't appreciate is you playing both sides, waiting to see who comes out on top. As long as we hold you until the construction is complete, your people can't take control, and won't make all of the money."

Marty thought about how much he loved money, how much he loved not struggling like he did so often when he was younger. His life was hard growing up. His dad worked 12 hours a day in a machine shop only to come home to see his wife in bed with the mailman, the milkman or the neighbor. He knew how stereotypical his upbringing sounded, which is why Marty spent his whole life being the least stereotypical as possible. "What're you going to do with me? You going to kill me after I did your dirty work? You too scared to come out of the shadows and show your face? You were quite beautiful as I can remember."

The two officers tasked with watching Marty let out a sigh, which was their way of saying they liked Marty, and probably could've been friends if circumstances were different.

"You don't think I could have any man I want? Please," sniped the voice who felt like she was being challenged, and had to end it right in its tracks. "I'm going to put you somewhere where nobody will ever find you, not even Goose. Whatever happened to him? You said he could be trusted, and look what happened to him. He ended up being exactly what you're fighting against. I'm done listening to you. Boys, take him to the black site within the black site."

Marty didn't know what the hell that meant, but he was sure it wasn't good. The officers held some respect for Marty as they were about to lead him out of the office building, that looked like it could have been situated in any strip mall across America. Was this where all the entities hideouts were Marty thought? If they had their fingers in all the pies, then hiding in plain sight on any street USA was the perfect way to do it.

"Later Marty. You were good in the sack, but I sincerely hope we never see each other again. I hate to use the tired line that my people are so much more powerful than yours, but they are. Money controls everything. You throw money into someone's face, and they'll do anything you want. How do you think I got you to kill for me? Take him away boys," exclaimed the voice abruptly from out of the loud speaker. The officers took him out of the office and into the front room.

Marty remembered this was the age of the internet, not the age when he stole the blueprint. Now was the time that information could end up around the world in a split second. This could lead to the world's downfall, but could also be its greatest gift if used in the right way.

The officers were just as cautious as Marty when they got into the waiting room of the office. They didn't know where the cameras were either. "Where does she want us to take him?" asked the older junior officer who didn't like taking orders from a youngster, but knew he had to respect the hierarchy or he'd end up like Marty.

"I have the directions in the car," responded the younger senior officer who knew his place and position because he played it very well; that's how he got to the place he was in life. What he didn't figure was the constant evolving and changing nature of the human mind. "Let's go outside, I think she sent it to my GPS."

The two officers walked Marty out to the black unmarked S.U.V. that looked like hundreds of other government vehicles. Since this particular office park had many secret government and corporate entities operating within it, there were many of them.

"Where did I park? I think it was over there," wondered the younger officer trying to throw off the older one.

"I told you, stop smoking so much weed, its starting to affect your memory. You don't think I've stayed alive this long without being completely clear headed do you?" inquired the officer who was showing his age. It wasn't because of the wrinkles on his face, or his propensity for using the name "Sonny". He just didn't have the energy to stand up anymore, and didn't want to die without anybody knowing it.

"Ha, ha, ha, ha Mr. Funny Man. Maybe you should smoke some so you'll calm down a little bit. I might not be clear-headed all the time, but there are times when I'm too clear-headed," expressed the younger officer as they both got in the front seat, after directing Marty into the back. Marty could have run because he wasn't wearing handcuffs and there wasn't a gun on him, and he thought there weren't any snipers. He was curious to see how the whole thing played out.

Marty was barely situated in the back seat, when out of the corner of his eye he saw the younger officer pull the gun from his shoulder holster, point it at the head of the older officer and pull the trigger. If brains splattered on the windshield for all to see wasn't a big enough problem, Marty wondered how unhinged this guy was.

"What the hell man, don't shoot me," Marty shouted scared for his life, but not as scared as he thought he should be.

"I knew I kept this silencer on for a reason, you never know when you're going to need it," chuckled the younger officer who now had Marty's complete attention. "This guy was going to rat me out."

"What do you mean rat you out? I thought you were on the same side," Marty already knew the reason for the shooting, but he wanted the guy to say the words.

"I agreed with everything you said to that bitch. She thinks she is all-powerful, all-knowing and that nobody will ever defy her. She's constantly testing her power and showing her strength, almost like she's compensating for something," replied the young officer who looked to be about Jason's age.

If he wanted to make up for lost time with Jason, make money on the pipeline and do good for humanity, Marty saw how he could accomplish all three goals at the same time. Even though this was a very dangerous situation, he knew that it was a synchronicity nonetheless.

"I hear that," Marty agreed, feeling commonalities with this man even though they had just met. Using violence to get rid of people standing in the way of what you think is right, was something he related to. "So what's next? Isn't she going to be looking for you if you don't show up, especially without Chuckles the dead splattered clown here?"

"That's a good one man. I wish we had more time. Some of our goals are probably the same. I originally thought the entities were the way to go because they talked about improving every aspect of human life. Now I know the truth. It's all about greed and exploitation. I want to make the world a better place. I have to figure out my own path."

Marty was starting too really like this guy. Since cars were pulling in and out, he knew half of them were probably entity vehicles. The happy moment needed a rain check. "I'd say give me a ride somewhere, but I think driving around with blood splattered windows might draw attention." Marty wondered if the entities were on to him yet. Then he remembered why he had called Jason to New York. Not only because he was his father. He knew Jason had a passion for unrelenting positivity and holding the world accountable for its transgressions. He also knew that Jason wanted to help the population fight back the onslaught of destruction that was coming if the entities got fully set up.

"You're right, I know of an old safe house from about ten years ago. The entities don't use it anymore. This guy named Jay or something found it. I think that's what that bitch called him. Anyway, he found it so the cover was blown. You should be safe there for the time being. I have an identical backup car for situations like this, with the same license plates, so cameras can't tell the difference between this one and the next."

"Sounds good to me. I wish we could do this thing together, sounds like you want to take them down just as much as I do."

"I never said I want to take them down, I just want to make sure they don't succeed in controlling this pipeline. I'll take you to this place, and I'll make sure the rest of your group will head there. I'll send them a message I know they'll catch."

"How do you know who my group is, and how do you know what signals they'll catch?"

"I've been following you under the direction of our bitch lady leader for years. I know about your group, about Cuba, about everything. I'll take you to the safe house, and make sure they're waiting for you when you get there."

Marty thought why should he trust a guy he didn't know from a hole in the ground. From the way the guy was looking at him though, he could see the inner battle going on inside his head. He remembered actions like these weren't based on trust, but based on mutual needs. As long as what they wanted was the same, they wouldn't get in each other's way; they both knew what would happen if they did. After the escape he knew he'd have more enemies than he knew what to do with, so Marty thought, what the hell.

"Let's do it."

Jason and his old friend Tim were getting reunited. They remembered why they had become friends in the first place, because their thought processes were very much alike.

"I like this guy. Can you tell me any funny stories about Jason that he might have forgotten to tell me about? You know, something really juicy and embarrassing," inquired Christina as she took a hit of the second joint that Jay lit when Tim walked over.

"I have a few, and they're doozies," Tim fired back as he laughed at Jason shaking his head, like here it comes. Bryan and Jay were just as intrigued by Tim's stories as Christina was. They listened so intently that all they needed was popcorn and you'd think they were watching a movie.

Just as Jay was going to join in the fun, and tell some embarrassing stories about Christina to help Jason out, his phone rang.

"What is that, is that a phone? I thought we got rid of our phones because they can be traced?" asked Jason, curious who wasn't telling the whole truth. He knew it was impossible to tell the truth all the time, we can't all be Gandhi he thought.

"I've had this satellite phone for years, and it's never been traced, even when I went into exile. I didn't think it was possible," replied Jay as he pulled the small phone out of his pocket; it had an antennae that was huge when fully extended. "Hell, maybe it's Goose calling to apologize and bring the troops to help."

As Jay looked at his phone, Christina scowled at him, like here comes another lie; something else he's covering up. Jay knew they shouldn't keep secrets from each other, so he just decided to see what would happen next.

He didn't recognize the number so Jay didn't pick it up. Five seconds after the phone stopped ringing, it buzzed with a picture message or a text; Jay never really knew the difference. He yearned for the days when a text message was something you wrote on a letter, before you put a stamp on it and put in the mail box.

"It looks like you have a picture message, dad," Christina explained because it looked like her dad was having a hard time deciphering it. "Let me see it."

Jay handed the phone to Christina who took one look at it, and saw a coded message she couldn't figure out. "What does it say? Who is it from?" Jay interrogated because he knew it would force them to take the next step.

"I'm not sure who it's from. The phone number isn't a real number, too many digits and letters. I don't even know how something like this comes up on a phone. Anyway, the text message says you were looking into me because I was looking into someone else. We thought we were each other's enemies but we aren't, we're both after the same thing. Come to the place you saw your first day in Detroit. When you eat a Coney dog around the corner, everything will become clear."

Jay thought about the words Christina read. He wondered who could have written them, but then it came to him, at least the meeting point did. "I could go for a Coney dog just as much as the next guy. I just wish they had Cuban sandwiches there I could really go for one right now. All that meat and melted cheese, mmmmmm," pondered Jay who knew what the message meant, but was also really stoned and hungry.

Christina rolled her eyes, Bryan, Jason and Tim's mouths started to water, but Jay didn't flinch. When his mind was focused on the betterment of the world, or a key part of the mission to get there, Jay was unrelenting; you might say he was a Madman for Good.

"That's referring to a place not far from that office park where we first met Marty," surmised Jay, not wanting to say too much right away.

"I'm not going back in there. The last time, my father held a gun to my head. Then I saw him shoot the President instead of me because he didn't want to take orders anymore," exclaimed Jason whose passion was high as ever because he was being honest about the best path forward. He wanted the pipeline built and for the water to flow to all the drought stricken areas that needed it. He just didn't want to get killed in the process. Not that he wasn't willing to die, he just felt like he had a lot more to accomplish before he did.

"Excuse me what?" asked Tim with a look on his face like the aliens had not only invaded, but they were coming over for dinner and bringing some really good alien beer.

"It's a long story man, the last ten years have been one wild ride, and I'll catch you up on all of it. Right now, that has to wait. Go on Jay, where's this leading?" queried Jason because he now had faith in somebody even though he hadn't in a very long time. He always had faith in Christina, but this was a different kind of faith. Like the faith that the pied piper had finally come to save the day, or maybe that was just the weed talking.

"You driving Bryan? Let's head over there. I have a feeling all our questions will be answered once we arrive," remarked Jay confidently as he looked at the rest of the group like come on, I haven't steered you wrong yet. Even though they knew that was true, they also knew they didn't have a choice. Bryan looked at Jason like should we do this, and Jason nodded.

That was all Bryan needed. He walked back over to the car and warmed it up. "What kind of car are you driving these days man? I remember the blue beast from back in school, that thing was awesome. Remember doing burnouts alongside the Camaro I used to have?" asked Tim, regaling one of his favorite stories, because it was one of Jason's favorites as well.

"Of course, how could I forget, we almost got caught by the cops every time." Jason laughed as he and Tim shared a moment that proved two old friends had come together for a reason, and it was time for that reason to be fully recognized.

Jason sat alongside Tim in the front bench seat, and Christina and Jay were in the back. "You guys making us sit in the back of the bus? What is this, 1954?" quipped Jay hoping his dated humor might strike a chord.

"Not especially, but you do have to keep the smartest people the most protected," replied Jason as he looked at Tim and Bryan who nodded in agreement.

Bryan started the Lincoln and they drove toward a place Jay hadn't told him the location of yet. "So where are we going man?"

"Go back to the office park where we first saw Marty. There's a small hot dog shack a half mile down a side street right before it. That's where we're going," blurted Jay, waiting to see what their secret messenger had for them.

"How do we know this isn't a trap?" inquired Jason. He thought it was a logical question because somebody had sent a message to a phone that isn't supposed to exist.

"This isn't a trap. The person who sent this transmitted coded message can be trusted."

Jason knew that just because the message was sent to Jay, didn't mean it wasn't somebody keeping Jay's friend hostage just to get information. He also knew that they didn't have much other choice at this point. They had to go where the signs were pointing. They had to follow.

"Onward James," Jason retorted to Bryan because he knew a witty remark wasn't too far behind.

"Do I look like a James? Do I look like I'm wearing one of those stupid hats?" Bryan surmised with a laugh. He knew that no matter how hairy things got, Jason keeping things light hearted was going to be the key to their success.

The Lincoln was getting close to the office park, when all of a sudden it started to rain. "Were we expecting any rain today? I wouldn't know, I haven't heard a weather report in forever with chasing worldwide government conspiracies and all," remarked Jason with another light hearted quip.

"I didn't hear anything either, we just have to deal with it. There's the turn, make that left up ahead. You'll see a run down, little brown shack looking thing down behind the trees," replied Jay happy that his hard work might finally be coming to fruition.

Bryan pulled the car alongside a broken down creaky building that looked like the roof would cave in at any second. "You sure this place is safe? With all the rain, I'll bet it has a million leaks," wondered Jason who was thinking out loud.

The Lincoln was the only car in the parking lot which would have only fit four anyway. If it weren't for the amazing smell of chili, walking into this shack would have been like walking into a horror movie where a serial killer was waiting to chop you up. Of course Jason knew it was possible the chili could have been made out of people, they couldn't be too sure.

"Come on Jason, this isn't a serial killer factory where they feed you soylent green," expressed Jay who knew Jason's thoughts because his contorted face told the whole story.

Jay opened the creaky door to see the old familiar face of Trevor, the guy who owned the joint. He couldn't be making much money off the place Jason thought, but it was the perfect place for a secret meeting, so he just went with the flow.

Trevor directed them to sit at one of the five tables spread around that needed paint more than the walls did. This hot dog shack needed some TLC, but more likely a bulldozer. They sat down at the middle table and Trevor brought them each a beer. "Here you go, guys and girl. You look like you could use it," remarked Trevor, the 75 year old owner who was too ornery to have a real job, but damn if he didn't make some of the finest chili around.

Jason sat next to Christina along with Tim, Bryan and Jay for five minutes with nobody saying anything, so Jason decided to cut the silence. "So, is this mystery person even coming? Do they even know where this place is?"

"Trust me, they know where it is and how to get here," Jay answered with utmost confidence. He glared at Jason like are you really questioning me at this point?

Just when Jason was going to return with an intellectual volley, the front door creaked open to reveal who they were meeting.

"Nice to see you Jay, it's been a while."

"It has. I'd introduce you to all my people here, but they already know who you are and vice versa. Good to see you Marty."

CHAPTER EIGHTEEN

If trying to figure out what side Marty was on was like a ping pong match, it would be the longest recorded volley in history. Human emotions can change as situations on the ground change, but nobody at the table could figure this one out, not even Marty himself.

"Marty, dad, I don't even know what to call you," stammered Jason as he blurted out the first thought that came to him. "What are you doing here? How do we know you aren't working for the entities? How do we know they aren't going to disappear us into some black hole somewhere?"

Jay wondered about Jason's line of questioning, even though the way Bryan, Christina and Tim were looking at him, he saw that they agreed. "Look I'm sure if Marty is here, and not locked into that black hole himself, he must have something important to offer," interjected Jay. He found it interesting how quick he was to defend Marty, even after investigating all his shady business deals. Maybe since they investigated each other, they felt a certain kinship; and the old saying rang truer now than ever, the enemy of my enemy is my friend.

A zillion things ran through Jason's head, and he wanted to blurt out all his thoughts at once because he needed an answer like yesterday. "I want to prove to you all that I'm on your side," expressed Marty to skeptical looks from the group. He knew that being skeptical was always better than being cynical, because being skeptical meant your mind was still open and evolving. "That blueprint I showed you guys at the lair was authentic. I have the infrastructure to not only get this pipeline built, but also to have this bio-analyzer do the work it was meant to, provide much needed water for the people."

Before Jason could respond, Trevor, the ever faithful restaurant owner for the last 45 years brought out some chili dogs that wafted heaven to the nostrils. "I can see why you use this place. It's out off the beaten path, and has some of the best food around," remarked Jason. His mouth watered as a pile of chili dogs and a mountain of fresh cut fries were set before them. What a way to fix the problems with humanity Jason thought, he always knew the mind worked best on a full stomach.

"Now that we've got this food, maybe we can talk about what our next move is," stated Marty who knew the entities were soon to be after them. Maybe they were already. They certainly would be if Marty got the bio-analyzer up and running. "How do we get this thing moving along? The quicker we get this thing built the better. Once the people see the pipeline working and are reaping the benefits, they won't want it to stop, and it will be harder for it to be handed back to the entities. Kind of like social security, once the people saw it working as intended, the program couldn't be abolished; even though the Republicans to this day are trying to privatize it."

Jason saw some of the original spark he witnessed when he stepped foot into Marty's office, as some of his truth of spirit was beginning to show. "I agree, but how do we know we can trust you?"

"You can keep asking me that over and over again, but if you don't trust me by now, I don't know what I can possibly do to change your mind," Marty fired back as he and Jason just stared at each other, sizing each other up. Bryan had some choice words as well. He had spent just as much time with Marty as Jason, probably more. He couldn't put his thoughts together right and since he and Jason were on the same page, he didn't mind having a microphone he could trust.

"Who is this guy, a new member of the menagerie?" Marty inquired while looking at Tim, who was playing the observer and not saying much, but only because he was thinking several chess-moves ahead. "Anything you'd like to add? I know what all these people think because I've seen and worked with them before. Tell me, why I should trust you?"

Jason looked at Tim like you don't have to answer this guy. "I trust you, and therefore the others will trust you because they trust me." Tim put up his hand like its okay man, I appreciate you coming to my defense, but I don't need help with this one. "I'm one of Jason's oldest friends, he's a brother to me," responded Tim, causing Jason to smile. "I've been doing a lot of work in this field."

"What field is that?" Marty asked, wondering if it was water, conspiracies, or if he'd been doing research on the best way to eat chili dogs, because the steaming pile of goodness in front of them was softening all their resolves.

"A little bit of everything. I've tracked overreaching government and corporate control, thinking up real world solutions to some of society's most pressing problems," retorted Tim like he'd been practicing for just this situation. Jason and Bryan wasted no time in inhaling the delicious bounty in front of them, so Christina and Jay followed suit. You might say they were enjoying their food with a free show.

"That sounds like a politician's answer, but I don't see a teleprompter anywhere. Have you served in office before?"

"You might say that."

"What does that mean?"

"Well, I guess we're all friendly here. I was investigating a pipeline that was supposed to carry snow and ocean water from the east coast to the west coast, turning it into drinking water by the time it got there. To make it all possible was something called a bio-analyzer that would desalinate and purify the water so it was potable when it got to its final destination."

Tim did seem to know everything going on, but questions remained. How did Marty know Tim wasn't a spy for the entities, meant to lull him into a false sense of getting ahead, only to pull the rug out at the last second? "How did you track it?"

"I tracked it through the public permitting process. Every time they needed a permit or to complete an environmental review, it would be posted in the public record. There has been lengthy legal disputes and public outrage over oil pipelines that have been built, and the ones still in the planning stages. I figured a water pipeline was something the people could actually get behind," mused Tim. He still felt like he had to prove himself, but that was okay; he'd sing for his supper.

"I like it so far, and yes a pipeline for water is much better for the environment than oil. The potentially small scale wars that could break out over water rights, scares the hell out of me. Lots of good people could lose their lives for something that covers 70% of the earth," Marty expressed from the bottom of his soul.

Jason was now on his second chili dog, while Christina and Jay were still finishing their first, and digging into the fries. "Man this is good Trevor. I'd say you were the king of the chili covered wiener if I didn't think you'd take offense," Jason cajoled, trying to lighten the mood, and show his appreciation for the grub in front of them. The ball was rolling, because once he got some food in him, he was always ready to go. "Hey Tim, tell Marty what you told me out at the lake."

Bryan, Christina and Jay's ears popped up as they put their dogs down, wiped their chili smeared faces and listened intently. "What did you tell him at the lake, and how stoned were you?" chuckled Marty with a smart-ass smirk because he knew Jason's love for a good joint in a beautiful spot, and he wanted to make sure this wasn't some sort of stoned confessional.

"We did smoke, and man it was good. It reminded me of the good old days," Tim reminisced as he smiled at Jason because they had many good times together, and he knew the best were yet to come. "We talked about my investigations of course, but also about the group I started once I found out who was building the pipeline. It took me a while to go through the spider web of shell companies on top of shell companies, piled inside of conglomerates then bounced around the world to a hundred different institutional mutual funds. When I figured it out, I knew I had to do something about it."

Marty's ears perked up, especially now that he was the entity's number-one enemy. He loved the idea of having a friend's group help fight them. Not that the other people sitting around the broken down chili covered table wouldn't, but he wanted to hear more. "What did you come up with?"

"A research project this big requires lots of eyes and lots of hands to see and find everything. I discovered a group called the six entities who were trying to take over the world one section at a time through full privatization:

labor, environmental, pharmaceutical, military, education and political."

Marty was taken back, how did he know? He felt like he finally saw a light, at the end of the tunnel; especially and hopefully because Tim and his guys weren't yet on the entity's radar.

"I grew up always wanting to do good for the planet and the people who live here, and everywhere for that matter. This group wanted to take over the world one category at a time. I knew I had to start my own group to take control from them in these categories, and to make them work how they were meant to work. To benefit the people, not just the money-changers behind the scenes," exclaimed Tim as the full fire of his soul was on display for all to see.

Jason devoured his second chili dog, and could have gone for a third because these were the Krispy Kreme's of chili dogs; you could eat a dozen and not even know it. He knew if he did though, he'd be farting all night and Christina wouldn't let him anywhere near her. This was evident by the way he went to grab another when she said with just her eyes, you've had enough; show this guy what's in that big beautiful head of yours, and let's start saving the world.

"Tim is one of my oldest friends and....." Jason began to state before Tim interrupted him.

"You don't have to talk for me man. We're old buddies and I appreciate how we've always had each other's backs, but

I can handle this one," replied Tim feeling the fire still building in his soul. "Since the group is called the six entities because of the six categories they need to control all of society, I decided to call my group the Anti-entities."

"Don't you think that's a little cliché?" wondered Marty, trying get under Tim's skin. Marty knew personally, that was when his passionate work was produced.

They all smiled when Jay added, "It might be cliché, but when you're helping the majority of the population get what a few powerful people are keeping from them, nobody will care about a name."

"I can see how something like that would work. Instead of them making all the money, we'd make the money. I like money, I'd be down for that," agreed Marty to the chagrin of Jason. He felt Marty always had his own well-being as priority one. After everything that had happened Jay was right. Marty always looked out for Jason no matter what. A person who killed the former President has to be serious.

"Let's not turn this into another money making scheme. We're not cogs in your machine," fumed Bryan who felt let down by Marty just as much as Jason. He also needed a lot more proof that Marty was on the up and up.

"So how can I prove that to you, to all of you for that matter? I wouldn't be here if my heart wasn't in the right place," Marty unloaded. He looked Bryan deep in the eyes and down into his soul. The group had many enemies out there. Marty personally got rid of a few of them. That didn't mean he wasn't in for the long haul. It was just going to take more than revenge killings to get the entities off of their backs.

"Well there is one way," Jason thought out loud. "It's crazy and it might not work, but it could. In the end, isn't that the most important part in any plan to save the world, believing it was possible no matter how hard it was? Put the whole thing under a non-profit umbrella. Make it so the people benefit from the new technology, and not have to pay a cent for it. If you want to do good after all these years and have something other than money to show for it, if you have any hope of a relationship with me, your son, this has to happen. This is how all of us can trust you."

Marty stared for a minute at each person sitting around the old, broken down table. He looked at Bryan, then Jay, then Christina and Jason, and then finally Tim. They all nodded they'd be okay with that. He thought it was interesting that when everybody is on the same page, they didn't have to use words; they knew what each other was thinking, because their hearts were screaming out for conscious change.

"I could make that work, but how would it be administered?" Marty queried, wondering how something like this would be pulled off. Then, he figured it out. "You want to use my infrastructure to build the pipeline?"

"Yes, all the permits are in place. All we have to do is use your construction contacts to outbid the entities, and then we should be scott-free," Tim responded, knowing it wouldn't be nearly that cut and dry, nothing ever was. He also knew such an answer would elicit other answers to help fill in other blanks.

"The way we fix that particular problem is with something I like to call honesty. How much will this pipeline cost to build, it has to be in the hundreds of billions right?" inquired Jason who knew the nuts and bolts were just as important as the philosophy behind it.

"Yes, and that's the thing, where are we going to get that kind of money?" Marty asked Jason who looked back at him like you already know the answer to that.

"Well you of course. I know you've acquired quite the fortune in untraceable off-shore investments and Swiss bank accounts. If I've learned anything about people and their fortunes, is that the only way to keep them is to make more money off the money they already have. Basically the same idea with people in power, you keep it by acquiring more."

"What are you getting at?"

"You know. Somebody like you always has secret funds, or investments somewhere that nobody knows about that could get this project off the ground. That's how you didn't even bat an eye when you were supporting me all those years."

"I supported you because you were my son."

"Maybe, but if you love me, I mean truly love me, you'll do this," Jason remarked. Jay looked at him, making Jason glad he let it all hang out. He thought about the sacrifices parents make for their kids to not only succeed, but also to contribute to a much better world than the one they entered.

"When I looked in on you all those years, I saw you had secret accounts scattered around many foreign countries. Some legal, some not so legal, and some nobody would ever think could be used with good intentions. Prove to us, the world, and most importantly yourself that you'll leave a positive mark when you exit the earth, not just a bunch of money in accounts that are nothing but numbers on a screen. Make them do something good, it'll clean out your soul," blurted Jay who felt his own soul open up. He thought of the sacrifices he'd made for Christina over the years, and how he had to prove to her the same thing Marty had to prove to Jason.

"Okay, okay, let's say I am able to pull the money together and funnel it to the right people. How do we get this project off the ground? We could give it to the Governors or to an ownership in trust to the people so they owned it. What about the legislators and office-holders the six entities have in their pocket? How do we know they won't step in the way?" asked Marty because it was a legitimate question.

"You guys almost done, it's late and I want to go home?" muttered Trevor whose back always started to ache when the sun was setting.

"Sorry man, we're about done," answered Marty who always liked Trevor, which is why he and Jay used this place countless times over the years. Trevor talked to Marty like any normal person, not a secret money funneler. Trevor knew about Marty's dealings because his ears were always open to what happened in his restaurant. If Trevor was still alive after all the secrets he'd been privy to over the years, Marty knew Trevor must be trustworthy. Little did Marty know, Trevor was about to prove it again.

"If you don't know which office-holders to trust, make your case to the people. If enough of them get angry and unite as a force, they will have more than a chance to defeat the entities. Find some friendly governors that aren't within their control, I'm sure you know some. Hell, I know some. Then once their people see the pipeline's benefits, other Governors and office-holders will stand up to the entities, because the people would support that. Any person holding office wouldn't be able to hold that office if all the people were against them, so they'll stand up against the entities also. They'll try to kill some people, and they'll probably succeed. What they won't be able to do, is kill everybody. Fear, intimidation and distraction can be a powerful tool, but not as powerful as the people when bread and circuses don't work on them anymore,"

Trevor explained in the most authentic down to earth voice any of them had ever heard.

"You sound like somebody we need in office, somebody willing to tell it like it is," remarked Jason happy to see that people could still see through all the bullshit.

"I thought about it when I was younger, but it's not for me. Life is a lot simpler when you make good food to make people happy. That's when I'm the happiest," expressed Trevor as he broke out in a smile, then walked back into the kitchen.

"Wow, I have to say, that's a great plan. Do you think it is possible?" Marty wondered, who was coming more on-board the more plausible the plan became.

"It has to be. Studying the pipeline route, a few friendly Governors might be willing to stand up to the entities that have probably made them incredibly lavish offers," replied Tim who felt like his path finally had a direction. What better way to do it he thought, than with the oldest friend he had.

"Okay, well then, that's that. Let's get out of here and make this happen. I am full with chili dogs and fries, and am ready to save the world, one more time," Jason exclaimed with an infinite passion.

"You never grow out of those stupid one-liners do you?" responded Bryan with a laugh.

"Sheeeeeeeeet up," Jason shot back who was smiling as big as ever because there was a light at the end of this particular tunnel.

"Thank you Trevor for everything, we'll never forget you," expressed Jason as he got up from the table. "I can't thank you enough for everything here."

Trevor didn't hear Jason's words because the sound of gun shots rang out towards the back of the restaurant. By the time Jason and the rest of the group went to see what had happened, they saw Trevor lying on the ground in a pool of blood, with a bullet hole to the back of his head.

"Did the entities have this place bugged? How'd they know?" stammered Jason, trying to figure things out lightning fast.

"They must have, you really think they didn't know about a place a half mile from Marty's old office?" Christina argued, feeling like her old self and the voice of reason even though she was still freaked out. "They must've heard what Trevor said and how he gave us a starting point."

"Why didn't they come in here and kill the rest of us? Why would they leave witnesses?" wondered Jason, who knew what these guys could do firsthand.

"Maybe it has something to do with that note by the body." Christina picked up the scrap of paper and read it aloud. "You've taken me down, I have come back. At one point I thought I could trust you guys, but after you killed someone that was like my brother, I'll personally see to it that you never succeed. You think you can find friendly Governors we don't already have in our pockets, good luck. Don't you know that we put down anybody who steps out of line? Don't make us put the rest of you down."

Christina handed the note to Bryan who reread the words as Marty spoke. "If I've learned anything to this point, it's that I shouldn't trust anybody. I've also learned there are people I can. This note could only have come from one person, the person whose cleaner I killed," remarked Marty with a calm but unseasonably happy voice when talking about the death of another human being.

Jason caught onto this, but it would have to be dealt with later. "I kind of wish that car explosion would have killed that stupid Congressman, he just won't give up. Do you think the entities are actually paying him, or is he just trying to get back on their good side?"

"At this point it doesn't really matter. Tim, how quick can your people talk to these friendly Governors and get them on board?" inquired Marty who was taking control, which was okay with the rest of them as long it was for everybody's benefit, not just his own.

"I just need to make a few phone calls. I've prepared them for a time when all the pieces fall into place. I told them to be ready once I got construction contacts under my wing.

They will have all the fast track permits in hand the minute they hear the okay," stated Tim who felt a surge of energy rush through his body because for the first time, he realized a better world was possible. He was about to be an active player in making that happen.

"Sounds good. Let's call them from the car, I don't want to take a chance in-case it wasn't Ridell. He must be trying to take my spot as enforcer, he was always a bumbling idiot," sniped Marty with an edge in his voice. "It's a good thing I was playing them the whole time, which is the only reason you guys trust me right?"

"Do we have to get into this again? Will it prevent us from ever having a real relationship, I don't know. What I do know is the entities are looking for you just like they're looking for us. We don't have to trust each other because we have the same enemy, we have the same wants," replied Jason looking Marty right in the eye.

"I realize I have a lot to do to earn back your trust, but this is a great starting point," Marty expressed sincerely, with a tear starting to form.

"You guys had enough of a chick moment, let's go out and do this thing. Afterwards, you can show me what a Cuban sandwich is all about," blurted Tim. He knew he met back up with Jason for a reason that was about to be fulfilled, so they might as well celebrate afterwards.

Jason agreed, so they all hurried out to the Lincoln that was more than big enough to fit them all. "I'm glad you found this thing back at the pad. I kept it nice in case I met up with you again. I wanted to show that I could take care of something important to you," Marty expressed proudly with a wink.

"Thanks dad," Jason shot back without a second thought. "Tim, do you have a phone for the calls you need to make? We had one but it got compromised?"

"The thing about that is, the phone got hacked by somebody that's now on our side," answered Marty, hoping it wouldn't elicit another "here we go again" from the group.

"How do you know that?" asked Jason thinking Marty was still hiding something.

"A guy helped me escape from the entities by shooting his partner in the head. He said the guy was going to rat on him, and that he was down for our cause. He shot him right in the car when I was in the back. The shooter hacked into the phone, which brought us together. He was able to pull it off because of the work he'd done for the entities over the years," Marty exclaimed speaking a million miles a minute, as Bryan fired up the Lincoln, smiling as it roared back to life.

"Oh you must be talking about Dave. I got to him years ago, and was able to change his mind by telling him why the entities were bad, and the Anti-entities were good," explained Tim. Bryan pulled the car out of the spot, went down the dirt road and back toward the highway.

"Wait, so you knew this guy? You turned him around how, by just talking to him? Is that how you turned around the Governors, by just talking them out of their support for the entities and toward support for your group?" inquired Christina who had been curious ever since Tim spilled the information.

"It's one of those things that's simple and not at the same time. I told them what they could look forward to with the entities, piles of cash and always looking over their shoulder. If they joined me, they'd still have to look over their shoulder, but their lives would be much more fulfilling with the majority of the public supporting them; more than any other politician has felt before.

I told them they could leave this world with a clean conscience no matter what misdeeds they've done if they do this. The evolutionary step this would bring would more than outweigh anything bad they put out there. Even if it couldn't, they would die happy knowing they did the best they could to be the best person they could be. Excuse me I have a few phone calls to make."

Jason and Marty were speechless, and Christina and Bryan didn't have anything to say either. Jay simply handed Tim the phone and he proceeded to call his contacts.

"I'm sure glad we went to that lake and watched the birds. Something great always happens when I open myself up to the beauty of the world. When we were lost, we opened up to anything that could help, and there sat Tim. Not only did my soul get filled because I saw a friend I hadn't seen in years, but he also provided us a path forward," remarked Jason with a smile that went from the bottom of his soul to the top of his head.

"Marty don't you have some calls to make as well, get your construction people on board?" Bryan asked trying to make sure Marty kept up his end of the bargain.

"I will as soon as Tim is done. The people will be in place once the permits are there. They'll build the pipeline, along with the first working model of the bio-analyzer that will be placed at the intersection point so it'll flow," answered Marty who finally felt like part of the team.

"You mean you've never built a working model? So you have had ones that didn't work? We have too much on the line for this not to work. If the bio analyzer doesn't work and the entities see us fail to take them down when we obviously have a leg up, it'll be that much harder for us to do anything. They will then come after us with everything they've got.

People think death squads and private armies only exist in other countries, think again. Money makes a strong point when trying to vanquish your enemies. Pay somebody enough and they'll flatten a village, wasn't that your way?" retorted Jay who had to get in another dig, because there was still something he didn't like about the plan. He looked into Marty for too long to not know the consequences of failure.

"We did tests and it tested okay, but nothing on this massive a scale. Just like anything in life though, there are no guarantees," Marty shot back. He then proceeded to pull out his phone to make the necessary calls.

"You have a phone too? How do we know it hasn't been traced and they aren't following us right now?" inquired Bryan who still wasn't sure if they should trust Marty.

"Of course, I never leave home without it. Don't worry though, it's untraceable because of moving cell towers into different positions, or repositioning them I don't know, my tech guy handled that. I don't know the scientific answer, but the short story long is that nobody will listen in," explained Marty as he dialed the first person he had to talk to.

Bryan piloted the Lincoln towards an unknown destination, while two different important phone conversations were going on that could change the fate of the world. If the water could really flow, with the ownership falling to the people, and if Marty was willing to make all that happen while not making a cent off it, maybe he could be trusted again.

"I hope those guys aren't trying to pull something again, but knowing my daughter and my ex, they probably are," barked the mysterious female voice. She spoke to Ridell through one of the many burner phones the entities provided so he didn't get caught, again. *"Don't screw this up again, I'll come after you. Not me personally, but the*

private armies I have at my disposal. I pay them, they kill for me. It's that simple. No wonder being a dictator is so much easier. You tell somebody to do something, and if they refuse, you kill them. No muss no fuss."

"I get it, the message that was sent was what you wanted me to do," replied Ridell as he tried to grab a quick bite to eat. He felt like he hadn't eaten in weeks because of running from one crisis to another.

"That's true, and thank you for mostly obeying my orders. You didn't plant that bug like I asked you to. It's a good thing we already had it planted before you got here, because I knew something like this would happen. That son of a bitch that murdered his partner, that's who I want you to kill. I'll have my private guys handle Jason and the rest of the Mad People for Good. No way could they ever be against the entities. Nobody is against the entities, and if they are we could just kill them anyways, so who cares."

"I'll let you know when its done."

The six entities started as a force for good with a very heavy profit motive. Anything with money as a number one priority always turns to greed, because it wants more power and more money and more power and more money. They always want more. Tim and Marty were ensuring this would never come to pass, at least not yet.

"Okay I've called my contacts; they're ready to sign as soon as I give them the word that Marty's guys are ready to start construction. We have to get them to start building before the signatures are dry. Once the construction starts, the entities will have to deal with the public fallout of trying to stop something that benefits the whole country," Tim explained, happy he was able to start doing his part.

Having just finished his calls as well and having heard what Tim had said, Marty agreed. "My guys are ready and in route now. Tim, call your guys back and have them grab up the permits. My crews will be there first thing in the morning," Marty replied with a warm heart because he was about to give society something it always wanted, honesty and clean drinking water for generations to come.

"Sounds good to me, I'll call them back right now," Tim responded, who was more than happy to help.

Bryan kept driving the Lincoln down the road, feeling like he was stuck in a Chuck Berry song; cruising and playing the radio, with no particular place to go was pounding in his head. He knew that wasn't true because they were headed in a very specific direction, and pushing humanity to its next evolutionary step.

"Just got off the phone with my guys, everything is in place. Building will start in the morning."

Just as Jason was about to say something about eating Cuban sandwiches to celebrate, a tire blew out on the Lincoln. It caused the car to spin out of control and hit one of many oak trees that were lining the highway they were driving on.

Nobody inside was hurt seriously, but when Jason got out of the car to see what they hit, he saw that was the least of their worries. A caravan of three Tahoes pulled up behind them, and out jumped twenty camo clad men with machine guns pointed right at their heads.

"You don't think you can just escape right? You think you can do everything to destroy our plans and nothing will happen?" barked the man at the front of the group who led the charge.

Jason thought the voice of the man sounded familiar, but he wasn't quite sure; then it hit him.

"Goose, is that you? Did you switch sides that quick?" queried Jason with some trepidation but not that much, it wasn't the first time he had a gun in his face.

"Shut up, you don't know me. Guys, they don't know me," stammered the head guy in charge to all the men behind him, who didn't believe a word he said.

"Why should we believe you?" asked the second in command very cynically.

"Let me talk to this guy and prove it to you," yelled Goose who knew there was no point in trying to prove anything to Jason, so he attempted to break it down for him.

The men behind Goose nodded their heads slightly, and Goose started walking toward Jason.

"Sorry it's to come to this, but I don't have much time. I started working for my old private security firm, who happened to pick up a contract held by one of the entities front companies. They know you're trying to start pipeline construction under their noses," whispered Goose at a 1000 miles an hour.

"So what do we do now?" Jason wondered because he saw how antsy the guys behind Goose were getting that he hadn't destroyed the target yet.

"I had to make it up to Jay somehow. I hate how I left things. The plan was to stop you here, shoot you all, and the problem would be handled. Having known that, I stashed a car about a mile or so from here. Run through the trees to the north until you come to a rock formation with three rocks. Make a left there, and go about another half mile down the trail and you'll see it."

"Goose, I can't thank you enough."

"Just go, and tell Jay I always believed in him and everything he fought for. I'll always remember him."

"What?"

"Just go."

Jason turned around and started walking back to the busted Lincoln, and immediately started hearing Goose's gun. He was spraying bullets all over the crowd and the cars behind him. Jason hurried over to the guys, and motioned for them to follow.

"What happened?" wondered Christina so scared she was about to piss her pants.

"No time to explain, there's a car stashed through the trees about a mile from here, we have to move now. Jay, Goose said thank you for everything, he believes in you, and he'll always remember you."

Jay smiled as he grabbed Christina and followed Jason, along with Tim, Bryan and Marty bringing up the rear. Goose was able to drop six or seven guys, blow out some windshields, flatten some tires and bust some radiators before he was brought down in a hail of bullets. The investigators that would later find his body, counted at least a hundred holes.

As the group ran through the woods, they looked back and didn't see Marty behind them. "What happened to Marty? Did he get shot, did they capture him?" Jason asked, out of breath from the running. He put his hands at his sides to give himself a little breather. When he did he felt a little scrap of paper in his pocket. Once they all made it safely to the car Goose had stashed, he read it aloud, barely able to make out the words because his heart was beating out of his chest. Running from men with big guns when you don't have any yourself will do that to you, but also when you're long lost dad is lost again.

"Jason if you're reading this, I might be dead. Or I might have had to escape. Either way, it's to your benefit. I'm too much of a liability for you and your people. I'm glad I could help get my people in line for you, but I can't risk the entities coming after you because I screwed them over. I'll find you again one day, on this earth or the next. Please know that I love you, and thank you for proving that raising consciousness isn't done from the end of a gun, but from the bottom of a heart. Good luck."

EPILOGUE

Jason waited a long time to have his friends, his woman and her amazing dad all together to chill with. He knew hanging out on a Cuban beach was a great place to start.

"Aren't you afraid the entities will catch us out here, didn't they find your place the last time?" wondered Bryan. He was worried, but not worried at the same time because the Madman for Good and the Anti-entities kept up their respective ends of the bargain.

Building the pipeline only took seven months, which wasn't fast enough to ease the summer drought, but was lightning fast when dealing with any sort of bureaucracy. Of course this wasn't any normal bureaucracy. The entities tried to stop construction by sending in one private security contractor after another.

Once the people saw armed people trying to stop something that would benefit them all, they stood up and said enough is enough, construction will go on. People saw how important this project was, and realized they couldn't all be murdered. The bio analyzer was successful in operation, and for the first time in recorded history all of the contaminates were taken out of ocean water and snow, turned into drinkable water, then delivered to people who were thirsting for it.

"I can't believe it worked. That device your mom came up with is truly saving the country, and will eventually save the world when people see how fast ocean water and snow can be turned into drinking water," expressed Jason with a gigantic smile on his face. Even Tim helped the situation by bringing Jason one of the finest rolled, giant joints he'd ever seen; although Christina Sherman and her dad weren't too bad at rolling either.

"Here man, smoke this," chuckled Tim as he handed Jason the joint. The day was as sunny and warm as the last seven months that seemed to fly by. Of course that happens when you're surrounded by good friends, family, and the best weed anywhere.

"Thanks man. Well I guess we should be thanking Jay for bringing us back to this beautiful island. I'm surprised you still had a place to hide out," remarked Jason as he took a deep hit, let out a huge cloud of smoke and handed the joint to Jay.

"The entities did find me that last time, but I have all different places to hide here in Cuba. Besides, they're dealing with private military issues back in the states," Jay shot back with a wink as he took an equally big hit.

"So where are these Cuban sandwiches I hear you talking about? I've been in Cuba for how long now, and I haven't tried one," Tim inquired as he grabbed the joint, took a hit which caused his mouth to water more than it already was.

"I guess we've just been enjoying everything else a little too much. Since it's more of a Cuban American thing than a Cuban thing, there aren't many places here that make them. A few do though, and they do them right, don't they Jay?" surmised Jason as he winked at Jay, who proceeded to pick up his phone to have some delivered to the beach, right where they were sitting.

The sun was at its highest point in the sky, with not a cloud anywhere to be seen, making it rather hot. Many people were out that day, just enjoying the water, the sun and the peaceful calm.

Twenty minutes later, a muscular Cuban man in his late twenties walked up with two huge bags in hand.

"I know what that is, prepare to be in heaven," explained Jason as he could smell Cuban sandwiches a mile away. He grabbed the bags, tipped the delivery guy and handed them all out.

"These things are pretty big, but man does it smell amazing," Tim added as he held his up. "Feels likes there's plenty of meat in it too."

"You always did like when plenty of meat was stuck in," Jason fired back, as he and Tim were practically rolling on the sand laughing causing Bryan to shake his head.

"There you go laughing about your meat again, something ladies do to you all the time right?" replied Bryan as Christina and Jay started laughing along with the rest of them.

Jay handed his phone to Christina to hold, because he knew how messy cubanos were, and didn't want to get melted swiss cheese all over his phone.

Just as Tim, Jason and the rest of the gang were about to bite into their sandwiches, the phone rang. Since it was sitting on Christina's lap, she decided to pick it up.

"You might have been able to control the water that we couldn't, or should I say stole our opportunity to do so. Taking away one of our main money making ventures really pissed us off. You think you can just stop our plans? You might have foiled the first entity, but you won't foil the rest of them. We have so much more in store it would shatter your tiny little brains if we tried to break down the complexities. We have control over private armies that could level whole cities, you don't think we can handle little nothings like you?"

Christina interrupted the rambling voice when she realized who the person was. "You couldn't handle us because we got the people on our side before you could scare them into submission. You couldn't handle me when I was a teenager either, could you, mom?"